God to renew your mind and spirit from these potential influences and to help you set new standards for yourself that will benefit your faith:

> *Heavenly Father, I know You said we would suffer persecution in this life, but I am weary from the constant warring. I have almost grown accustomed to the discouragements, depression, fatigue and rejection, but I am expecting to see a shift as of today. I know that You will never reject me. I know that You are my encouragement and my strength. I also know that I can be confident because You are the glory and the lifter of my head. In Jesus' name, Amen.*

Correlating Physical Detox

Today we finish cleansing the muscular system. Repeat yesterday's meal plan, experimenting with this section's colors.

Closing Blessing

May God finish detoxifying your muscular system as you grow into the person He has created you to be, strong enough to withstand anything. You are an overcomer!

DAY 29

Spiritual Toxin: Copy and Paste (Will the Real Me Please Stand?)

There is so much pressure on this generation. Pressure to perform. Pressure to achieve. Pressure to have the perfect body. Pressure to be the perfect spouse. Pressure to stay young. Pressure to make good grades. Even pressure to be the perfect Christian. All this perfecting can take you miles from the original you and leave you wondering who you really are underneath all the exterior perfections.

If, however, you are hoping that that opener means this is a devotional about slacking off and giving up on becoming the best you, well, you are going to be disappointed. Besides, I think deep down inside you *do* want to be the best you. Why else would you have made it this far in this book?

The difference is all in the perspective. If you are changing and bettering yourself without first confidently knowing who and whose you are, the foundation is unstable and all the changes will not be successful. Nor will you. If, however, you start with the footing of being rooted and grounded in Christ, accepted unconditionally by Him but ever reaching and growing to become more like Him, then your progress and process will be much more fruitful and far less superficial.

I get very frustrated with people who never change or grow. Some of them seem so laid back, easygoing and humble, but the "what you see is what you get" or "this is me; take it or leave it" mindset is the most self-absorbed, narcissistic, vain, self-admiring, egotistical alibi in the world (and yes, all those synonyms were for effect).

So this devotional will not be about never changing due to your love for the original you, but about loving the original you enough to change.

In fact, the "best you" *is* the real you, and that is the person you should be fighting to protect. That person is already within you right now. Michelangelo said, "Every block of stone has a statue inside it and it is the task of the sculptor to discover it." So imagine that the real you is already inside today's you and that God's chisel is merely bringing it definition. With that perspective, from here on out I am going to be addressing *that* you.

Do you even know who that you is? Even if you like the current you, are there ways you can look more like your heavenly Father and be more forgiving? Productive? Loving? Creative? Joyful? Merciful? Disciplined? Sabbath-keeping? I like the current me, but she has a way to go in looking just like her Father. I want to change every single day. I like today's me. I am going to like tomorrow's me even better.

But I remember once when yesteryear's me asked God to please let me be somebody else entirely. Times were hard and I was weary. So hard that food was scarce for the eight of us, and the task of providing it (and the repeated failures) began to make me lose sight of how blessed I already was. Who would not want the blessing of six kids, right? Well, you might say, "Not I!" But if you met my kids, you would want them all. Jessica's strength, Julian's humor, Jhason's steadiness, Jeorgi's loving-kindness, Jude's hair (just kidding; Jude's magnetism) and Jenesis' invincibility. Who would not want a strong, funny, steady, loving, magnetic, invincible household? But all of that was so eclipsed by my struggles that in a pool of tears one day on my knees in my closet, I begged God to let me be somebody else.

What I did not realize was that God *was* turning me into somebody else. The new me was emerging. And once I realized that the new me was the real me, it felt much less like achieving and more like receiving. And of course, I have repented for my tearful wish and thanked God repeatedly for letting me be and keep becoming "me."

I once read that in computing, the phrase *whoami*—which is a concatenation of the words *Who am I?*—is a utility command for a certain operating system. If you have forgotten your username, you merely type in *whoami* to the command prompt window and your identity is revealed, along with your privileges.[2]

Would it not be nice if you could do the same in life? To type in *whoami* and find out who you are? Well guess what? You can!

All you must do is ask God. He will reveal your identity to you, along with all its privileges. You are the only one privileged enough to be you. And you need to know who you are so that when others ask, you know how to answer.

Personally, I like Jesus' mode of operation. He answered questions with questions. ("Who do you say that I am?") In fact, some of His most profound questions came as a reply to someone questioning Him. But He was not asking due to an identity crisis. He knew who He was. He *was* I AM. He still is.

Have you ever been through an identity crisis? According to psychologists, they happen in adolescence. Ever had a midlife crisis? Evidently, those come somewhere from age 37 to mid-fifties. Ever been a victim of identity theft? It is said that more than nine million people each year will!

But with Jesus, you do not have to experience any of these internal crises. He is the giver, definer and protector of your identity. Why? Because He is secure in His. And when you are secure in yours, you can help others find theirs, too. You can help them stay confident when tested. You see, Jesus knew who He was because God affirmed Him. Upon Jesus' baptism, His Father spoke and said, "This is My beloved Son, in whom I am well pleased" (Matthew 3:17 NASB). Jesus left there and went immediately into the desert where Satan tested Him. Satan said, "*If* you are the Son of God, command that these stones become bread" (Matthew 4:3 NASB, emphasis added). Satan wanted to plant doubt in Jesus' mind about His identity. But it did not work. We do not see Jesus saying, "Okay, check out what happens when I zap this boulder." No. Jesus knew that Satan was questioning His identity to get Him to question everything else God had ever said. He did not get caught up in performance to prove who He was. He merely sat there looking like His Father, the great I AM.

If you are going to be a copy-and-paste of anyone, let it be of your heavenly Father. Maybe your earthly father never affirmed you the way God did Jesus at His baptism. Sadly, I hear this repeatedly from broken people all the time. They never heard in their childhoods, "This is my son (or daughter), in whom I am well pleased." In fact, many years ago Chris and I were asked to minister at a large citywide conference on a presbytery prayer team where people lined up to be prayed over. There were three tents designated for this prayer time: one for healing, one for finances and one to receive the Father's blessing. Chris and I were assigned to the last. I remember thinking, *Oh, man! I wish they had put me in the healing tent! That is where all the action and crowd will be.* But to my surprise, the line for the Father's blessing tent was the longest of all three. It wound outside the tent and all the way down the hill. I was shocked. People wept when we merely spoke the love of a father over them.

I speak that blessing over you right now in the name of your heavenly Father—the best father on earth and in heaven—the great I AM. Because of Him, you can know exactly who and whose you are!

Corresponding Emotional Toxins

People who suffer with identity often struggle with feelings of insecurity, anxiety, timidity or fear. Let's pray now for God to renew your mind and spirit from these potential influences and to help you set new standards for yourself that will benefit your faith:

> *Lord, who do You say that I am? I will not be satisfied with becoming anything less. I give You any insecurities, anxieties, timidity and fear. You know my heart better than I do myself. Make me into the "me" You designed me to be. In Jesus' name, Amen.*

Correlating Physical Detox

Today and tomorrow we cleanse the sensory system.

Breakfast	Come to Your Senses Smoothie
Mid-a.m. Juicing	Warrior Tonic
Lunch	Pick Six Detox Soup
Snack	snack liberally from your oranges and greens
Dinner	choose one green and one orange fruit or vegetable (see Recipes for prep ideas); pair with brown rice or quinoa tossed with section spices and section nuts or beans
Nightcap	Detox Tea

Closing Blessing

May God cleanse your sensory system starting with your eyes—physically and spiritually—so that you can see the brand-new you!

DAY 30

Spiritual Toxin: You University

Congratulations! You have reached Day 30 of *The 30-Day Faith Detox*! This book was intended to shake off whatever doubts ailed your faith and spirit, heal your emotions from their residue, and mend your body from its physical manifestations. You have had a whole month to focus on just you, as if you were going back to school at You U! Section 8 will be full of questions about what you have learned so that you can measure your own outcome. It is a no-pressure assessment but is necessary so you can see how far you have come. Plus, we want to determine what you are going to do with all this new and improved faith so that you can begin influencing others with it.

But first, I want to take a look back at what you have done this month. It is quite a lot!

In Section 1, we talked about the force of faith, and you weighed and measured your faith's current condition. I hope you realized that without healthy faith you cannot believe in the miraculous or the supernatural. In fact, without faith, you are not a Christian at all, since it takes faith to become one. In this portion of the book you were reminded that you are made up of three inseparable parts: spirit, mind and body. You also learned that there is a link between what you eat and what you think, between what you think and the condition of your faith, and thereby, there is a very probable food-faith link. It is my prayer that if you were chemically propelling yourself toward doubt through poor food choices, this detox has helped you set better dietary habits and moved you to a majority diet of living foods vs. dead ones.

In Section 2, you set some ambitious goals for the month. How did you do with them? Were you able to give God a tithe of your waking hours and spend an hour and a half working through this book, praying and just listening to Him each day? Did you sleep nine hours each night? It is very likely that you could not do that every night, but at least now it is on your mind to try to make sleep more of a priority. Did you try new vegetables if you were a vegetable hater? And how did you do with those occasional Epsom baths and skin-brushings? Maybe you even bought a portable sauna. The bottom line is that even if you were unable to meet each day's goals, you made *some* changes, and *some* changes lead to even more changes.

In Section 3, you took back control over all of your appetites and unhealthy environments. You examined the media you ingest, which might be infecting your faith. Congratulations if you

229

pruned them from your life. You also learned to avoid ungodly counsel, break soul-ties, keep standing when your heroes fall, avoid church splits and their aftermaths, and I hope you even got a more well-rounded perspective on world catastrophic events and natural disasters. You confronted emotions of doubt, anger, agitation, lust, disillusionment, confusion, uncertainty and fear, and asked God to heal your mind. Finally, you cleansed your digestive, excretory and urinary systems, including your liver. Your bodily filters are now clean! Just imagine what a healthy position that puts you in if you will only maintain it.

In Section 4, you tackled those pesky financial toxins that rob your peace. You learned ten traits of promoted people as evidenced in God's Word. You learned not to sin against God by withholding your tithes from His storehouse, which calls down a curse upon your life and finances. You even learned the ten things *not to do* if you want to stay stuck and never get ahead in life. We prayed a blessing upon your efforts to have and maintain your own home, and you were challenged to have a "stuff liquidation" and redefine "enough." I even shared with you my top twenty Scriptures on what the Bible says about finances so that you can be convinced God is concerned with what you do with them. You faced your fears about money as well as your frustrations, jealousies, anger, rejection, stress, confusion, failures, embarrassments and despairs. In the meantime you cleansed your endocrine, nervous, and reproductive systems as a powerful statement that you are regulating healthier responses to financial strains, increasing your productivity and retraining your brain to embrace the success God has called you to be!

In Section 5, you tackled the health-related toxins with which the enemy has sought to take down you and your faith. You learned the Ten Healing Commandments, which are the cure for sick and tired. Did you memorize them? Never too late! You learned the difference between healings and miracles so that you can understand and not be discouraged when healing takes time. We explored what I believe is false teaching—that Paul's thorn was a disease or affliction God refused to heal him of— and learned how to make your persecution-afflictions work for you and why God allows them to begin with. Then we learned about that little *sozo* word with the big promise of salvation, healing and deliverance, and how the war on wellness is actually a war on your very salvation and on the global Gospel itself. You eradicated the sources of your weariness, disappointments, grief, impatience and anger, while simultaneously detoxing your immune, lymphatic and respiratory systems, signaling to the enemy that you are now more immune to his attacks on your spirit, mind and body.

From Section 6, on relationship toxins, you gleaned the skills to hold your head high and refuse rejection and estrangement with family members and friends. You learned how to pray for your unsaved loved ones and how to respond in unhealthy environments where physical or verbal abuse is present. As a single, single-again, widowed or divorced person, you learned that there is a difference between loneliness and being alone. If from a failed marriage, you gained insight on the seven steps toward finding healing for your heart. And if you lost a loved one too soon in life, you learned to hold on to the healing Gospel and to trust it despite what you saw or see, knowing that God has a plan and is still at work to use the situation for His and your good. You worked through your sorrow, bitterness, rejection, betrayal, loneliness, sadness and more, and since we were discussing the people you love (those in your heart and those who get under your skin), you cleansed your cardiovascular, circulatory and integumentary systems for a fresh start all around.

Finally in this section, Section 7, you asked God about your purpose and identity. You discovered what might be delaying your deliverance, and how to stay on the "up and up" concerning your unanswered prayers and unfulfilled prophecies. You learned how to wait on God, how *not* to wait on God, and how to hold on to Him during the many faces of persecution (which Jesus said would come to us). You even learned about finding your identity in Christ so that no identity thief can steal your purpose for being on this earth. You have tackled your insecurities, frustrations, despondencies, discouragements and embarrassments and taken them down! You are even fresh on the heels of the detoxification of your skeletal, muscular and sensory systems, reminding you to stand tall and see yourself as the "you-nique" person God has created you to be!

As you now move into Section 8, I am going to ask you some inspiring questions, and you can determine how effective you think this detox was for you and where you should go from here. If you feel you did not complete a particular faith-detox offered to you during a devotion, the good news is that you can go back at any time and repeat that day, and I encourage you to do the accompanying bodily detox regimen and pray the prayers for emotion healing, too. In fact, you can isolate any portion of this book at any time for a booster shot in your faith. Are you ready? Let the results begin!

Corresponding Emotional Toxins

People who complete a thirty-day faith-building devotional guide for the spirit, mind and body are filled with hope and resolve! Expectancy and faith! So this time, I am going to pray for *you* so that we can guard what you have accomplished and hear from the Lord on what to do with all this newfound faith. You ready?

Right now, in Jesus' name, I ask God to put a hedge of protection around your spirit, your mind and your body. You have taken the initiative, invested the time and resources into this book, prayed the prayers, prepared the detoxes, and now I am asking God to add His super to your natural and bless your efforts. Father, bless these efforts! You say in Your Word that without faith it is impossible to please You, so, Father, reward this obvious display of obedience with newfound faith! And add to that newfound healing, opportunities, love, promotions, finances, wisdom, wellness, unity and answers. Thank You for the journey, God, and now I entrust my friend to You in this new season. In Jesus' name, Amen!

Correlating Physical Detox

Today we finish cleansing the sensory system. Repeat yesterday's meal plan, experimenting with this section's colors.

Closing Blessing

May God finish the cleansing of your sensory system—your sight, hearing, taste, touch and smell—while increasing your spiritual senses to be able to discern His direction for your new faith-filled walk with Him.

SECTION 8

Day 31

In these thirty days, you have evaluated your faith and the trials that have bombarded it in five main areas of your life: (1) social influences, (2) your finances, (3) your health, (4) your relationships and (5) your identity. Before that, in Sections 1 and 2, you learned some new things about total temple health and how what you eat affects how you think, which then directly affects your faith. You have been challenged, spirit, mind and body!

Now it is a new day. Day 31! It is the first day of your life with a toxin-free faith that is spiritually sound, emotions that are healed from previous pains and a body that is detoxified and has set new habits! You are now a stronger, sharper, more focused child of God. The sky is the limit for you!

With that exciting progress in mind, I want to ask you some thought-provoking questions about your journey. You listened to me for thirty days, and now you need to listen to yourself.

You need to have a frank conversation with the new you about where you are going from here.

The following questions are conversation starters. You can convey the answers in one of three ways:

1. Write them down in a journal.
2. Speak them aloud to God in prayer.
3. Discuss them with a friend, one at a time.

While I can see the benefit of each, I suggest that you include #3, even if you choose #1 or #2. The reason is that it builds accountability so that you might maintain everything you have worked so hard to accomplish this month. Maybe you even went through this thirty-day detox with a friend, as suggested, so that you can continue to process your results together.

The questions are simple. The answers may be simple, too, but do not let your simple answers eclipse the profound outcomes. Are you ready to look at the fruit of the last 720 hours? I am excited for you to see the answers!

I hope you will also share some of your answers with me. Remember to go to my Facebook author page wall (www.Facebook.com/LauraHarrisSmithPage) and let me know what God has done in you these last thirty days—spirit, mind or body. Let the world know! Here we go.

Q&A

Section 1: Look at your old diet and determine the ratio of living foods to dead foods. Review these definitions, if necessary. In the last thirty days, your percentage has been 100 percent living food! So after one month of eating whole foods, can you tell a difference in the way you feel or think? And has your unclouded thinking led to unclouded faith? Explain. And post your thoughts for me!

Section 2: What were your favorite new foods from this month? What is the most significant change you have seen in your body in the last thirty days? Greater energy? Weight loss? Clearer skin? More rested? Better digestion? Greater immunities? A changed palate? List all changes and make note of the new foods that will become part of your weekly grocery list.

Section 3: This important section's faith-detoxing devotionals were not only the first but the longest. Name any changes you have made in your media intake. That includes all television, music via radio or devices, talk radio, magazines, books, news and all forms of social media. Which new changes can you make?

Section 4: What did you learn about your finances this month? About promotion? And what about sharing, gifting or selling your "stuff"? Finally, what did you learn about tithing? Are you a tither? Why or why not?

Section 5: Did you have any health-related breakthroughs this month? Did you learn the cure for "sick and tired"? Do you feel able to give a defense for why Paul's thorn was not a chronic disease or affliction? Finally, see how many of the Ten Healing Commandments you can remember. And memorize the rest so that you will know what to do when sickness comes knocking!

Section 6: Did you experience any new insights about the relationships in your life? About how to handle rejection, abuse or loneliness? Are you praying the Scriptures listed over your unsaved loved ones? Finally, has your faith healed from losing that loved one too soon in life?

Section 7: Do you feel you now have more faith to address your unanswered prayers and unfulfilled prophecies? Do you feel more educated on deliverance and persecution? Finally, what new things did you learn about yourself in this section, and in this last month?

Remember, I want you to post your victories, recipes, break-throughs and feedback: www.Facebook.com/LauraHarrisSmith Page.

A Well-Deserved Blessing

I want to leave you with a blessing. You have earned it! I am so proud of you for embarking upon this journey, and humbled that you would trust me to accompany you. If I were with you now I would lay my hands on you and pray for a fresh filling of God's Holy Spirit. If you are able, get somewhere quiet and let me pray this final blessing over you.

In the name of the Father, Son and Holy Spirit, I speak a newfound energy to your spirit, mind and body. He is three, and so are you, in His image. I declare that what you started here, you will continue, and that Christ will complete the good work begun in you. I declare that your social influences are pure, your finances are plenty, your health is sound, your relationships are whole and your identity is secure in Christ Jesus. You are clean! Your faith is strong! "Now may the God of peace Himself sanctify you completely, and may your whole spirit and soul and body be kept blameless at the coming of our Lord Jesus Christ" (1 Thessalonians 5:23). In Jesus' name, Amen.

Recipes

Experts' opinions vary greatly on which color vegetables and fruits benefit which organs, but I have arranged and assigned them to the body systems based on my personal research as a starting place for your easy remembering. The good news is, all colors and their nutrients are represented in this book, so you will benefit from every one by the end of it!

Make sure to review the "Yes, Please" and "No, Thanks" lists from Section 2.

BREAKFAST SMOOTHIES

Stevia is my preferred choice for these recipes because it is a natural, zero-calorie sweetener, so use it to bring extra guilt-free sweetness to any dish, especially my smoothies and shakes (or experiment with small amounts of agave, honey, coconut crystals or grade B pure maple syrup).

Yogurt is chock-full of living enzymes, but I generally do not include it in smoothies for two reasons: (1) new studies show that blending disrupts and destroys its living enzymes, and (2) a banana and a milk provide the same consistency and are more flavorful. Substitute with 1 cup yogurt if you prefer, but fold in after blending other ingredients.

Smoothie Base for All Smoothies

½ cup   milk or water (milks: organic 2%, unsweetened almond milk, coconut milk; waters: coconut water, aloe water or filtered water)

1 Tbsp.   olive oil, flaxseed oil or coconut oil (each provides different flavors, so experiment)

½ cup   ice

Note: Blend all smoothies on high until smooth, using additional milk or water if necessary. Consider adding a raw egg for morning protein if you are worried about feeling weak. I don't ever find I need one, but if you do, choose organic. Never store smoothies; drink fresh.

The Yummy Tummy Trimmer Smoothie

Smoothie Base (choose a milk)
1   banana
½   avocado
½ cup   fresh pineapple
juice of 1 lemon
¼ tsp.   chopped ginger root
2 Tbsp.   honey
(for more sweetness, add stevia or agave)

Bottoms Up Detox Smoothie

Smoothie Base (choose a water)
handful of spinach
2   yellow apples with peel, sliced
½   a peeled lemon
⅛ tsp.   cayenne pepper
½ tsp.   turmeric

The New Kidney on the Block Blast

Smoothie Base (choose a water)
2 bananas
2 peeled kiwis
15 cranberries
½ cucumber (with peel)
½ a peeled lemon
¼ tsp. chopped ginger root
1 Tbsp. cilantro (or parsley)
½ tsp. turmeric
1 Tbsp. honey
1–2 tsp. powder stevia
(blend until kiwi seeds disappear)

Endocrine Energy Boost

Smoothie Base (choose a milk)
2 bananas
30 coffee beans (regular or decaf)
2 raw brown eggs
1 tsp. powder stevia
4 tsp. grade B organic maple syrup (or blackstrap molasses)
½ tsp. cinnamon (optional, but cinnamon boosts the endocrine system)
(more stevia for sweetness)

Brain Boosting Banana Choco Chip Smoothie

Smoothie Base (choose a milk)
2 bananas
2 square inches dark chocolate bar (at least 75% cocoa)
(optional 20–30 coffee beans, regular or decaf)
2 Tbsp. honey
(for more sweetness, add stevia or agave)

241

The Hormone Fixer Elixir

Smoothie Base (choose a milk)
½ cup   cashews
2   bananas
1   brown egg
1   cup kale
½ tsp.   cinnamon
¼ tsp.   turmeric

Love Your Lungs Smoothie

Smoothie Base (choose a water)
2 cups   purple (or red) grapes
1 cup   pomegranate arils*
3 drops   peppermint flavoring or oil or 3 peppermint leaves

*It is next to impossible to separate the pomegranate seeds from their yummy pulp. These are called "arils." So toss your pomegranate arils in the blender first, blend on high, pour off the liquid and trash the gritty seeds. Then return juice to blender and add other ingredients. This is one of the most uniquely flavored smoothies I have created and I want you to enjoy it.

Lick the Spoon Immune Purple Slurp

Smoothie Base (choose a water)
1 cup   seedless concord grapes (or just purple or red grapes)
1 cup   blueberries
1   cubed plum
1   banana
½ cup   almonds or pistachios, etc.

The Clean Spleen Cider

The spleen loves warm foods. Cold or frozen foods mean more work for this body filter and result in what some call "spleen damp." So to target and nourish the spleen, foods must be cooked or at least brought to room temperature. With that in mind, today and tomorrow's breakfast smoothie is not a smoothie at all, but a cider. I have also placed this spleen detox to fall when you are enjoying your Pick Six Detox Soup for the next two days. Your tonsils and lymph nodes will enjoy the warmth, too!

No Smoothie Base today. Fill blender with:

2 cups	purple (or red) grapes
1 stalk	celery, chunked
½ tsp.	cinnamon
2 tsp.	powder stevia

Warm 2 cups cranberry juice on the stove (not juice cocktail)
Pour over berries in blender
Blend and sip

The Heart Beet Berry Smoothie

	Smoothie Base (choose a water)
2 cups	strawberries
1 cup	red grapes
¼	of a large beet
¼ cup	almonds, pistachios or walnuts
¼ tsp.	cayenne

The Chocolate Cherry Circulation Smoothie

	Smoothie Base (choose a milk)
1 cup	pitted cherries
1 cup	red apple slices
1 cup	strawberries
2 square inches	dark chocolate bar (with at least 75% cocoa)
1 tsp.	powder stevia

243

The Bright Skin Blend

	Smoothie Base (choose a water; coconut water is great for skin!)
1	avocado
1	banana
1 cup	kale
1 cup	fresh pineapple
4	mint leaves
	juice of 1 lime
1 Tbsp.	honey
½ cup	almonds
½ cup	or more water

The Bone Fuel Boost

	Smoothie Base (choose a milk today for bones; almond milk has about 15 percent more calcium than dairy)
1	orange
½	grapefruit
1 cup	kale
1	banana
1	large romaine lettuce leaf
1	large carrot
1	raw egg
½ cup	almonds
3 heaping Tbsp.	honey

The Muscle Flex Protein (Espresso) Smoothie

	Smoothie Base (choose a milk)
2	bananas
1 Tbsp.	nut butter of choice
1	raw egg
20	coffee beans (or more peanut butter)

Come to Your Senses Smoothie

	Smoothie Base (choose a water)
1	large carrot
1	peach
1	orange
½	avocado
½ cup	spinach
3 tsp.	stevia powder
	add ½ more cup water
	(add any of this section's "hearing herbs" if you suffer from hearing loss or ringing in ears)

JUICINGS

(sweeten with stevia if desired)

Laura's One-Two Punch

Using your section colors, juice 4 cups each of 1 vegetable and 2 fruits. Drink immediately, but do not gulp.

Four-of-a-Kind Juice

Using your section colors, juice 4 fruits, add 1 section spice and drink immediately.

Warrior Tonic

Using your section colors, juice 1–2 cups each of all (or a majority) of the green vegetables and add 1 Tbsp. apple cider vinegar (raw and unfiltered). The tonic will not be sweet, but add an apple or two for flavor.

245

LUNCHES

Sixcess Salad

Dice 1 cup each of 6 of your section color's fruits and vegetables and combine with 6 cups of a dark leafy green lettuce of your choice. For dressing, drizzle with olive oil, apple cider vinegar (raw and unfiltered) and fresh citrus juice of choice. Sprinkle with any of your section spices and sea or Himalayan salt.

Take-Five Stir Fry

Choose 2 cups each of 5 vegetables from your section's list. Dice and sauté until tender in skillet with 2 Tbsp. olive oil and ½ cup water. Add sea or Himalayan salt and section spices or herbs to taste, or for international versions, try:

Italian: oregano, basil, garlic, rosemary, thyme, bay leaf
Asian: turmeric, ginger, chilies, wheat-free soy sauce (Tamari brand)
Mexican: cumin, onion powder, cilantro, coriander, chilies

Pick Six Detox Soup

Select 3 cups each of 6 vegetables from your section's list. Place in large pot and fill 3 inches above vegetable line with filtered water or low-sodium chicken broth. Add sea or Himalayan salt, along with your choice of the section's herbs and spices. (Refrigerate second serving for next day.)

DINNER MEAT ENTRÉES

As I have said, during this detox, it would be beneficial to your body to abstain from meat (including fish). Remember that only organic chicken, turkey and fresh fish or fresh frozen fish from healthy sources are allowed.

Meat (Poultry) Entrées

Lean poultry (chicken or turkey) should be baked, sautéed, grilled or broiled. Whichever meat and method you prefer, drizzle with olive oil, add any section spices or herbs and cook with medium heat.

Reed's Nut-Encrusted Fish

Anne Reed, M.S., N.C.

1 lb.	any variety fish cut into 3 oz. fillets
½ cup	nuts, finely ground (pecans, almonds, walnuts . . .)
3	egg whites
	spices (Herbamare or section's spices)

Rinse and pat very dry. Rub in spices of choice. Dip fish in egg whites then roll firmly in nut meal, baking at 275º for 20–30 minutes. Fish is done when it flakes easily with fork.

EXTRAS

Godfather's Healing Soup

Dr. Rucele Consigny

In a slow cooker, lay a 3–4 lb. whole chicken on a bed of:

1	sliced onion
4	celery pieces, halved
2	carrots, halved
3	whole garlic cloves

Add 1 cup chicken broth.
Dribble desired olive oil over chicken.
Sprinkle with Worcestershire sauce.
Dust with salt and fresh-ground pepper.

Slow cook on low 8–9 hours. Remove chicken, saving broth and ingredients. Peel off meat and return bones and unwanted chicken pieces to broth. Add 2 cups water or broth and bring to boil. Simmer covered for 4 to 5 hours. Strain with colander and discard solids. Strain again with fine sieve or strainer. Add to the clean broth:

4	carrots, sliced thickly
2	potatoes, diced
½	onion, diced
2 Tbsp.	fresh parsley
1 tsp.	red pepper flakes
1 Tbsp.	dried chives
	pulled chicken, to taste

Bring to boil and simmer for 13 minutes or until carrots are tender. Salt and pepper to taste.

Tam's To-Your-Health Roasted Vegetables (use for any veggie combo)

Tamara Rowe, The Wellness Coach

Drizzle 2 lbs. of beets, Brussels sprouts, onions, etc. (small pieces/wedges of any vegetable) with 1 Tbsp. extra-virgin olive oil. Sprinkle with sea salt/pepper to taste. Place in 425° oven for 40–45 minutes. Use for any veggie combo!

Sautéed Vegetables

See "Take-Five Stir Fry" for ideas on stovetop preparation of vegetables.

Fruitful Salad

Janice Harris

1 cup	orange sections
1 cup	pineapple cubes
1 cup	seedless green grapes, halved
½ cup	blueberries
1 cup	unsweetened shredded coconut

Dressing (whisk together):

2 tsp.	lemon juice
1 tsp.	grated orange rind

2 Tbsp.   honey
1 cup   yogurt

Stir into fruit and refrigerate for at least an hour.

Then add:

½ cup   sliced strawberries
1   banana
    toasted almonds

Quinoa and Brown Rice

As a delicious side dish for evening meals, prepare 1 cup of brown rice or quinoa per package instructions and in final 7 minutes of cooking add pine nuts, chopped garlic and section herbs or spices. Quinoa is preferred because it is a complete protein, meaning it provides all nine essential amino acids necessary for good health. Gluten-free, its nickname is "the mother grain."

Cashew Rice and Peas

Dr. Jim Sharps, N.D., H.D., Dr.N.Sc., Ph.D.

brown rice
curry powder
roasted, salted whole cashews or cashew pieces
cooked peas

Cook the brown rice using the package directions or the rice cooker directions, but use canned vegetable broth instead of water and use olive oil instead of plain oil. Add curry powder to the rice water before you cook the rice. When the rice is done cooking, stir in the cashews and cooked peas and serve.

Orange Jasmine Rice

Dr. Elisa Ramirez-Sharps, N.D., C.C.H., C.N.C.

2 cups   jasmine or brown rice
1 14-oz. can   vegetable broth
½ cup   orange juice
½ cup   water

2 Tbsp.	sesame oil
1 tsp.	powdered ginger
¼ tsp.	sea salt
¼ tsp.	onion powder
¼ tsp.	garlic powder

Put the rice in a fine sieve and run water over it until the water coming out of the strainer is clear, not cloudy. Allow the rice to drain for a minute. Put all ingredients in a rice cooker and cook until the rice is plump and tender.

SNACK SHAKES

All shakes are blended until desired consistency using additional milk or water if necessary.

Shake Base

½ cup	organic milk or almond milk
1 Tbsp.	honey
½ tsp.	powder stevia (more to taste)

Baby Banana Split Shake

	Shake Base
1	banana
6	strawberries
½ cup	pineapple (optional)
¼ cup	nuts of choice
1 tsp.	unsweetened cocoa powder
1–2	fresh cherries on top

The Carrot Cake Shake

	Shake Base
2	carrots, chunked
1 tsp.	cinnamon
½ tsp.	nutmeg and cloves

| 1 tsp. | vanilla extract |
| 2 Tbsp. | walnuts |

Peanut Butter Jelly Time Shake

	Shake Base
½ cup	no-sugar-added grape juice
4	strawberries
2 Tbsp.	creamy peanut butter (or PB2 powdered peanut butter)

Good Mornin' Sunshine Shake

	Shake Base
½ cup	papaya
2	large oranges
	(add ½ cup cantaloupe for a tropical flavor)

DRINKS

Nanny's Fruit Punch

Janice Harris

2 cups	unsweetened apple juice
2 cups	unsweetened pineapple juice
1 cup	fresh orange juice
¼ cup	lemon juice
	lemon slice and mint to garnish

Trish's Cleansing Potassium Broth

Trish Beverstein

To remove toxins from the body, alkalinize and re-mineralize the system.

| 3 | jalapeños, deseeded |
| 4 bulbs | garlic, peeled |

2	large onions
4 stalks	celery
5 lbs.	carrots
1 bunch	kale
3	beets, with greens
3 lbs.	potatoes, with skins

Bring a large pot of filtered water to boil. As water heats, fill with *chopped* veggies, including favorite spices and sea salt. Water should cover veggies.

Cover and simmer gently for 1 hour. Remove from heat; leave lid on pot. Let sit for another hour.

Strain and sip on liquid all day, as desired.

Fountain of Youth Detox Water

(Counts toward your daily water quota.)

1	cucumber, thinly sliced
1	lemon, sliced
1	orange, sliced
10	mint leaves

Add to 1 pitcher filtered water and let sit overnight.

Nightcap Detox Tea

Brew 1 tea bag each of dandelion root and milk thistle in 1–2 cups water and add 1 Tbsp. honey or stevia. Sip before bedtime. Add a bag from any tea recommendations on your section's grocery list, or sip them during the day.

Dandelion is known in Persia as "the little postman" because it always brings the body good news, gently cleansing it whenever sipped. Traditional Medicinals makes a healthy Roasted Dandelion Root Tea.

Milk thistle's main ingredient is silymarin and is both an anti-inflammatory and antioxidant. Alvita makes a hearty milk thistle tea.

Celestial Seasonings makes a Natural Detox Wellness Tea containing both dandelion and milk thistle, plus echinacea, red clover, roasted barley, licorice, roasted chicory and sarsaparilla.

TRUXTON WHISKEY

A ROUTE 66 MYSTERY

by

MICHAEL ALLAN SCOTT

Cover art: Copyright © 2024 - Michael Allan Scott

Cover design by Michael Allan Scott

Cover photography by Cynthia A. Scott

Cover background photo © North2south

Logo design by Michael Manoogian of Michael Manoogian Logo Design

Author photograph by Cynthia A. Scott

Published by MAS-9375

Version: 2024.11.13

ISBN 13: 979-8-9920008-0-1 (paperback)

Contents

Dedication

T HIS SERIES WAS INSPIRED by and is dedicated to my mother, Shirley
  S. Scott.

Preface

R OUTE 66, WINDING FROM Chicago to L.A., and memorialized in song as "the highway that's the best." These days, as a tourist destination, it's easier than ever to get your kicks. Back in the day, it was a workhorse, paving the road to progress.

On its way through Arizona, historic Route 66 opened the doors to Winslow, Flagstaff, and Kingman, along with several whistlestops along the way. Oatman, Hackberry, and Truxton are but a few.

It was the late 1940s when Sara arrived in Kingman permanently, as the new bride of Sam Wayland. At age twenty, she sparkled with ice-blue eyes over a perfect smile. Tallish at five-foot-six, she was lithe and shapely, with long golden locks framing her angelic face. An aircraft mechanic during the war, Sam was tall at six-foot-three. Above a ruggedly handsome face, he sported a full head of black hair slicked back into a loose pompadour. Though his teeth weren't perfectly straight, his smile was genuine with blazing hazel eyes that captured her heart. Sara and Sam were a pair.

In 1970, the crew of Apollo 13 survived an explosion in deep space, Simon & Garfunkel's, "Bridge Over Troubled Water" topped the pop music charts, and Route 66 was in the throes of decline, largely abandoned or paved over with new Interstate freeways.

By that same year, Sara and Sam and their two boys had worked through hard times, made good friends, and enjoyed their hard-won success. At age forty-four, Sara thought things would be easier from here on out. She still had her looks. The boys were grown. She and Sam were very much married, a tight-knit couple, comfortable with each other. Good partners, Sam ran the show while she covered the bases—hand in glove. And, with their house and vehicles paid off and money in the bank, life was running fairly smooth.

With Sam busy most days, Sara filled more of her free time with her closest companion, Rocko. Having more or less inherited her youngest son's large yellow lab when he left for Arizona State University, she couldn't imagine what she would do without Rocko. Intuitively smart, he was her sixth sense. He couldn't be more dear.

As we begin, Route 66 holds still as a snake, its crippled back cracked and crumbling in the Arizona sun. Up the road, new adventures await Sara and her sweet boy, Rocko.

April 5, 1970

Bryant & Wamaya

MAKING OFF WITH A near-empty bottle of Old Grand Dad from Mom's cupboard, the pie-faced Bryant Watachka, a gangly thirteen-year-old Hualapai, left early this morning, hiking miles through the high desert southwest of Peach Springs, sipping little tastes of whiskey as he wandered off the reservation.

Bryant tried to steal Mom's whiskey before, but it's not easy. When she's home, she carries the bottle around like a child with her blanket. When she's not, she keeps it locked in her closet. To find it in the cupboard was a windfall; she must have forgotten. He was after some Twinkies when he found it—what luck.

Bryant thought about taking it to school, hiding it in his locker, but then he would have to share. He decided he would finish off the bottle, then tell his schoolmates he drank the whole thing, showing off. They would have to drink their own bottle if they wanted to be like him.

Late in the day, at the edge of the reservation, a blood-red sun drops behind a rose-banded rim snaking along the Lower Granite Gorge. Alone and miles from nowhere, Bryant drops to his knees gasping for air. Thick mucus flows from his nose, his eyes blurred with streaming tears, his dark skin burning, his lungs on fire. Less than fifteen minutes ago, when it blew up in his face, the boy went into shock and has been running for home ever since.

Chest heaving, Bryant wails as he pours the last of the whiskey over his head, frantically rubbing his face, trying to wash off the stinging pain. Clutching the empty bottle to his chest, he bursts into another coughing fit. He struggles to his feet, gasping as he stumbles to the edge of a deep arroyo. Losing his balance, the boy tumbles down the steep bank, rolling to a stop in the tall brush at the edge of the sandy bottom—his heart, stopped dead.

·········

Forlorn, Wamaya Watachka, an obese young woman with skin the color of coal dust, slumps at her tiny kitchen table. The round-faced Hualapai mother stares out the little window of a shabby single-wide through the fading twilight. Her son has been gone all day. Not all that unusual, but it is getting dark, and she can't find her whiskey. She has a fifth in the closet, unopened. But Wamaya is sure she left the last of a bottle in the cupboard. There wasn't much, but she wants to finish it off before she cracks open her next bottle.

Another worthless day evaporates, leaving her empty. Anxiety creeps up on her like a ravenous demon. Wamaya doesn't dare think about how she ended up like this: alone with her unruly son, trapped on the reservation, living in a tin can on a sub-poverty subsistence doled out with a long list of caustic rules by the white man's Bureau of Indian Affairs.

Bryant's father, Jasper, left the reservation years ago to go it alone. Living in Kingman, he chases white women, works odd jobs, and wastes his meager pay in the skid row bars, playing the white man's clown. Wamaya can't care anymore. He gets what he deserves as far as she is concerned.

Times like these, Wamaya wishes she had a phone. Waddling to the closet, she unlocks the flimsy door and reaches for her last fifth of Old Grand Dad. She needs her whiskey, needs to drown out the despair, keep the hopelessness at bay. She twists off the cap and takes a big swig, worry clawing at her like a rabid badger. Where is her son?

Eight Days Later

Burma Shave

Aʙᴏᴠᴇ Mᴇᴛᴄᴀʟғᴇ Rᴏᴀᴅ ᴀᴛ the top of Spring Street, the two-and-a-half-story Wayland home perches on the steep face of their three-acre hillside lot. Across the wash and down a piece, the highway hums with traffic. Cobbled together from surplus barracks after the war, the house faces southeast into a gusty breeze. Cool and fragrant with wildflowers, the air is pregnant with the promise of renewal. Springtime in Kingman has its moments.

In their boxy kitchen at a little past eight a.m., Sara Wayland sets a big mug of fresh coffee on the plastic placemat in front of her husband. "Here you go."

Sam looks up from this morning's Mohave County Miner with a quick smile. "Thanks, Mom."

"Not much of a mom, these days," she says wistfully. Sara turns back to the spotless linoleum counter to grab her coffee. "I miss 'em."

"We knew they were gonna leave someday." Snapping his paper as he turns the page, Sam raises an eyebrow. "Think of all the free time you've got to paint," he says amiably.

Sara holds up a chew bone for a hefty yellow lab with an eager grin. Rocko lifts onto his hindlegs and snaps his morning bone out of her fingers.

"Yes," she says as she sits. "Speaking of which, Rocko and I are going on a field trip. I'm going to try a watercolor landscape. I'll be gone all day. You don't need the truck today, do you?"

Rocko lays down next to her feet, pins the chew bone with a paw and begins to gnaw.

"Take the truck. I'll be in the step van all day." Sam folds his paper, lifting his gaze to Sara. In their twenty-four years of marriage, she has never ceased to amaze him. She abandoned her artist's life to stand by his side, help him build their business, and raise their two sons. At forty-four, she may have some miles on her, but that same ol' magic still shines. Smart and tough, and what a beauty. He's lucky, and he knows it.

Sara sips her Folgers as their eyes meet. Twisting her cup between her hands, she lowers it to the table and smiles. "Good." Sam has been rock-steady, he'll never change. Thank the Lord, she still has Sam. She thought once her oldest boy, Jack, left home, she would acclimate before it was Timmy's time. She simply wasn't expecting such a pernicious void when Timmy left for college.

Sam takes a swig from his earthen mug and smacks his lips. "Where ya headed?"

"I think I'll take a drive out to the reservation, somewhere around Truxton."

Sam nods. "Wide-open spaces... You know Truxton is just a mile or so this side of the reservation." He pushes back from the table and stands. "Have a good day." Heading for the back door, he stretches to pluck a light jacket off the coatrack. "And make sure your pistol is loaded."

"Bye, Honey." Sara reaches down to rub Rocko's head. "See you tonight."

Sara watches him close the back door on his way out, wondering how many times she has seen her husband leave for work. At forty-six, he cuts a manly figure, tall and rugged. And predictable, one of the many things she loves about him. She feels safe in her life with Sam, knowing he'll always be there for her.

Smiling, Sara recalls a time when Sam was showing young Jack how to handle his Woodsman .22 pistol. When Sam offered to teach her, she had never fired a gun, never been around guns growing up, didn't like the idea of guns or killing people. Sam changed all that with the first lesson. His motto: 'Better to have a gun and not need it, than need a gun and not have it.' Learning how to target-shoot was fun, confidence-boosting and great sport. They used to go to the range out in Slaughterhouse Canyon about once a month. They haven't been in ages. With the boys gone, maybe that will change.

······•·····

Rocko stands by the driver's door of their tall, four-wheel-drive truck, vigorously wagging his tail while Sara secures her new collapsible easel, her paintbox, and a small ice chest in the bed. At five-foot-six, she's not short, but every time she has a load of groceries or anything that needs to go in the bed, she wishes they had a step-side. Sam said they needed the larger-capacity fleet-side for work. The reliable, go anywhere, 1960 Ford F250 is her daily driver. She doesn't care much for the tan paint scheme, but it's easier to keep clean. They bought it with low miles several years ago. Sam does all the maintenance himself and it runs like a top. Mr. Fix-it won't let anybody else touch it.

It's nearly nine and she's as eager as Rocko to get going. The trek out to Truxton is a good forty-five-minute drive, and there are only so many usable hours of daylight. When she opens the driver's door, Rocko leaps into the cab and takes up position on the bench seat at shotgun. Grabbing the armrest with one hand and the door frame with the other, she stretches to brace a foot on the rocker panel. Sara climbs into the tall pickup with a grunt, plops down, and pulls the door closed. Leaning across Rocko to the glove box, she checks for the holstered .357 Magnum and the box of ammo—good to go. Pumping the gas once, she shifts to the brake pedal and stabs the stiff clutch with her other foot. The big V8 rumbles to life when she turns the key. She wrestles the tall shift lever into reverse and backs out on Spring Street.

Coasting down Metcalfe, Sara squints through the morning sun, forming a picture in her mind of the perfect spot to paint. Sam's right. She needs to broaden her horizons, take her mind off the boys, though she can't help wondering how they're doing. Well, Jack, she knows. Much like his father, he's a workaholic. Recently promoted to foreman, he takes his construction job in Phoenix seriously. Timmy is a little less predictable. And, from time to time, she catches herself worrying. He should be all right though, once he settles in. ASU is a top university, though its reputation as a party school concerns her a bit. Timmy can be a wild one.

Sara works her way through town, downshifting as four lanes of Andy Devine curve to climb up a deep cut through a rugged volcanic escarpment. At the top of the hill, she upshifts, changing the landscape painting in her head from a broad expanse of prairie covered in wild-flowers to rolling hills dotted with scruffy juniper.

Keeping to the fast lane, the offroad tires roar while the V8 growls. The Hilltop Motel to the left, the El Trovatore to her right, up ahead Corky's Barbeque, the City Café, and the Smokehouse, an all too familiar scene. Once they put the new freeway through, everything will change.

Sara scolds herself for not paying better attention to her oh-so-familiar surroundings. Her artistic instincts push her to observe the world around her. It's the details that bring out the authenticity in her paintings. Seeing the beauty and bringing it to life with colorful brushstrokes on paper, she needs practice. Though she dabbled in Fine Arts at UCLA, watercolor is a new medium for Sara. With the boys gone, she often wonders what life would have been like if she hadn't met Sam. A fateful night, one dance at the USO... then another.

As the gas stations and storefronts drop away, Andy Devine narrows to two lanes, dropping the honorary name and returning to Route 66. On the outskirts of town, railroad tracks of the Santa Fe pace the highway, straight as an arrow firing into the morning light. Having seen enough, Rocko stretches out to lay his head on her lap.

Ahead, the airfield rises out of the middle distance. Enormous aluminum tails of mothballed bombers stick out between the mammoth hangars like silver shark fins. Sara smiles at the memory of Sam flying his World War II trainer from Kingman to L.A. to court her on weekends. He swept her away.

As the last building disappears in Sara's mirrors, traffic thins to an occasional semi and a rare car or two. Green prairie surrounds the two-lane strip of worn asphalt. Fenced on both sides with barbwire, the paving forms a dark scar. Passing the other way, a mile-long, four-engine freight train rides the rails parallel to the road. The high desert blooms, alive with a patchwork of purple lupine, golden poppies, and fiery Indian paintbrush. Sara cranks her window down another inch, letting the wind fill her senses. She hasn't seen a wet Spring like this in years.

To her left a jagged ridge of dark basalt floats in a vast expanse of wildflowers like a gigantic Gila monster warming itself in the sun. The rare beauty of the flowering desert inspires Sara, capturing her imagination, holding her breathless with exhilaration. Broad vistas, boundless prairie, blue mountains at the horizon's edge, they are scenes unmatched, lasting for an instant then replaced, never to be repeated; this is why she loves painting landscapes.

Reaching the edge of the prairie, Route 66 rises to curve around the worn humps of the Peacock range. Crowding the horizon, the Music Mountains drop gnarled ridges from halfway to the sky, while puffs of cottony clouds parade high above. Her pulse quickens with the prospect of what's to come. Sara hasn't been out this way in a long time. In the early days, Sam used to take her on his vending route, servicing his jukeboxes, cigarette and pinball machines from the Shooting Star Café all the way to the Peach Springs Market. When Jack was old enough, he took over, riding with Dad as his hired hand while Sara held down the fort and did the books. Their vending business has always been a family affair. Sam took care of everything, the boys pitched in, learning the business and earning their keep along with a small allowance. Sara took care of Sam and still does, the love of her life. Sam, being Sam, works all hours nearly every day of the week and their business thrives.

The wildflowers lose their foothold as the big four-by-four rumbles through dark foothills covered with broken boulders of lava rock. The tall offroad tires thump on cracked concrete as she crosses Truxton Wash. Then the road narrows, swinging side-to-side, the curves tightening as it climbs the steepening grade. Sara rubs Rocko's head with a spare hand. He's Timmy's dog, left behind when Timmy moved to Tempe. While Timmy and Rocko are great pals, Sara raised him from a pup, seeing to Rocko's every need: food and water and his carefully guarded toys, rare trips to the vet, and loving on him every chance she gets. With Timmy off to college, she and Rocko are inseparable.

The red flying horse logo sits atop the antique Mobil sign in front of two old-timey gas pumps. As she passes, Sara smiles, knowing one of Sam's cigarette machines sits just inside the door of the Hackberry General Store. An old Chevy Corvair sits in front of a ramshackle shed next door. With a soft spot for the old ways—people with character and integrity—she lets nostalgia carry her away. She would stop, but she's on a mission, the itch to paint driving her farther up the road.

Her tan pickup powers up the slope through sharp cuts in the massive rocks, the road curving under thousand-foot-tall volcanic escarpments, the normally barren slopes alive with patches of green and red and gold. In awe of its grandeur, Sara can't stop grinning. What a beautiful day for a drive. She wishes Sam could see it. They don't spend the time together they once did, but she suspects that's how family life evolves. And with the boys grown... She strokes Rocko's neck, refusing to dwell on it. *What a good dog.*

Passing to her left, the remains of the Valentine township hug the base of the rugged hills. The Truxton Canyon Training School, a two-story brick schoolhouse, stands boarded up, fenced off, and abandoned since the late 1930s. Located on an isolated exclave of the Hualapai reservation, it serves as a monument to the misguided policies of the Bureau of Indian Affairs. Sara winces at the manner in which the Hualapai are routinely treated: second-class citizens, social pariahs, frowned upon for their public drunkenness. On the wrong side of the tracks, back off the road in Slaughterhouse Canyon, the Talotones and a few other Hualapai families huddle in rundown shacks. Sara came to know Squibby Talotone as one of Jack's schoolmates. Skin as dark as charcoal, hair thick and straight and blacker than night, he was a sweet boy, always polite, though timid, his spirit broken. She felt sorry for him. It broke her heart when they found him dead from alcohol poisoning in the alley behind Dinty Moore's skid row bar.

Climbing through the scrub juniper in Crozier Canyon, Sara surveys the hills for a site. She could stop anywhere along here and have several landscape vistas from which to choose. Topping out on a high plateau, the highway straightens, gently undulating across the prairie. Meadows covered with wild grasses stretch to stands of evergreen juniper, full bodied and rich with their forest green foliage. Tempting, but Sara pushes on. Truxton is just a few miles up the road.

A narrow, roadside sign pops into view. Red with white text, it reads 'IF YOU DON'T KNOW.'

Within a minute the next sign appears, 'WHOSE SIGNS THESE ARE.'

Then another, 'YOU HAVEN'T DRIVEN.'

And another, 'VERY FAR!'

Sara gives a crooked grin when she passes the last sign. '*Burma Shave.*'

Relics from an earlier time, rough and tumble. She wonders if Burma Shave is still in business these days.

No Buffalo

T HE SKY WIDENS, BRIGHT and blue as the eyes of Sara's first born. Tiny clumps of fleecy cumulus crowd the far horizon. Flattening out, the plateau stretches away from both sides of Route 66, leaving the rambling mountain ranges to fade to purple in the distance. Barely a wide spot in the road, Truxton comes into view. A small highway sign announces her arrival. To her right, a rundown motel and coffee shop squat on a dirt lot. From the state of their decay, Sara reckons they were built just after the war. Sam had a jukebox and cigarette machine in the coffee shop until they became unprofitable. Sara recalls the burnt coffee and high prices. She hasn't been inside for years.

Slowing, she signals for a left turn across the oncoming lane. Rocko perks up to watch through the windshield. Sara turns onto the dirt shoulder as her F250 rumbles into the Truxton Trading Post. Across the facia, tall red letters outlined with flashing neon read "GAS and LIQOUR." As she pushes in the clutch to coast, she remembers Sam explaining that Ol' Billy Sutter had to locate the liquor store at least a mile away from the reservation, and that his trading post is just a touch over a mile this side of the line.

The customer bell rings as she pulls up to the first of two elderly gas pumps. She gazes at the front of the store, waiting for an attendant. Through the windows, there doesn't appear to be anyone in the store, though it's hard to tell from this angle. She doesn't need gas all that bad. She had a little more than half a tank when she left Kingman. She could make it back, but she'd be running on empty.

The engine ticks as it cools. Sara gives it another minute or two before climbing down out of her truck. "Wait," she tells Rocko. Cutting between the pumps, she crosses the dirt drive and pushes through the storefront door. The little bell above the door tinkles as she enters the empty store.

Sam's cigarette machine stands just inside. According to Sam, it's the best machine on his northern route, claiming Ol' Billy, and Cora, his Apache wife, are doing a land office business selling liquor to the Hualapai.

Sara moves to the soda section and pulls a frosty bottle of Seven Up from the cooler. Working through the aisles of candy and snacks, she walks up to the register, sets her Seven Up on the glass-top counter and looks around. "Anybody home?" she says loudly.

"Coming," a thin voice says.

Sara turns, catching the young half-breed as he appears from the back.

The boy is tall and lanky with skin like dark butter. His almond-shaped eyes sit wide in a face shaped like a heart. Lionel Sutter scurries spider-like around the end of the counter, rushing up behind the big National cash register with a timid smile. "Hello," he says politely as he eyes her soda. "Is that everything?"

"I need gas, too."

Lionel looks up, his smile broadening with a hint of recognition in his eyes. "Do you want to pay now?"

Sara digs in her purse, counts out three ones and hands them over. "This is for the gas. Please fill it up," she says. "How much for the soda?"

Lionel eyes her up and down. "Do you have a dime?"

Fishing around in her purse for change, she looks up to catch him staring.

"I think I know you," he says softly.

Sara gives him a big smile as she hands him a dime. "Of course. You are the Sutters' son, aren't you? I'm Sara Wayland. You know... The cigarette machine... Sam."

Lionel bobs his head. "Yeah."

"I haven't seen you since you were a little boy," she says beaming. "What's your name, son?"

Unwinding, he straightens up, laying his long fingers on the counter. "Lionel, ma'am."

"Just call me Sara, Lionel."

He dips his pointy chin. "Yes ma'am." He starts back around the counter. "Lemme fill 'er up for ya."

Sara takes a sip of icy Seven Up as she turns for the door. Following him out to the truck, she asks, "How are your parents? I haven't seen them in ages."

"They're in town, picking up supplies," Lionel says over his shoulder. "They should be back before noon."

"Tell them hi for me."

Rocko scoots over, wagging his tail as she climbs into the cab. Sara cranks down her window and settles in to watch Lionel work. Grabbing the nozzle, he turns on the pump. In a flash, he removes her gas cap, inserts the nozzle, squeezes the handle and sets the catch. Turning to the cleaning station, he pulls the squeegee out of the soapy water and snaps off the excess with a flick of the wrist, then pulls two paper towels out of the dispenser. She smiles as he attacks her windshield. Stretching on tiptoes, he barely manages to reach all the glass. She admires his effort as he thoroughly wipes away the streaks.

As the nozzle clicks off, Lionel returns the squeegee and grabs two more paper towels. He moves to the front, reaching under to pop the hood. He twists the radiator cap, checking for pressure before releasing the cap. "Coolant is good," he says peering into the radiator.

Through the gap beneath the hood, Sara sees him draw out the dipstick, wipe it down, reinsert it and withdraw it to check the oil.

"Oil is okay," he says as he wipes down the dipstick and slides it home.

Sara is tickled by this young man. Good help is so rare, these days. It's refreshing to see after the rash of tourist rip-offs at Kingman service stations along 66. Slashing tires, squirting oil on perfectly good shocks... Kingman gained a sordid reputation as a tourist trap. Shameful. She heard it made national news when a handful of the more notorious fraud artists were finally caught. Sam felt he had to pull his machines from those locations, despite the high revenues.

Greed, avarice, why? It makes her sad how some people will do anything for money. Money isn't everything. Doesn't everybody know that? It's only a small part of a decent life. Sure, people who work hard deserve to live well. And it wasn't easy when she and Sam started out. Sometimes, it still isn't easy. But to lie, cheat, or steal can't result in living a good life, no matter how much money one has. As the world leaves the 1960s behind, a lot has changed, and not all for the better. Sara remains hopeful that young people, like her sons Jack and Timmy, and this boy, Lionel, will have the same opportunities she and Sam have enjoyed.

Lionel drops the hood, shoving it down to make sure it latches. He rounds to her door. "You're all set," he says smiling. "I'll bring you your change."

Sara returns his smile. "Thank you, Lionel. You keep it." Pushing in the clutch, she turns the ignition key. "Be sure to tell your parents I said hi," she says as the engine fires up.

"Thank you. I will," he says as he waves and turns toward the store.

·····•·•····

Heading northeast, Sara pulls out on Route 66, intent on finding the perfect spot for her first landscape watercolor. The highway sign reads "Entering Hualapai Indian Reservation" as she passes. Peach Springs is less than ten miles up the road. Within a couple miles, the pavement curves, and she slows. Without a sign, a dirt road shows up on her left, heading the direction of the Lower Granite Gorge, just this side of the Grand Canyon. She would go all the way to the Canyon, but she wants to tackle something a little tamer for this attempt. With the wind in her hair, her confidence swells. It's a beautiful day. She has a feeling she will find the right setting.

Through the cattleguard, the dirt road quickly deteriorates, the little-used offroad trail petering out to a cattle track. Sara lets the big truck lumber through the ruts and over the scrub, looking for a place to give Rocko a break and lock the hubs. Smiling to herself, she thinks of Sam. Out here, she may not need low-range four-wheel-drive, but it's like the gun: better to have it and not need it, than to need it and not have it. Sam, pragmatic, dependable, it's like a religion with him. Locking the hubs will only take a minute.

Shifting into first, Sara nurses the truck up a tall berm, letting the big tires seek their footing. As she crests the edge, she spots the greenish water in the bottom of a small cow pond. She jerks the wheel when Rocko breaks out in a fit of barking. Across the pond is something Sara thought she would never see out here. Big as a house, the bull buffalo eyes her truck, irritated by Rocko's outburst. No one will ever believe this: a buffalo in Arizona. She brought her Polaroid, but it's in her paintbox. Scrambling out of the truck, she stiff-arms Rocko. "Wait," she says, as she shuts the door.

Before Sara can grab him, the big yellow lab leaps off the seat, through the open window, and out of the cab, charging flat-out around the edge of the pond, heading for the huge buffalo. It's happening so fast, she can't think.

"Rocko!" she yells as she runs after him.

Sprinting around the pond, Sara watches Rocko run up on the buffalo, barking, bounding back and forth.

Tossing his head, the buffalo flinches. He trots off, as though the noisy dog is no more than a nuisance.

Rocko gives chase as they approach a long span of barbwire fencing.

Sara gasps, running after Rocko, convinced that when the buffalo is cornered, he will turn on him. Rocko has never seen a buffalo; and now that he has him on the run, he won't back down. *Gawd, no!*

The buffalo takes the barbwire fence in stride, over it and gone without a backward glance.

Rocko slides to an abrupt halt at the fence and Sara stops cold, her world suddenly bright with wonderous relief. She claps her hands. "Rocko. Here, boy."

Panting, Rocko turns, his tongue hanging. With a huge smile, he trots to Sara, supremely pleased with himself.

Sara can't stop shaking and smiling all at once. When Rocko reaches her, she bends to grab his head, ruffling his fur with affection. She gives him a hug. "Dang it, Rocko. You had me scared half-to-death. Don't do that, okay?"

As though waking from a dream, Sara gazes past the barbwire as the last puff of dust settles, marveling at a stand of junipers on a rocky hillside where a mystical buffalo vanished before her eyes. Shaking her head, she turns for the truck, snapping her fingers for Rocko to heel. "Nobody's gonna believe this."

Grim Discovery

W ITH THE HUBS LOCKED and Rocko holding station next to her, Sara shifts into first gear and eases the truck down the face of the berm. Back on the cattle track, heading toward the Canyon, she shifts to second in high-four-wheel-drive, letting the F250 lumber over the rough terrain at a tolerable pace. A light breeze gusts through her window. Fresh air full of Spring aromas sharpens her senses. Spade-shaped junipers, dressed in their finest sprigs of forest green, dot the landscape. She scans the horizon as the plateau rises into the low hills.

Skirting a mound of broken rock, the truck trundles up a gentle slope. The vista opens, exposing banded rims of salmon, pink, and lavender: the Lower Granite Gorge. She pushes in the clutch with a deep sigh, letting the light, the colors, and the wide-open horizon fill her senses. Marvelous, the only place on Earth with this view, unique in all the world, its natural beauty a work of art. She found it. This is it.

Sara sits for a moment, gazing at the scenery, taking it all in before shutting off the engine and bailing out.

Rocko leaps to the ground, eager for new adventures, wagging his tail as he sniffs around the truck's perimeter.

Sara shuts her door and lifts a hand to shade her eyes as she looks for a likely spot to set up her easel. Ahead and to her left, a reasonably level patch of brush-free ground looks likely. On tiptoes at the side of the bed, she grabs her gear, leaning the easel and paintbox against the fender while she retrieves her folding seat. Arms full, she carries everything to her spot, wondering where the heck Rocko went. As she sets up her easel, she glances around expecting to see Rocko.

Sara's ears perk at his bark. Out of her line of sight, Rocko barks louder, more insistently. He made a discovery; she can tell from his bark. She hopes he hasn't cornered another buffalo or a rattler or... Laying her gear on the ground, she dashes to the truck and retrieves her pistol. No sense in taking any chances.

Sara trots off, pistol pointed down. "Rocko," she calls, following his barks.

The ground slopes to the edge of a steep arroyo. She spots him several yards down, at the bottom, barking.

He paces back and forth in front of a strip of thick weeds rising three to four feet from the edge of the sand.

Sara works her way down the bank, calling to him, "What is it, boy?"

Rocko turns and runs up to her, his tail wagging, a gleam in his dark eyes.

"What is it?"

Sara cautiously follows him into the arroyo. As she approaches the tall weeds, she makes a face, getting a whiff of something rotten: a dead animal odor wafting up the arroyo. Closer, the stench is worse, but she doesn't see anything. It must be hidden in the weeds. She can't imagine what it could be, a dead bird, or a rabbit, or maybe a coyote. Whatever it is, it has been dead awhile. She slowly approaches the weeds, the odor thickening. As she closes on the source, a swarm of flies boils out of the stinky weeds. Whatever it is, it's bigger than a bird or a rabbit, maybe a dead cow.

Rocko leaps ahead and she calls to him. "Here." Obediently, he trots to her side. "Wait." She points down and snaps her fingers. "Sit. Wait." Rocko reluctantly sits and starts to whine. "That's enough, Rocko," she says as she creeps toward the smell. Gun raised, she slowly walks an arc around the offending area, peering at a clump of tall weeds, trying to locate the source of the stench.

Gasping, Sara nearly drops her pistol when she spots part of a pantleg in the deep weeds. Horror rips through her as she gets another glimpse of grimy jeans. She quickly turns away to catch her breath, nauseous. Without closer inspection, she scrambles up the arroyo, headed for the truck. "Rocko, come."

· · · • • · • · · ·

Sara grabs her gear on her way to the truck. Tossing everything in the bed, she jerks the door open. "Rocko. Let's go," she says as she holds the door. "Get in."

Rocko leaps onto the seat, pads to the passenger window and sits, panting as he watches through the windshield.

Sara jumps in, tucks her pistol in the glove box and fires up the engine. Shifting through the gears in four-wheel-drive, she pushes as hard as she dares. The big truck rocks and bounces over the rough terrain, searching for grip. Sara hangs on to the steering wheel, her butt sliding around the bench seat like a shuffleboard puck.

Rocko slides off the seat into the footwell, eyeing her with trepidation as he braces with all fours.

The closest phone is the trading post, several minutes away, if she hurries. Though Sara isn't sure why she is in such a hurry. She can't save anybody. Whoever it is, they're dead and that body has been there a few days, at least. Easing up, she lets the truck settle into a more natural rhythm. That corpse isn't going anywhere. *Gawd!* Stumbling across a dead body out in the middle of nowhere—she can't imagine. So much for her watercolor landscape.

As the cattle track broadens into an offroad trail, her mind races. *Who do you call out here?* Is she on the reservation or still in Mohave County? Through the cattleguard, she upshifts and hits the gas, bouncing the three-quarter-ton Ford onto Route 66 back to Truxton. The axles roar as the tires grind. In her panic, she forgot to stop and unlock the hubs. Now she can't shift out of four-wheel-drive.

Full bore, the engine thunders as her speed tops out just under sixty. Passing the Hualapai Reservation sign, she grits her teeth at the horrific howl coming from the drivetrain, hoping she's not tearing up the gears. It will have to wait until she reaches the trading post. It's an emergency. And it seems like it's taking forever.

Finally, the trading post appears on the near horizon. Sara hustles the big truck onto the dirt shoulder, pulling into the drive and sliding to a stop in front of the store. Eyeing Rocko, she grabs the door handle. "Wait." She says as she kicks open the door and hops out. She sprints to the storefront door and runs in. "Lionel," she yells, looking around. "Where are you?"

"Right here, ma'am," Lionel answers as he hustles out of the back.

"I need to use your phone," she says as she rushes up to him.

Lionel swings around behind the counter. "Over here," he says as he scurries to the phone. Alarmed, he slides the phone across the counter.

Sara grabs the handset and stares at the rotary dial. Looking up, she asks him, "Who should I call?"

Stupefied, he replies, "I don't know."

"There's a dead body... I found a dead body out there," Sara says frantically.

"Out where?"

Sara eyes him, then looks away, thinking how to explain. "I better call the Sheriff," she says as she dials "0" and puts the handset to her ear. "Yes, Operator. Can you connect me with the Sheriff's Office? It's an emergency."

Tribal Police

S ARA STANDS AT THE top of the bank overlooking the arroyo with
Rocko by her side. The Mohave County Sheriff, George Bailey, and
his deputy, Tom Adams hike down the steep bank toward the weeds.
At the bottom, the portly Sheriff pushes the brim of his Stetson up his
forehead as he makes a face and crouches next to the tall weeds.

In his wrinkled uniform, the lanky Adams holds his nose and squints
as he peers over the Sheriff's shoulder. Suddenly turning away, he scrambles up the bank, breathing hard.

"He's dead, alright," Sheriff Baily says as he stands and brushes off his
hands. "Looks like a boy, maybe a Hualapai, badly decomposed, hard to
tell," he says as he hikes back up the bank. At the top of the bank, he
meets Sara's fearful gaze. "I think we're still on the reservation, out of
our jurisdiction," he says. "I'll radio in, have dispatch call the Hualapai
Police."

"Then what happens?" Sara asks.

"They're up the road, in Peach Springs," the Sheriff says. "Shouldn't
take 'em long. We'll wait till they get here. I'm sure they'll have some
questions for ya."

"What do you think happened?"

"No idea, Sara," the Sheriff says, scrunching his chin. "And we don't
want to touch anything. We'll leave it for the tribal police to investigate."

Sheriff Bailey and his deputy stand at the top of the arroyo, mumbling
and shaking their heads. With Rocko at heel, Sara heads back to her
truck. She opens the door for Rocko, then climbs up to slide behind
the wheel. Closing the door, she leans an elbow on the window frame,
saddened by the idea of a boy, dead. How does something like this
happen? Did he die of thirst, a snake bite, was he lost? A tragedy... Losing
a son... Sara's eyes fill as she tries to not think about the poor mother.

Wiping her eyes, Sara leans her head back against the seat, catching the glare of the late-day sun. She sits up and drops the visor, annoyed. Taking in the view, she lets her thoughts wander as her heart sinks. It would've made for a good watercolor in this light: the tall dark bluff to the north, thrusting out of the hillside like a blackened forehead; the pastel pinks and purples of the Lower Granite Gorge, its rims puffed and snaking like the lips of a giant clam. She would've enjoyed the attempt. Now this. *What a day... and it's not over.*

At the sound of an engine, Sara turns to catch a silver Jeep outfitted with an emergency light bar up top, and a pair of whip antennae at the rear fenders. As it wanders up the trail to park next to the Sheriff, the tribal police emblem shows on the door. She decides to wait, stay out of the way, and let them come to her if she's needed. The last thing she wants is to go anywhere near that corpse.

Sara squints through the brightness as the driver and a passenger climb out of the Jeep. Closest to her, the dark-skinned passenger is a double-wide, round-faced and rotund, in a black and grey uniform, with a black-leather gun belt. Under a thick shock of black hair, his dark eyes cut to her, then flick away. From the look in his eyes, she knows he's the Chief. A younger version, less certain and less obese, shuts the driver's-side door, hitching up his gun belt as he rounds the front bumper. She has heard of the tribal police, of course—just never seen them in action. They don't look friendly. She watches them walk up on the Sheriff and his deputy, everyone nodding and talking just out of earshot. When the conversation wanes, they disappear into the arroyo.

The second-hand ticks around the face of her watch as though in slow motion. It's getting late and she's getting hungry. She is sure Rocko is, too. In the back, she has a ham and cheese sandwich and a small bag of Laura Scudder's chips in the little ice chest, as well as a couple of chunks of cheese for Rocko. Glancing at her watch again, she debates whether she should eat now or wait. About the time she is ready to climb out and grab the ice chest, the Police Chief trundles out of the arroyo and heads up the slope toward her truck.

Sara recoils when the big man sets his meaty hands on her window frame and leans in. Up close, the acne scars on his dark cheeks become apparent. His scent wafts through her open window, strong and alien, almost off-putting. His breath smells of burnt coffee and rancid meat.

Hackles raised, Rocko growls low, then barks.

"Rocko, off," she says.

Rocko quiets and sits, keeping a watchful eye on the dark stranger.

The Chief gives her a half smile and hands her his card, as though resigned to a measure of courtesy. She can tell it's a strain. Maybe it's the circumstances. The Hualapai tribe is very small, a few hundred people, last she heard. And to lose one of their own, a boy, must be devastating. Or maybe, it's him—too long on the job. Either way...

The Chief focuses his gaze, meeting her eyes with a dark glare. "Sheriff Bailey tells me you found the body," he says in a gruff voice.

Sara nods. "That's right."

"What were you doing out here?" he says, accusatively.

"I came out here to paint."

The Chief looks down and away, nodding. He looks up to lock eyes with her. "You're an artist," he says matter-of-factly.

Sara holds steady. "I try. It's a hobby of mine."

"You live in Kingman."

She nods. "That's right."

He cocks his head, eyeing her. "And you came all the way out here to paint—on the reservation."

"It's pretty country," she says a bit too quickly. "Is there some reason I shouldn't?" she asks defensively.

He gives his head a small shake. "The visitor center is just up the road in Peach Springs. But you didn't think to check in?"

"I didn't think I needed to," she says. "I wasn't sure I was still on the reservation."

The Chief nods, thick jowls tightening on his dark face, as though he's heard it all before.

Her eyes narrow as she watches the Chief.

"How did you find the body, if you were out here painting?"

"Rocko found it," she says, taken aback.

Pulling his hands off her window frame, he steps back. "Show me."

In a huff, Sara leans back and grabs the door handle, a small frown gripping her face. She turns to Rocko. "Wait," she says as she opens the door and climbs out.

Rocko vibrates on hold, hackles up, a low growl in his throat.

With a flinty glare, Sara straightens her sleeves. She didn't do anything; and he's treating her like a criminal. This isn't going the way she thought it would—unsettling and a little scary. Sara gives the Chief a sideways glance. "Show you what, exactly?"

At the start of the Sheriff's Blazer, Sara snaps around to watch him wave. As he backs out and turns for the cow path home, blood drains from her face. With a sinking sensation, she turns to the Chief.

Hualapai Nation Police Chief, Wendel Watonami, glares at her, waiting.

Sara clears her throat and marches to the spot where she planned to set up. Pointing to the ground, she says, "I was setting up my easel here, when I heard Rocko bark." She leans on one foot and puts her hands on her hips, giving the Chief a firm look.

Chief Watonami holds his glare, giving her a quick nod, his black eyes shining. "Then what?"

Sara points to the edge of the arroyo. "I grabbed my pistol and went to see why he was barking."

The Chief cocks his head. "Your pistol?"

Clenching her jaws, she nods. "I keep a pistol in the glove box."

"What kind of pistol?"

She squints one eye, looking him over, wondering if it was a mistake to mention the pistol. "Smith and Wesson, three-fifty-seven magnum."

Chief Watonami nods. "Good weapon," he says under his breath. Turning for the lip of the arroyo, he motions for her to follow. "You went this way?"

Reluctantly, she joins him at the top of the bank. Sara shades her eyes with her hand, looking down the arroyo to the Chief's driver. Crouching next to the weeds, his back is to them. "There," she says. "We found the body there, where your officer is."

He glances at her. "We?"

"Me and Rocko."

"The dog," he mumbles as he shifts his gaze to his subordinate.

Head down, the Chief waves for her to come along as he starts a slow hike sideways down the steep bank, his feet sliding in the loose dirt as he balances heavily, one leg at a time.

Hands locked behind her back, feet apart, Sara stands at parade rest at the edge of the arroyo, watching the big man work his way down at an angle. Misgivings arise as she debates whether to follow him. When she thinks about the mother of that poor child, she doesn't mind lending a hand, answering his questions, as long as he's not trying to pin it on her. After all, she doesn't know anything. If it hadn't been for Rocko, she wouldn't have found it. A decomposing corpse, she can't fathom how anyone could get used to such a thing. Awful. And she doesn't want to get anywhere near that horrible stench. Her stomach clutches just thinking about it.

Chief Watonami reaches the bottom and stops to catch his breath. Looking over his shoulder, he eyes her. "Coming?"

Sara smirks. At least he asked, better than ordering her around like some sort of criminal. "I'm not getting close to that thing," she says as she starts down the bank.

"The boy is dead," he says as he lumbers toward the weeds. "Can't hurt you."

"It stinks," she says defiantly. "I'm not going near it."

As she nears the bottom, her curiosity piques. "You're sure it's a boy?"

Without turning, the Chief nods.

"You know him?" she asks as she edges closer.

As the Chief turns his head, she sees deep sadness in his eyes. Regret floods her, hitting hard. Such a small tribe, close knit, they are probably related—the boy might be his son. How could she be so thoughtless, so callous?

"We think this could be the boy who went missing a week or so ago," he replies.

Sara slows to a stop, still several feet away from the Chief and the scene. "I'm sorry. I didn't mean to..." She lets the words die on her lips.

Turning away, the Chief waves her off. He taps his round-faced subordinate, Henry Natomi, on the shoulder and Natomi stands. The Chief leans in close, pointing at Sara while he quietly gives Natomi instructions.

Natomi nods and heads toward Sara with grim determination. "Ma'am," he says as he walks up. "Let's go back to your truck." He walks past her and starts up the bank with long strides.

Sara follows, hustling to catch the younger policeman, relieved to get away from the scene. Matching pace with Officer Natomi, she stumps up the slope and hikes past the Chief's Jeep to her truck.

Rocko comes unglued as they approach, his head out her window, barking fiercely, ready to leap.

Sara holds out her palm. "Rocko, off," she snaps. "Sit."

Rocko whines as he backs down, his tail wagging as he sits.

Natomi veers off, turning back for the Jeep. "I need my notebook," he says over his shoulder. "I'll be right there."

Sara leans in the window and rubs Rocko's head. "Good boy." Turning, she catches the officer walking up behind her. She watches him stop and pull his pen and flip open a small notebook. "What can I do for you, Officer?"

Natomi blinks, tension gripping his dark face, his mouth a tight scar. "Call me Henry, ma'am."

"And you can call me Sara."

"Yes, ma'am."

She smiles at his deference.

"The Chief asked me to ask you…" Henry straightens as he thinks it through. "We need some information."

Squinting at him in the late-day sun, Sara leans an elbow on the driver's side window frame. "What do you need, Henry?"

Looking at his notepad, Henry scribbles awkwardly. "Your name is Sara Wayland, and you live in Kingman, right?"

"That's right."

"Can I see your driver's license and registration, please?"

Sara grabs the door handle. "Certainly." Turning to Rocko, she says, "Wait," as she opens the door and climbs in. She sits behind the wheel and leans for the glove box, fishing out the registration. "You knew that boy, Henry?" she asks as she straightens. Bending, she retrieves her purse from the footwell. She sits up and hunts through her purse for her wallet. Not wanting to pry, she hands him her driver's license and registration and tries again. "Henry? Did you know him?"

Henry reaches for her documents. "If it's who we think it is, yes ma'am." He shifts her license and registration to his other hand, clasping them between his fingers as he scribbles.

"When do you think you'll know?"

He continues to scribble, head down, concentrating heavily on his notes. "Don't know, ma'am. We'll have to wait and see what the Medical Examiner says."

Sara waits until Henry looks up to hand her back her documents. "Can you tell how he died?"

Henry crimps his lips as he looks down and shakes his head. "Looks like alcohol poisoning, but we won't know until we get the ME's report." He looks up at her sheepishly. "The Chief said you have a gun... Can I see it? I need the serial number."

"Of course." Sara stuffs her license in her wallet and leans to the glove box, tossing in the registration and grabbing her Smith & Wesson .357. Smiling, she hands her gun to Henry, butt first. "Be careful. It's loaded." She watches him pull her pistol from the holster, turning it over to locate the serial number. "Why do you think it was alcohol poisoning?"

His eyes snap up to her. "What?"

"You said alcohol poisoning."

He holsters and returns her pistol, puts his nose in his notes, then scribbles. "I said we don't know yet. It's under investigation. I can't talk about it."

"Henry, come on. I found the body. You can tell me."

Henry looks up, chewing his bottom lip as he gazes off past the horizon. "I don't know," he says, dropping his head and giving it a small shake. "The empty whiskey bottle... I just don't know."

Country-Fried Chicken

S ARA STOPS THIS SIDE of the cattleguard, steps on the parking brake, and leaves the 4X4 truck in neutral. Still rehashing the odd events of the day, she hops out, unlocks the hubs and climbs in. She ruffles Rocko's fur, his smiling face a comfort after all the ugliness. Pulling out on the highway, she turns for home, upset at the treatment she received from the Chief, disillusioned. But that's not at the heart of it. A boy child, missing for days, his body decomposing in the middle of nowhere, how did it happen? Alcohol poisoning? How long did he lie out there suffering or unconscious? Why couldn't they find him in time? Why did he have to die?

Pushing the three-quarter-ton truck to seventy, she barely notices the highway sign, 'leaving the Hualapai reservation.' Coming up fast on the Truxton Trading Post, she debates whether to stop. Maybe Lionel knows something. She figures he attends high school in Peach Springs, he might know the boy, or heard he was missing, or... She can't imagine losing a child.

No. She's not going to think about it. Her boys are fine. It's not important anymore. Anyway, it's not really her business. Sara wants to go home, clean up, wash off the faint odor of death clinging to her clothes—forget about it as best she can.

By the time Sara sees the Kingman Airfield emerge from the far side of the flats, she has gone numb from thinking about everything. The smell, the flies, the ragged pantleg, she can't get them out of her head. Painting a watercolor never enters her mind.

Pulling into her driveway, she doesn't remember driving through town. She shuts down the truck and slumps, fingers gripping the steering wheel, her head resting on the back of her hands. What a horrible day. The thought of the poor boy... She struggles to put it out of her mind.

Rocko scoots next to her and gives her a kiss on the cheek.

Sara laughs as her tears dry. "Okay, boy." She turns to him with a grateful smile. "Thank you."

·········

Out of the shower, fresh and clean with a change of clothes, Sara feels more at home, the dark events of the day, behind her. She focuses on rustling up dinner for Sam as she feeds Rocko.

By the time Sam walks through the back door, the fried chicken batter is turning a golden brown.

Sam's eyes light with a grin. "Umm, smells good," he says as he grabs Sara from behind and hugs her. He lets her go and takes off his thin jacket to hang it on the coatrack. "Have a good day?"

Expertly wielding the tongs, she turns a chicken breast in the iron skillet, hesitant to say.

"How did the painting go?" he prompts.

"It didn't," she says with a slight catch in her voice.

Sam moves to her side and puts his arm around her shoulders. "What happened?"

Sara shuts off the burner and sets down the tongs. Turning, she wraps her arms around Sam's neck and buries her face in his shoulder to shake her head, her eyes welling. "You won't believe it."

Sam pushes away, holding her at arm's length to look into her eyes. "What?"

Sara wipes her eyes with her hand, turns back to the skillet and grabs her tongs. "The chicken is ready. I'll tell you while we eat." She shakes her head. "Honest-to-Pete, you won't believe it."

Sara hastily sets two places. Since the boys are gone, she and Sam use the cozier kitchen table rather than the dining room. She serves up her extra-crispy fried chicken and helpings of fried diced potatoes with bell pepper and onions for both her and Sam, setting the steaming bowls of food between them.

Sam returns from washing up, savoring the aromas of his wife's country cooking. Rubbing his hands together, he takes his chair. "Can't wait."

Sara sits and snaps her napkin, tucking it in her lap. "Dig in."

"Looks great." He smiles tenderly. "But what I meant was, I can't wait to hear about today."

Sara nods, looks him in the eyes, then at her food. With her fork, she spears a bite of potatoes and pops it in her mouth. Looking at Sam, she nods as she chews, then swallows. "I don't know where to start," she says, casually waving her fork.

Sam picks up a hot and crispy chicken breast, takes a big bite, then nods. Chewing big, he swallows. "Start wherever you like but tell me *something*."

Laying her fork on her plate, Sara takes a swig of lemonade. "Well... We made it to the reservation. I found a good spot with an amazing view of the Lower Granite Gorge—would have been great." She picks up her knife and fork and cuts into a chicken breast. "Then Rocko... He was busy today." She takes a bite and chews.

Sam watches her expectantly as he twirls the chicken breast between his fingers and takes another bite.

"I heard him barking. You know how he gets when he's onto something... I found him in the bottom of an arroyo, barking at the bushes. I could tell there was something in there. When I went to look..." Clouding up, she swallows hard and looks away. She takes a drink and turns to face Sam. Shaking her head, she holds up her palms, keeping the memory at bay. "Anyway... It was a dead body."

Sam drops the chicken breast on his plate. "What?"

"I called Sheriff Bailey," she says, looking him in the eyes as her story unfolds. "He followed me out to the place where I found the body. He said it was out of his jurisdiction and called the tribal police."

Sam drops an eyebrow and tilts his head. "What happened?"

"They wouldn't tell me. The tribal cop, Henry, said the body was in tough shape and they couldn't tell what happened. But it was a young Hualapai, a boy who they thought had gone missing."

"Oh no," Sam says, sitting back in his chair. "Dang it..." He slowly shakes his head. "That's a shame. How did he die?"

Sara fills her mouth with another bite of potatoes and chews, wagging her head. "The cop, Henry, told me they wouldn't know until the Medical Examiner did his thing." She looks up, squinting as it occurs to her. "Then he said something about an empty whiskey bottle..." She waves her fork. "I don't know."

Sam retrieves his half-finished chicken breast and pulls the rest of the white meat off the bone with his teeth. Chewing, he watches her uneasiness take hold, waiting to see if she has anything to add. He swallows and locks eyes with her. "George and his deputy... What's his name? Tom, I think. They're usually at the City Café for coffee, weekday mornings. I'll try and catch ol' George tomorrow—see what he can tell me."

Turning morose, Sara barely nods as she munches on her chicken. "Wish I knew..."

Digging into his potatoes, Sam says, "You had quite a day. No wonder you didn't get any painting done."

They eat without saying more as Sam works another chicken breast and Sara finishes hers.

Sara pulls a thigh out of the bowl, carves it off the bone, slices it up, and feeds it one piece at a time to her enthusiastic yellow lab—his mood lightening hers. Wiping her fingers on her napkin, she turns her gaze to Sam. "Oh... I forget to mention Rocko's run-in with the buffalo."

Sam pulls in his chin with a sour look. "You're right... Unbelievable."

"No, really," she says emphatically. "Rocko chased off a buffalo. It was on the way out there. We stopped at a cow pond. I didn't know there are buffalo in Arizona."

"Where was this?" he asks. "On the reservation?"

"I think so." She pushes her plate away, pulls her napkin off her lap, and tucks it under the edge of her plate. "You should've seen Rocko. He scared me half-to-death. That buffalo was huge, the biggest thing I've ever seen on the hoof. And Rocko ran straight at it," she says, shaking her head. "I thought he was gonna get gored or trampled. You should have seen the size of that thing."

"What did he do... the buffalo?"

"When Rocko went after him, the buffalo trotted off like it was no big deal, heading for the fence. I thought he would turn and charge Rocko, but he didn't even slow down. That buffalo went right over the fence like it wasn't there. He didn't even break stride."

Sam cleans the last of the potatoes off his plate and leans back to chew. He swallows and pushes back from the table, grinning. "Makes sense."

"What, that there's a wild buffalo roaming the reservation?"

Sam lifts his chin as he gives a short laugh. "Not exactly." He tosses his napkin on the table. "I heard about this. It's quite a story." He eyes her mischievously. "What's for dessert?"

"Oh no you don't," she says with a grin. "No dessert until you tell me the whole thing."

Sam throws up his hands in surrender. "Here's what I know. That buffalo probably belongs to the Drake Ranch. Dennis Drake leases grazing rights from the BLM. That lease land borders the reservation to the north. The story goes that ol' Dennis bought a bull buffalo for breeding. You've heard about beefalo, right?"

"I've seen it in the meat case at Central Commercial, but I don't know..."

Sam shrugs, "Supposed to be good, better than beef. Apparently, Dennis paid a small fortune to buy this breeder buffalo and transport him down here from Montana or some durn place. Anywho, he made a big investment in this beefalo project of his."

Sara smirks. "I'll bet he can afford it."

"Yeah." Sam sits forward to lean his elbows on the table. "So, the truck arrives, and they unload the buffalo into a holding pen, away from the cattle. The way Dennis tells it, his prize bull buffalo looked around for a couple minutes, snorted once, then took off, clearing the fences on his way." Sam sits back, grinning. "Dennis said the last he saw him, that buffalo was headed northeast at an easy lope."

"Oh no!" Sara breaks out laughing, slapping a hand on her thigh.

Sam chuckles as he shakes his head. "Wait 'til I tell ol' Dennis you saw his prize buffalo on the reservation."

Leave It Alone

WISPY CLOUDS HANG ABOVE the western horizon, their pow-
derpuff complexions turning cotton candy pink. Golden-orange
streaks line their bellies as the sun sinks behind the volcanic escarpments
of Coyote Pass.

On her back patio at the end of a long day, Sara relaxes with her sketch
pad in the thick cushions of her favorite chair. Sara whips out pencil
sketches of desert plants from memory as she sips her Salty Dog. A blue
agave dominates the page, a short yucca leans to the right with a small
Spanish Dagger bristling in the bottom left corner. She has yet to tackle
a landscape with watercolors, but feels drawn to it, refusing to let it get the
better of her. However, when it comes right down to it, Sara doesn't know
what she'll do.

Content to stick close to Mama, Rocko lies on a folded-up horse blanket
between chairs, panting in the late-day warmth.

Sam left early this morning on a service call. The jukebox at the El
Mohave Mexican restaurant was on the fritz again. That on top of his
normal route makes for a long day. He should be home anytime now. He
said he would fire up the grill and char a couple of thick T-bones for dinner.
Sara whipped up a fresh batch of potato salad as a side for the steaks early
this afternoon. She half wonders if Sam saw Sheriff Bailey.

As the light fades, the Sky Chameleon shifts from scarlet-banded gold
through puffs of orange chiffon with lavender and plum pastels, fading to
deep-sea blues and eggplant purples. When she hears the step van pull into
the driveway, Sara puts up her colored pencils, closes her sketchbook, and
climbs out of her chair.

Rocko pops up to follow, tail wagging.

Sara smiles as she holds the screen door for her yellow lab. "Steak tonight,
boy."

Rocko's tail wags faster.

·····•••·····

After dinner, Sam holds the screen door for Sara and Rocko. He flicks on the back patio lights on his way out.

"Please leave them off," Sara says as she finds her seat. "I want to see the stars."

Sam obliges. "No problem." With his Seven & Seven in an icy tumbler, he walks by to sit in his chair.

Ambient light from the kitchen leaves the couple in silhouette as they sip their drinks with Rocko taking up his spot between them. Sara sets her drink on the side table and leans back to gaze at the night sky. Stars glisten in the velvet darkness. She imagines they are angels, shining brightly for all who would care to see. They tug at her, smiling, showing the way. Is the Hualapai boy one of them?

She turns to Sam. "You said you talked to Sheriff Bailey, but he didn't know anything. Did he say when he would?"

Sam shakes his head in the dark. "He said he hadn't seen Doc Pratt. The way George tells it, the tribe didn't have anyone to examine the body, so they sent it to the Kingman morgue. Even though it's not his case, George figures he'll hear about it anyway. 'Ol Ham Pratt isn't much for secrets."

"But he didn't have any idea when?"

"George kept saying it was out of his jurisdiction, but he would look into it for you." Sam lifts his drink and sips, then swirls the ice. "He apologized for leaving you there—a couple times."

Sara nods. "It kinda threw me for a loop. I wasn't expecting him to take off like that."

Sam sucks on an ice cube then crushes it between his teeth. "I would give him a day or two. If he doesn't call, I'll give him a nudge."

"I wonder what Sheriff Bailey would think if I headed back out there."

"I don't think George will care one way or the other," he says. "But if I were you, I'd check with your tribal cop buddy, first."

"*That* doesn't sound like a good idea," she says as she smirks.

Sam scrunches his eyebrows. "Why do you want to go back out there?"

"I don't know that I do," she says pensively. She glances at her half-empty glass and swirls the ice. "It doesn't feel right... Like I forgot to do something, or there's unfinished business."

Long moments pass uninterrupted, only the faint sound of highway traffic and the whisper of the cool breeze.

Sara brightens, shifting to smile at Sam. "Anyway... the view is magnificent. I want to capture it in watercolor."

Sam turns, catching the glint of starlight in her eyes. "My hard-headed woman," he teases.

·····•·•·····

The morning after next, in their downstairs office, Sara sits hunched over a cloth-bound ledger and a neat stack of vending machine sales receipts. She transcribes Sam's hand-scrawled numbers onto the proper ledger line and column for each location and amount. She and Sam are a good team. Sam has the know-how to get things done and keep them running smoothly. She runs a tight ship. Once a week, she brings the accounts current. Doesn't take long, an hour or two. She'll do a few chores before she leaves. Then off to run errands. She needs a few things at the store. Routine perhaps, but the sense of accomplishment is reward enough. More than satisfaction, she takes pride in what she does for her family. The boys, Sam, and Rocko make it worthwhile. They are the dearest parts of her life.

Halfway through the receipts, Sara sits up and grabs her earthenware mug, looking over her entries as she sips tepid coffee. Everything checks out. Machine receipts are up, so far. Promising. Looks like April will be a good month. She'll wait and see, maybe treat herself to a new pair of summer shoes. Leaning back, she yawns, stretching her arms above her head, her shoulders sore from sitting.

At the end of the desk, curled up on one of his old horse blankets, Rocko looks up and wags his tail expectantly.

"Not yet, boy," she tells him with a smile. "A few more minutes and we'll stretch our legs. We're going shopping later."

Rocko drops his chin to his paws, giving her sad-puppy eyes.

She shakes her head as she lifts the next receipt off the stack. "You are so abused," she says. "I can't believe it."

·····•··•·····

Backing the hefty F-250 out of the driveway, Sara contemplates her afternoon. Groceries. She checks her back pocket for her list as she motors down Spring to Metcalfe.

Head out the window, Rocko watches from shotgun as she pulls onto Beale Street.

Sara keeps left, heading past Locomotive Park. Downshifting, she slows, staying under the speed limit behind Dunton's service garage and Western Auto. She brakes for a Greyhound pulling out of the bus depot, then swerves to miss a Chevy station wagon backing away from the curb. Hitting her blinker, she slows for 4th Street. She rounds the corner at Penny's, catty-corner to Central Commercial, her grocery stop for later. The engine chugs as she lugs past the theatre, Alex's Toggery, and her dentist's office.

Beyond the Elk's Club, the Mohave County Courthouse looms at the end of 4th St. Built in 1915, three short years after statehood, it's a chunk of local history frozen in time. Its neo-roman dome rides high behind the gabled masonry. In the neoclassical style, the massive portico, supported by four colossal columns, rises two stories above the top of the broad entry. Sara has to chuckle. Its sister building, the jail, might be architecturally compatible, but it doesn't hold prisoners worth a darn. She wonders if they still lock up drunks and vagrants in there.

Sara cranks the wheel, swinging the pickup into an angled parking slot in front of the courthouse. "Wait," she tells Rocko as she hops out. In fresh-pressed Levi's and a breezy top, she takes in the warm scents of Spring. Her sunny mood matches the cheerful blue of the sky. A persistent smile stretches her face as Sara steps over the curb, up the steps, and along the sidewalk to the Sheriff's Office. She pushes through the heavy door and walks up to the vacant reception window. Shifting toe-to-toe, she looks at the empty desk in the stark little office behind the glass. Usually, Janet Benson works the reception desk. Sara taps the service bell on the narrow counter, letting it ring, running through what she wants to say to Sheriff Bailey. As the rear door opens, she turns to face the reception window, watching Janet slip through the narrow doorway.

Her brassy blonde locks piled high with hairspray, Janet bustles up to the window. "Hi, Sara. What can we do for you?"

"Is the Sheriff in?"

"He is," Janet says as she scans the logbook. "Do you have an appointment?"

"Not really," Sara says. "Is he real busy?"

Janet gives a perfunctory smile. "Let me check. Can I tell him what it's about?" she says, turning for the door.

"It's about that boy on the reservation."

Janet nods as she slips out.

Sara pushes away from the counter, chewing her lower lip. Wondering if the Sheriff will see her. It's been two days. She slowly paces in front of the reception window. She could say, ...*on my way to the store, I thought I would stop by*...

Janet pops her head around the end of the counter, motions her in, and points down the wide hall. "You know where it is."

"Last door on the left," Sara says as she heads down the hall. "Thanks."

As she raises her knuckles to knock, the Sheriff swings the big mahogany door wide.

"Hello, Sara," he says with a twang, his corpulent face grinning under the brim of his Stetson. Sweeping an arm toward a pair of chairs in front of an acre-wide mahogany desk, he says, "Have a seat."

As she eases down on the burgundy leather, he moves behind his custom-made desk. He drops into his high-back chair and swings around to face her. Resting his forearms on the blotter, he gives her a sincere smile. "Let me start by apologizing," he says. "I didn't mean to leave ya out there."

Sara waves it off. "It's okay, Sheriff."

The Sheriff's grin tightens. "That ol' boy, Chief Watonami, he's somethin', isn't he? He didn't give ya a hard time, did he?"

"No big deal, under the circumstances."

The Sheriff shows his palms. "Well, again... Let me say I'm sorry."

"Apology accepted." She smiles as she leans forward. "I was on my way to the store and I... Well Sam said you might know more about that dead boy."

Sheriff Bailey rocks back, nodding his head, interlacing his fingers on his large belly. "You know that's not in my jurisdiction, don't ya?"

Sara nods. "Yes, I know, but..."

The Sheriff leans forward propping his elbows on his desk to look her in the eye. "Sam probably told you Doc Pratt did the examination."

She nods.

"I caught Ham at coffee this morning. He said the condition of the remains prevented a full autopsy. He said it might have been something else, but as close as he could tell, it was probably a combination of alcohol poisoning and exposure. That boy had been out there quite some time. Ham figured he'd been dead a week or longer."

Sara tilts her head. "Do you think Doc Pratt would talk to me?"

The Sheriff slowly shakes his head. "I doubt it. That kinda stuff is supposed to be confidential."

"Did they identify the boy?" she asks.

The Sheriff shrugs. "Beats me. Like I said, not my jurisdiction. Why do ya wanna know?"

Sara pushes straw-colored bangs out of her face and rubs her forehead. "I guess I just want to know what happened... and about his family."

"If I were you, I'd leave it alone," the Sheriff says as his eyes narrow.

An Evening Walk

S ARA LOADS THE LAST of the dinner dishes into their five-year-old dishwasher, pours in soap, closes the front, and presses the on button. The GE is her first undercounter dishwasher. And with Sam around, she figures it's the last dishwasher she'll ever need. He has already replaced the impeller and rebuilt the pump motor. It works better than new.

Wiping off her hands, she looks out the kitchen window. She can still see Spring St. drop into the wash in the early evening light. Watching the nightlights of MCUHS campus wink on, she speaks up, "Let's take a walk."

In the front room, Sam grins at Sara's gentle reminder. In his late forties, it's harder to keep the weight off than it used to be. "Thatta girl," he loudly replies. He remembers complaining to his mom on their last visit. She simply nodded, remarking, '*Wait 'til you're in your sixties.*'

Sam tucks in the flap of the book cover to hold his place. He's about a third of the way into his new Michael Crichton book, The Andromeda Strain. It's getting interesting, but it will have to wait. After a big dinner, they both need their exercise. Laying the book on the side table, he pushes out of his overstuffed armchair. "Let's go," he says, stretching.

The faint astringency of the desert in full bloom shifts in a light breeze. Evening air mellows with the fading light. Rocko leads the way down the steep face of Spring St. with Sara and Sam, hand-in-hand, bringing up the rear.

"Beautiful evening," Sara says looking up and around.

Sam nods. "Indeed."

She brushes her long blonde hair away from her face after a gust. "We should do this more often."

"Sounds like a plan," he says, grinning in the dusky light. "How far you wanna go?"

Feeling sixteen, Sara half skips, swinging their hands high. "Until we don't want to go anymore."

"You're full of it tonight." Sam lengthens his stride to keep up. "Durn, woman. What got into you?"

Laughing, Sara drops into an easy rhythm. "I can't believe you're going for a walk."

"Hey." Sam grins. "Nothing like an after-dinner walk... Better than some ol' book, any day."

"You love it out here," she teases.

He nods as the asphalt dips at Metcalfe. The streets are quiet, they haven't seen a car since they left the house. Crossing Metcalfe, they walk along the rounded curb at the backside of the County Yard. The light fades, draining the color from the maintenance buildings behind the ten-foot chain-link fence. On the other side of the street, a broken row of houses backs into the shadows. Curtains glow in their neighbors' windows. Sara has known these folks for years, watched their children grow up alongside her boys. It's a comfort.

"It's getting kinda dark," Sam says. "You wanna keep goin'?"

"We'll turn at the wash. We can go back on Gold Street."

"Sounds good." He bumps hips with her. "You know George caught me coming out of the bank this afternoon."

"Before or after I saw him?"

"After."

Sara squeezes his fingers. "What did he tell you?"

Sam nods as they swing hands. "He said he was afraid he gave you the wrong impression."

"Really."

"Yeah. He said he didn't want to give you the idea that he can be much help. It's not his jurisdiction."

"He made that perfectly clear, several times," she says with a smirk. "What else did he say? Bet I can guess."

"I'll bet you can." Sam saunters down the street with Sara, two steps to her three. "Ol' George talked around it plenty. He thinks you need to stay away from the reservation—steer clear of the tribal police."

"Yup," she says bunching her lips. "I heard that one loud and clear." Glancing up, she gazes at the lights of downtown Kingman, a smattering of glowing yellow dots against a backdrop of swirling indigo. If she were painting, she'd use acrylics.

They walk in silence with Rocko trotting ahead in the darkening shadows. Crossing the street, they start down the steep slope into the wash. As the tail of Gold St. strings along the rim, it curves down, dumping into Spring St. Approaching the narrow lane of asphalt, they climb the short bank to head up the steep slope out of the wash.

Hiking up the bend, Sam pulls her close. "He has his reasons."

"I'm sure," she replies half-heartedly.

"Do you want to know what I think?"

"You're going to tell me, anyway. Aren't you?"

"Yup," he says smiling.

They crest the slope and walk along the edge of the wash. Side yards, hidden in the shadows, line the other side of the one-lane street. They pass a dark alley, then the house on the corner with its tall pomegranate bushes rustling in the light breeze.

"The Hualapai Nation has its own laws," Sam says.

"I know this," she says defiantly.

"They are not subject to our laws unless they go off the reservation."

"Painfully obvious," she says, sarcastically. "And they've acclimated so well."

"Hey," Sam says. "There's more than enough blame to go 'round. Let's not go there."

"So, what are you saying?"

Sam bunches his chin as he looks up the street. "They have their own problems. They may not appreciate you nosing around."

Sara stops and drops his hand. "I don't see..."

"Sara," he interrupts. "They are a sovereign nation; they don't answer to the Sheriff or anyone else. They have their own jail up there in Peach Springs. And from what I hear, it ain't the Ritz."

Sara snaps her fists to her hips, arms akimbo. "I won't break the law. I'm not going to jail."

Sam shakes his head in the dark. "How do you know? Do you know what their laws are?"

"I just want to help the family—find out what happened to that poor boy. How can *that* be against the law?"

"What if they resent your help? What if a white woman sticking her nose in tribal business *is* against their laws?"

Sara kicks at the pavement. "Okay. I see what you're saying. Maybe I can find another way."

"I think you should listen to the Sheriff and leave it alone."

They trudge up Gold St. with the home turf dogs barking fiercely, charging up and down behind their gates. Rocko works the dogs on both sides of the street, casually lifting his leg on their fenceposts, then trotting off.

Sara shakes her head, grinning at Rocko's antics.

Sam gives her a quirky smile and reaches for her hand. "That boy of yours is a real troublemaker."

"Aren't you all," she says, taking Sam's hand.

He takes her hand without another word. After this many years with this woman, Sam knows when to keep his mouth shut.

Sara fondly watches Rocko's shadow shift in the dimness of the porch lights as he swaggers up the street. "Dogs will be dogs."

By the time Sara follows Sam into the house, she's spent. It was quite a hike, uphill all the way home.

Rocko follows them panting happily as though he was the guest star on The Ed Sullivan Show.

Sam heads into the living room and drops into his armchair.

Sara stops at the kitchen cabinet to pick out a glass. "You want ice water?"

"Please."

Sara grabs another glass, retrieves a metal ice tray out of the freezer, and breaks out the ice. Ice waters in hand, she heads into the living room and delivers one to Sam before plopping in her favorite spot at the end of the couch. She takes a big swig and sets her ice water on an end table. Glancing up, she takes in her large oil of the broken-down ore chute at the Emerald Isle ghost mine. The weathered planking, the rotting timbers half-buried in a pile of broken rock beneath a blustery sky, it's one of Sam's favorites. That and her other large oil of Ed's Camp. The Emerald Isle won a 1st-place blue ribbon at the County Fair three years ago. If she were to paint it again, there are a few things she would improve. They are never perfect, none of them, ever. Her thoughts wander off to other paintings, other places. She imagines the colorful bands running along the lips of the Lower Granite Gorge and how she would capture them with watercolors.

Sam studies her look. "If you stayed on BLM land," he says thoughtfully.

Sara swirls her ice. "You said Drake's Ranch, the BLM land, borders the reservation, didn't you?"

Sam nods. "I'm sure it's okay with Dennis. Just let him know before you go."

Sara glances back at the Emerald Isle oil. "I wonder how close I could get to the Lower Granite Gorge?"

"We'd have to check a map," he says crimping his lips. "But I bet it would be close enough."

Sara takes a long drink of ice water and sighs. "At least I could finish what I started."

El Mohave

AFTERNOON SUN FILTERS THROUGH the lace curtains of Sara's art studio. Converted from an upstairs bedroom, it's smallish. More so, due to the self-inflicted clutter: works-in-progress, one on the easel and five leaning against its legs, a menagerie of paint supplies, brushes soaking in jars of diluted turpentine, and stacks of finished works, each waiting for a frame.

Parked on her stool, Sara sets down her palette, wipes off her brush, and turns away from the easel. She gazes at shifting patterns left on the wall by the broken sunbeams, then turns to the window. There is so much light, so much color, so much life to see. And it's there for the taking, miracles in the making, constantly changing. Capturing it on canvas is the hard part.

Sara has set her painting aside more than once over the years. With Sam and the boys, it had been easy, a great excuse to keep everything stashed away downstairs, her creative urges saved for another day. Giving Rocko a critical look, she stands and stretches. "Whaddaya say we get outta here?"

Rocko unwinds off his horse blanket, yawning, wagging his tail as he stands and stretches.

Sara plucks a business card out from under the corner of her paintbox. On her way out to the hall, she examines the card: Hualapai Nation Police Chief, Wendel Watonami stretches across the center in bold letters. The tribal emblem dominates the top left corner. A phone number is centered across the bottom. She taps the card against her pastel pink nail on her way to the kitchen. Laying the card next to the phone, she lifts the handset and dials the number.

In a gruff tone, a woman answers, "Hualapai Police."

"Is Henry Natomi there?" Sara asks.

"Who's calling?"

"This is Sara Wayland. I…"

The woman interrupts. "Are you that white woman?"

"White woman?" Sara replies.

"The woman who found Bryant?"

"Was that his name?" Sara asks.

"Bryant Watachka. You're the one who found his body?"

"I guess so." Sara pauses, unsure. "Can I talk to Henry, please?"

"Hold on."

Sara runs through all the things she should say as she hears the woman yelling for Henry in the background. A long hum of silence ensues. As Sara is about to hang up, the woman says, "Hold on. He's coming."

"This is Henry."

"Hello, Henry. This is Sara Wayland. Do you remember me?"

"Yes," Henry says with a formal tone. "How are you today?"

"I'm so sorry about Bryant. I just wanted to find out if there is anything I can do for his family."

"Not that I know of, Mrs. Wayland."

"Could I call them? Do you have their number?"

"You mean, his mother, Wamaya?"

"Would it be okay to call her?"

"She doesn't have a phone."

"Oh."

After hanging up, Sara stares at the phone. That didn't go at all the way she thought it would. So uncomfortable, as though these people... the way they must live their lives, separate and apart from anything she knows... secretive, strange. Maybe Sam is right. Maybe she should leave them alone.

It's confusing, but somehow that can't be right. Something is happening out there, yet everyone seems determined to ignore it—pretend it doesn't exist. An attitude? The Sheriff, the townspeople looking down on anyone that doesn't fit the norm? The tribal police... And the tribe wanting white folk to stay away, to leave them alone? It's all tangled up.

Sara turns away from the phone, her feelings hurt. Sure, she might have been prying a little, but all she wanted to do was help. Why, though? Because she feels sorry for them? When she looks at it that way, she can see why the Hualapai would be offended. Makes sense, no one with any pride would take kindly to sympathy. Still... Bryant's mother...

·········

When he shows up early, Sam surprises Sara. He pecks her on the check on his way to wash up.

"What are you doing home?"

"You're not happy to see me?" he shouts from the bathroom.

"I don't have anything ready for dinner."

"Let's go out," he says as he enters the kitchen. "I was working on that cantankerous jukebox down at the El Mohave and got a hankerin' for Mexican food. Whaddaya say?"

Smiling, Sara gives him a hug and a kiss. "El Mohave sounds great—a combo plate. Let me get cleaned up."

·····•·•····

Sam drives while Rocko keeps an eye on things at home.

Trying to remember the last time they went out to eat, Sara cracks the wind-wing but leaves the window up to protect her hair.

The El Mohave buzzes with hungry Mexican food lovers. The aroma of spicy salsas and carne asada on the grill fills the restaurant with a heady warmth while on the jukebox Glen Campbell croons his tune, Galveston. Sam escorts Sara to a booth with his hand at the small of her back.

Seated, menu in hand, Sara scans the list of combo plates, ready to try something new. When the busboy shows up with two icy bottles of Modelo Negra, a big bowl of tortilla chips, and bowls of hot and not-to-hot salsa, she decides to stick with her usual: a #1, two beef tacos, a cheese enchilada, rice and beans.

Orders taken, menus surrendered, Sara scoops up a bite of the not-so-hot salsa with a crispy chip. She eyes her husband as he drinks his beer. "How did I get so lucky?"

Sam contains a burp and sets his beer down. Looking into her eyes, he smiles. "Easy day. Off early," he says as he generously salts the chips.

"You deserve it." She cocks her head and winks. "So do I."

Sam dunks a chip in the hot salsa. "I ran into Dennis Drake this afternoon at Buddy's Texaco." Sam chews a bite and washes it down with cold Modelo. "He was getting gas while I was filling the cigarette machine."

Sara fishes out another chip and daintily dips it in the hot salsa. "What did he say?"

Sam munches a chip drenched in salsa. "He asked about my gorgeous wife," he says grinning.

"That man is incorrigible," she says, shaking her head.

"And one of the wealthiest men in Mohave County," Sam says. "When I mentioned where you wanted to go, he said, any time—mi casa, su casa—just let him know."

"You told him what I wanted to do?"

"Yup." He takes another swig of beer. "I told him about your buffalo sighting," he says, grinning. "Dennis got all riled up—wants you to show him where."

Sara works her neck, frowning. "Why? What did you tell him? That buffalo is long gone. I watched him take off. He's not mad at Rocko, is he... for chasing it?"

Sam shakes his head. "No. You and Rocko are fine," he says as he snags another chip. "Ol' Dennis has got it in his head that after his prize buffalo lit out for the hills, the tribe wrangled it. And he wants it back."

"Would they do that?"

Sam shrugs. "The tribe runs their own cattle on the reservation. I guess if a stray buffalo showed up... Who knows?"

"But you told me his buffalo ran away." Sara narrows her eyes. "They didn't steal him."

Sam lifts the cold Modelo to his lips and finishes with satisfaction. "Like I said, who knows? I'm goin' off what Dennis told me. Besides, you know how touchy ranchers get about their livestock."

"I don't know..." Sara twists her face. "I'm pretty sure that cow pond is on the reservation."

······•·•····

Sara squints at the morning light through the kitchen window. With the days growing longer, the sun has been up nearly two hours. Eight a.m. seems late. Handing out the morning chew bone to her enthusiastic yellow lab, she can't help smiling. Rocko is such a handsome devil. She rinses off her hands and wipes them on her apron. Turning to her Coffeematic, she pours a cup of the new Yuban she's trying. Mug full, she moves to the table. "How do you like it?" she asks as she pulls out her chair to sit across from Sam.

Nose buried in the Daily Miner, Sam nods. "Better than the Folgers."

Elbows on the table, Sara holds her mug with both hands. She blows across her coffee and takes a tentative sip. "Tasty," she says. "You don't need the truck today, do you?"

"Nope," he says without looking up. "You gonna show Dennis the spot?"

"Not today," she says. "Rocko and I are going to Peach Springs."

"Take your pistol," he says as he turns a page.

Indignance creeps into her voice. "Don't I always?" She takes another sip. "Speaking of which, when are we going shooting?"

Sam Shrugs. "How 'bout one of these weekends?"

"Timmy might come home this weekend," she says wistfully. "We could go then. He'd like that. It'd be fun."

"You goin' out to that same spot?" Sam asks.

"The chief said I should check in at Peach Springs before I go out there to paint."

"Good idea... If that's what you want to do," he says as he looks up from his paper.

"I'm not breaking any rules. I'll get their permission."

Sam lifts his coffee, takes a swig and sets it down. "If you get stuck out there, call George," Sam says as he returns to his paper.

"Ha! Our sheriff made it very clear. The reservation is out of his jurisdiction." Sara takes a sip and frowns. "Besides, I don't see a problem. They seem like decent people. The Chief is kinda surly, but I won't have any trouble."

Grinning, Sam peers over the top of his paper. "I believe it."

"I'll take some pictures of the cow pond with the Polaroid—see if I can find Dennis Drake's rogue buffalo."

Sam crimps his lips. "I'm in the shop later, if you need me."

Peach Springs

ROLLING ON ROUTE 66. Clear skies and a view that goes on forever. It's late morning when Sara crests the rim of Crozier Canyon. Truxton is a dot in the distance. Peach Springs is eight or so miles up the road. She feels good about this: a chance to finish what she started. She can't fault herself. Things can happen out here. Matters of life and death are everyday occurrences. It is the desert, after all: barren, no water, no food, no shelter, nobody around for miles. Most folks who live around here have learned from long experience: out here, you are on your own.

Approaching the Truxton Trading Post, Sara downshifts, and Rocko sits up, ready for action.

Sara hopes Lionel is working, it would be good to see him again. An ice-cold Seven Up would be nice, too.

Puffs of dust follow her four-wheel-drive truck across the gravelly hard-pan like dirty demons. Coasting past the gas pumps, she parks in front of the entrance. Sara shuts down the truck and drops the keys in her purse. Turning to Rocko, she holds out her palm. "Wait." She cranks her window down a couple inches, then climbs out, leaving Rocko on guard. Walking in, the store is empty, nobody behind the counter. "Lionel?"

"Coming."

Sara moves to the cold cases and grabs a frosty bottle of Seven Up as Lionel rushes out of the back. "Hey Lionel."

Lionel's eyes light. "Hi, Mrs. Wayland."

"Call me Sara, please," she says as she heads to the counter. Dropping her purse next to the register, she sets the sweating bottle on the counter, smiling at the shy boy. "How are you doing?"

Lionel nods. "Good, ma'am." He rings up the soda. "Do you need gas?"

"I'm good," she says as she pushes a dime across the counter. "Tell me something."

"Sure," he says, nodding as he picks up the dime.

"You go to school on the reservation, right?"

"Yeah, high school, part-time, but not today."

Sara nods thoughtfully. "Did you know that boy, Bryant?"

"I knew who he was," he says, closing the register. "But I didn't hang out with him. He was younger and... I'm not Hualapai. I don't really hang out with anybody at school." His eyes grow wide as he steps to the side of the tall cash register. "The whole school knows you found him," he says, softly.

Sara crimps her lips as she nods. "Rocko and I." She smiles. "Word gets around fast out here."

"Yeah, I guess," he says sheepishly. "It's just that... well, everybody kinda knows everybody."

"Do you know Bryant's mom?"

"Wamaya is a regular customer," he says. "She cashes her checks and buys her liquor here—Old Grand Dad."

Lionel's frankness gives Sara pause. *A regular... cheap whiskey...* She glances away, her eyes searching the empty highway outside. The image that comes to mind is Jack's friend, Squibby Talotone, dead from alcohol poisoning in the alley behind Dinty Moore's. She banishes the thought as though crumpling up a hurtful photo.

For a split-second Sara wonders, do the grocery clerks at Central Commercial share customer purchase information, such as products and brand names? Do they talk about what kind of booze *she* buys, or how much, or how often? Is that anybody's business? Not in Sara's book.

Suspicious of Officer Natomi's quick denial, Sara turns back to Lionel. "Does she have a phone?"

"I don't think so," Lionel says. "I can check her customer card."

She eyes him curiously. "You have a customer card?"

"They're in the back. I'll go check." Lionel scoots out from behind the counter. "I'll be right back."

Sara lifts the tall green bottle to her lips. Taking a swig of frosty Seven Up, she sets it on the counter, her eyes watering from the cold carbonation. She scans the glass cases on the wall behind the counter. Floor to ceiling, they run the length of the store. Except for one small shelf for assorted cigars and chewing tobacco, the glass cabinets are filled with booze, from sixpacks of beer and quarts of malt liquor and gallons of cheap wine, to a variety of pints, and fifths and half-gallons of cheap whiskey. There aren't a hundred people living in Truxton. Roadside business from long-haul truckers and tourist travel on 66 couldn't come close to this much liquor. Sam has told her more than once that Mr. Sutter's business catered to the tribe. But looking at all this booze on their shelves... She had no idea.

Lionel bursts out of the back, startling Sara. He scurries around behind the counter, waving an index card over his head. "I found it."

Fidgeting, she gives him a condescending smile. "You have her phone number?"

Shambling up behind the counter, Lionel gives his head a few quick shakes as he lays the customer card on the worn glass. "Wamaya Watachka, we don't have a number for her," he says, turning the card around for Sara's inspection.

Sara stoops to examine the card: Wamaya Watachka, her tribal ID card is checked, the phone number line is blank, the residence address given is 9697 Canyon View Dr., Peach Springs, AZ. She digs in her purse for a pen. Looking up, she asks, "Do you have something I can write on?" she smiles. "I want to copy down her address."

Lionel ducks behind the counter and pops up with a small scratch pad. "Will this work?"

"Yes, thank you," she says, taking the pad. She jots down the name and address and pushes the customer card toward Lionel. "Do you know where this is?" she asks, waving the address.

Lionel gives her a tentative grin. "Peach Springs."

Sara smirks. "Yeah, but where?"

Lionel looks baffled for a moment. "That's the back side, off Diamond Springs Road, where the trailers are. I don't know which one she lives in."

·····•·•·····

Sara rolls the three-quarter-ton Ford across the dirt shoulder at an angle, heading for the highway. When the tires bounce onto the pavement, she shifts through the gears into fourth, hitting sixty. Rocko lays down, taking up the rest of the bench seat as she sails over the border. Straight as an arrow, 66 climbs a long slope headed to the sky. She's in Hualapai country now, their rules, their laws.

Peach Springs is just up the road. It's hard to see how it's going to go when she gets there. How could a boy like Bryant end up dying like a skid-row drunk in the bottom of a wash, out in the middle of nowhere? She half-suspects the empty whiskey bottle belonged to Bryant's mother.

Officer Natomi—the police station, she needs to stop there first. But what if Officer Natomi tells her no? She'll have to leave. Maybe she should stop in on Bryant's mother first. What if they catch her? Intuition tells her it will be all right—a deep abiding faith. Sometimes, faith is all you have to go on.

As she crests the slope, Sara pushes the pickup to sixty-five, the big offroad tires roaring like a grizzly. Blanketed with wildflowers and stippled with scrub juniper, low hills rise to undulate alongside the highway. Off to her right, railroad tracks mirror the road. To her left, carved into the foot of a steep bluff, holding pens and a makeshift roping arena border the highway. It has been a long time since she was last in Peach Springs. It might have been their rodeo, with Sam and the boys, years ago. She forgot how it feels, foreign yet familiar.

On the outskirts of town, the highway cuts through the foothills. Leafy oaks spring up along the side of the road, their tall branches dropping shady spots on the asphalt like horse apples. Up a steep ravine, a derelict barn with half its roof missing, stands forlorn. A weathered clapboard box perches at the top of a bluff, empty sockets where windows once shone, its swayback porch on the verge of collapse.

Widening, the highway adds a center turn lane. Sara slows to the speed limit, keeping a watchful eye for the tribal police. An ancient rock wall appears on the far side of the highway, leading to a two-story rock-walled building, dark and empty as a mausoleum. Boxy, with thick rock pillars in front, the whole thing is constructed out of rocks, thousands of small stones. She can't tell what it used to be, but it looks abandoned. Next door, a small rock house sits in shambles, its door and windows boarded. Right on the main highway, how could business be so poor? She doesn't understand. She guesses a good location isn't everything. And in Peach Springs, who knows how the local laws and ordinances govern businesses? Watching both sides of the road, she looks for the Diamond Springs intersection. The post office, the market, she should be getting close. There's Osterman's old garage and gas station on the right. She must be close.

Spotting the street sign, she hits the blinker and swerves into the center lane, downshifting for a left turn.

As she swings across 66, she questions if this is the right move. The Hualapai Police Department has a Diamond Springs address. She might end up driving right by the police station on her way to Canyon View and Wamaya's trailer. Working her jaws, she upshifts and follows the narrow road up a low rise between two steep desert hills. A pair of cottonwoods spring from a roadside ditch, their big, spade-shaped leaves flutter in a light breeze, a rich emerald green. "Here we go, Rocko." She wonders what they would do with him, if they arrest her.

The big truck chugs uphill as Sara downshifts, slowing for a school zone. Tall weeds, thick with the spring rains, hug the power poles at the edge of the pavement. Back off the street, the red-brick schoolhouse hides in the trees. Beyond, modest homes are scattered along the street, interspersed with vacant lots. Empty dirt plots tufted with weeds hint at decay. Small block houses with pitched roofs sit on little hillocks at odd angles, their backs turned to traffic. More than a few are boarded up. At the next corner, a dead tree hides a yard full of junk: a ruined table on its top, an empty washing machine box, its cardboard rotting in the weather, and a pile of broken toys.

Despite the pleasant day, a quick shiver shoots up Sara's spine. All this time she was under the impression that the Hualapai Tribe were living normal, everyday American lives. Isn't that what the Bureau of Indian Affairs does? Aren't they there to make sure these people have what they need to live decently?

The street straightens and the incline eases. Back from the road, stark houses thin—nothing but weeds and dirt in between. Holding her breath, Sara passes the police station without incident. She glances in her mirrors; afraid she should go back and check in. But the trailers at the edge of town are within sight. No turning back now.

Hard To Hear

Rocko watches Sara through the windshield as she approaches the dilapidated mobile home. When she knocks on the door, he huffs and lies down on the seat, resigning himself to another nap.

Standing in front of the door, at the top of the rickety steps, Sara shades her eyes with a hand, looking around: the old single-wide sits on a narrow lot, a hundred feet off the rough-graded street. A beat-up old pickup sits next to the dirt road. A rusty bicycle lies on its side near a brittle roll of tar paper. No car anywhere. No yard, only bare dirt and sharp rocks.

Sara turns to the door and knocks louder. She drove by twice and still isn't sure this is the right address. There is no house number. And it doesn't look like anyone is home. As she turns to leave, the dented door opens a crack.

Beneath a thick shock of raven hair, hooded eyes peer out from behind the door. A blade of sunlight slices across a slash of a mouth in a pudgy face the color of charred wood. The young woman flinches, then grunts.

Sara dons her friendliest smile. "Wamaya?"

A sour look twists Wamaya's face as she pulls back from the door. "Who are you? What do you want?"

Looking at her hands, Sara twists her fingers, uncertain what to say. Maybe she shouldn't say anything, just leave. She eyes Wamaya sympathetically. "I don't know what to say."

Wamaya starts to close the door.

"Wait," Sara cries.

The door remains open a tiny crack. One eye squints at Sara with disdain. "What for?"

"Uh... I'm the one," Sara stutters.

"One what?"

Sara looks down, her fists clenched. "I'm the one who... found Bryant."

The door slams shut with a bang.

Startled, Sara stumbles backward down the steps. She stares at the door, stunned. She is not sure what she was expecting, but to have the door slammed in her face... Why is it so hard to help someone? She gives her head a quick shake as she turns away, heading for the truck. She isn't supposed to be here, anyway.

Sara hears hinges creak and turns to see Wamaya poking her head out of the doorway.

"Wait," Wamaya says gruffly.

Looking up, Sara takes in the young Hualapai woman. Expressionless, Wamaya's face is a thin veil of contemptuousness, trying to mask the hurt in her dark eyes.

"Would it be all right if I came in?" Sara asks.

Wamaya pulls back inside and waves her in.

Smiling, Sara slowly takes the stairs. She steps into the dim trailer, craning her neck as she looks around: dark carpet of an undetermined color, matted with grime; a ratty couch pushed up against warped paneling; a yard-sale coffee table with a cracked leg. Sara edges toward the couch. "Can I sit?"

Wamaya grunts and points at the couch.

While Sara clears a spot, Wamaya rustles through a cupboard in the kitchen. Curious but not really wanting to know, Sara sits, glancing at Wamaya's back while she rummages around. She waits patiently as the obese woman works her way into a chair across from her.

Settled in, Wamaya eyes her suspiciously.

Hesitant, Sara watches her for a moment. "I'm so sorry for your loss."

Wamaya's expression turns stoic.

Sara lets the moment stretch, waiting for a reaction.

Fusty air in the cramped trailer thickens as seconds turn into minutes. Finally, Wamaya lifts her chin, looking down her nose at Sara. "What do you know about it?"

Stricken with compassion, Sara shifts her gaze to her hands, horrified at the prospect of losing a son. She can't imagine... "I don't." She shakes her head. "Again... I am so sorry..."

Wamaya juts her chin at Sara. "That's all you got to say?" she says accusatively.

Sara opens her hands and looks up. "Well, I... wanted to see if there was anything I could do."

Wamaya's features darken. "Like what?"

Sara shrugs. "I don't know." Leaning forward, she looks Wamaya in the eyes. "Do you need anything?"

Scowling, Wamaya turns away. "You mean, like my boy back?"

Sara's heart breaks all over again. Torn, she wonders if she should be here at all. It's not doing poor Wamaya any good. "If it were in my power to bring him back, I would," she says. "But it's not." She tilts her head, looking to restore eye contact with Wamaya. "I can't even tell you what happened out there."

Wamaya glances around the tiny living/kitchen area, avoiding Sara's gaze. Struggling out of the chair, she waddles over to the open cabinet next to the old fridge. She grabs an unopened fifth of Old Grand Dad off a shelf and toddles back to her chair. Twisting off the cap as she plops down, she grunts. She lifts the bottle to her lips and tilts her head back as she takes a big swig. Wiping off the top with her sleeve, she extends the whiskey bottle, offering it to Sara.

Sara eyes the whiskey, then smiles. "Thanks, but I'm driving." She waves it away with her fingers. "You go ahead."

Wamaya's eyes narrow with her tight grin. Taking another long drink, she drains the bottle by half.

Aghast, Sara watches the woman soak up whiskey like a sponge.

Stupefied, Wamaya stares straight ahead and burps. Loosely gripping the bottle of Old Grand Dad by the neck, she leans back and closes her eyes. "He was a good boy." She struggles forward, her eyes snapping wide. "And I *know* what happened," she says, waving the bottle emphatically. "It's not what they say." She slumps back, eyes closing. "Bryant was a good boy." Old Grand Dad dribbles down her chin as she slurps the whiskey.

Sara wonders if it's the whiskey talking. "I'm sure he was a good boy."

Her fiery eyes pop open. "My boy was *not* drunk."

Tempted, Sara almost lets it slide, but she is here for Wamaya, whatever the poor woman wants to talk about is fine. "Who said he was drunk?"

Wamaya flings an arm, spittle flying from her lips, furious. "Chief Watonami told me Bryant died drunk, and it was my fault, I killed him." She collapses back into the chair, moaning.

Sara moves off the couch to crouch next to Wamaya. Gently placing her hand on Wamaya's arm, she tries to assure her. "No. It's not your fault." Though she half-believes it could be true. "That isn't right. He should never have said that. You would never harm your son."

Wamaya leans her head back to pour whiskey down her throat. Blinking, she sits up, catching Sara with a sorrowful look. "He took my whiskey bottle, I know it," she says bewildered. "But it was empty." She pauses to belch. "Barely any left in the bottom."

Sara perks her ears. "The empty whiskey bottle... it was empty?" Everything stops as all the explanations of Bryant's death grind to a halt. Unbelievable. "Did you tell the chief the bottle was empty?"

Wamaya wags her head. "He wouldn't listen to me. He kept saying I killed him—Bryant, my son." Little sounds escape her throat, like baby animals dying.

Sara's eyes well as she fights the tears. What could be worse than losing her son? The Chief of Police accusing her of killing him. Sara's heart thumps, panicky, trying to ward off the evil, the horror. No mother should have to live with this. "What if I go to the chief? Tell him we talked—that the bottle Bryant had was empty to start with?" She shakes her head. "This isn't right."

Burgers & Fries

S ARA PUSHES HARD ON the handle, shoving the door open. Marching up to the reception desk of the Hualapai Nation Police Headquarters, she looks the withered old Hualapai woman in the eyes. "Chief Watonami, please," she says, crossing her arms.

The old woman gives her a dismissive glance and resumes her paperwork. "He's not here."

"When will he be back?" Sara demands.

"He's out on patrol," she says as she sorts forms into small stacks.

"What about Officer Natomi?"

The old woman slides a stack into a file folder without looking up. "He's with the Chief."

Sara bunches her chin, perturbed. "And they will be back when?"

Wearily, the receptionist cocks one eye. "Won't be back for hours. Whaddaya need?"

"I need to talk with the Chief," Sara says, her fists pressed tight on her hips.

The woman twists her mouth, gazing sidelong at Sara. "I can radio him if it's an emergency."

"Okay. Radio him."

The old woman tilts her head, eyeing her like a crow. "You're that white woman, aren't cha? What's the emergency?"

·········

Sara fumes all the way back to Kingman, the hour-long drive a blur of red mist. Motoring down the hill through town, she chides herself for not waiting, but she figured it wouldn't do much good. Last they spoke, Officer Natomi was cold as ice. And the Chief never listened to her anyway.

7070707070

MICHAEL ALLAN SCOTT

Why? Because she's a woman? A white woman? It isn't right. What they are doing to Wamaya, that poor woman, it isn't right.

Approaching the cutoff to Beale Street, Sara bats around the idea of going to the Sheriff. Not that he could do anything. Instead, she slows in thickening traffic, following Andy Devine past the old tanks and water tower next to the tracks. The modern Texaco and the Kingman Drug pass to her right, with the Territorial arches of the old Santa Fe railroad station to her left.

She and Sam made Kingman their home, raised their boys here. She has never questioned their decision. And grinding a life out of the barren Mohave Desert has toughened her up. Sara downshifts for the light at 4th Street, coasting through a yellow, past the Hotel Beale. The thing is, she can't get Wamaya out of her mind. She has never given much thought to the plight of those less fortunate. Figured she didn't need to. Not that she doesn't care, everyone has their hardships, she simply didn't realize it was that bad. She lugs the Ford in third, chugging past the Brunswick Hotel, the El Mohave, and Dinty Moore's. *Booze, what kind of life is that?*

Dunton Motors glides by on her right. Shiny new cars in the showroom go unnoticed as she rounds the curve. With her speed up to 35, she cruises past the busy A&W and the Liquinox plant high on the bluff. She downshifts, signaling to turn on Metcalfe.

Sara powers up Spring St. and whips into her driveway, skidding to a stop. Rocko bounds out when she opens her door. Grabbing her purse, Sara jumps down, checks the tarp over her painting gear, and turns for the shop.

At the end of the long driveway, Sam's step van sits squarely in front of the shop's tall rollup door. Their shop stands on a narrow ledge, scraped out of the hillside with a borrowed bulldozer. Running to the north edge of their property, the steeply gabled steel building stands forty feet high. Sam bought the metal structure in a kit with forged beams and precut corrugated sheeting. She couldn't believe it when he had it delivered. With help from the boys, he built the foundation and poured the floor, then did the steelwork, assembling most of it himself.

Her footfalls echo, floating up to the high metal roof as Sara walks by the long workbenches toward Sam. Rocko follows her in, tail wagging, his nails clicking on the concrete.

Welding hood down, Sam works away, making a heck of a racket as a spray of bright sparks shoot off the grinding wheel.

"Hey, honey!" Sara hollers over the noise.

Sam backs away, flips up his hood to give her a grin and shuts down the grinder. "Hey, babe. You're home early. How did it go?"

"It didn't," she says, clipping her words.

As she approaches, Sam sets his bracket project on the bench and removes his hood to give her a hug.

When the phone rings, they go quiet, looking at each other.

"I'll get it." Sara walks down, leans across the workbench, and snatches the handset off the wall phone. She turns to look at Sam as she answers, "Yes?" Sara turns away from the workbench, leaning back against it, wrapping the coiled phone cord around her finger. "Oh, hi Peggy." Sara nods as she listens. "Sure. That sounds great." She eyes Sam as she turns to the wall phone. "I'll see you when you get here." Untangling the cord, she hangs up the handset. "Peggy's on her way," she says, glancing at Sam. "She wants to take me for a ride in a Corvette. We're going to the Kimo for burgers and fries. You wanna go?"

Sam gives her a look. "Corvettes only have two seats."

Sara shrugs. "You could meet us there."

Sam grabs his hood and fits it on his head. "No. You go on. We'll talk when you get back. Say hi to Peggy."

Sara leans down to look Rocko in the eyes. "Stay here with your daddy," she says as she pats him on the head. Waving, she heads for the rollup doorway.

"Hey." Sam waves his arm to get her attention.

She turns and takes a step backward. "What?"

"Bring me a cheeseburger and fries, will ya?"

"Okay," Sara says, giving him a thumbs up on her way out.

······•·•·····

Sara sets her paintbox on the stool, the last of her painting gear out of the truck bed. Moving to the studio window, she holds the lace curtain open as she watches a gold Corvette Sting Ray pull up in front. She can't help but grin.

A raven-haired beauty and a young mother of two, Peggy lives one street over on Gold St. Peggy's high-octane husband Ralph, is the Sales Manager at Dunton Motors. He brings a new car home almost every week. Peggy says he uses them for test drives, and she gets to test-drive them all. Two weeks ago, Peggy was driving a Cadillac Coupe DeVille, sapphire blue with a white convertible top—the lap of luxury. The thing was huge, and a little ostentatious for Sara's tastes. But it's always a hoot to go on 'test-drives' with Peggy.

Sara grabs her purse on her way out the front door and trots to the Corvette rumbling at the foot of the walk. Grabbing the handle, she tugs the door open. "Hi Peggy," she says as she climbs in.

"Hey Sara." Peggy grins as she revs the engine. "A big block," she says, "a 454. Sounds cool, huh?"

Sara hunkers down in the low-slung bucket seat as Peggy guns it and drops the clutch. The rear tires smoke as the Vette fishtails into the middle of the street. "Are you sure this is okay with Ralph?" Sara asks.

"What he don't know won't hurt him," she says with a country twang. Laughing, Peggy backs off and cranks the wheel. "Wanna take it out on Stockton Hill, see how fast it'll go?"

Sara wags her head, squirming in the thinly padded seat. "No thanks. Let's go get a burger."

Peggy nods. "Yeah. I'm hungry." Doing a U-turn, she heads for the Kimo Café. "You know this thing cost almost six grand new? You should see the commission Ralph gets for selling one of these," she says grinning.

"How many has he sold?" Sara asks.

"None, so far," Peggy says defiantly. "But he will."

Sara scrunches her chin. "I'm sure you're right." She watches Peggy speed away from the stop sign, motor roaring. "Don't let me forget," Sara says over the engine noise. "I need a cheeseburger and fries to go."

Peggy bangs second gear and chirps the rear tires. "Sounds like Sam is hungry."

Sara slowly nods. "High school lunch hour is over. The Kimo should be about empty."

"Yeah," Peggy says. "We can talk. I haven't seen you in a coon's age, girl."

Sara laughs. "We had lunch the other day. How long do coons live?"

Peggy breaks up, laughing loud as she whips the Vette into the potholed Kimo parking lot. The Vette bounces and scrapes its nose. Peggy nurses it to a space next to a window and kills the engine.

Sara struggles out of the bucket seat, closes the car door and follows Peggy inside. The Kimo never ceases to impress Sara. She would bet that if she looked up 'greasy spoon' in the dictionary, it would show a picture of the Kimo Café: a small row of stools at a short counter under the service slot to the kitchen, a few booths next to the filmy windows, the air saturated with deep-fried grease, cigarette smoke, and burnt coffee. And they make the best burgers; the French fries are hand cut and cooked to perfection, a light golden brown.

Peggy takes a booth in the far corner near a window and Sara slides in across from her.

"Yeah, but that lunch was before I got this Covette," Peggy says, grinning.

Without a word, a teenage busboy in a stained white apron expertly sets their places with tin flatware wrapped in paper napkins, and thick ceramic coffee cups upside down on their saucers.

Sara gives Peggy a wry grin. "Yeah, and before a few other things. The last few days... You wouldn't believe."

After serving them ice water out of a plastic pitcher, the busboy hustles off, disappearing into the kitchen.

Her rayon uniform rustling, Loretta, a wiry middle-aged woman with a pencil over one ear and a fresh pot of coffee, appears at their table. She turns over their cups and pours. "What'll ya have?"

"The usual," Peggy says.

"Two burger baskets with fries," Loretta says.

"Before we leave, I need a cheeseburger and fries to go," Sara says.

"Comin' up." Loretta winks as she turns away.

The two women watch the waitress walk behind the counter to place their orders with ol' Bill, the day fry cook. Within seconds, they hear patties on the grill and the deep fryer sizzling.

Peggy stirs sugar into her coffee. "So, what's going on?"

Between sips of cooling coffee, Sara tells her about the strange events of recent days: the dead body of a boy named Bryant, the Sheriff, the Chief of the tribal police, the poor mother, and the mysterious cause of death.

Peggy's eyes widen as Sara's story unfolds. Habitually stirring her coffee, she listens with rapt attention.

Animated, Sara throws her hands in the air. "All I wanted to do was try my hand at a watercolor landscape."

Peggy cocks her head. "But Sheriff Bailey told you not to go back out there."

"That's not all," Sara shakes her head. "There's the buffalo..."

"My Lord! Buffalo?" Peggy pulls back, hands braced against the table. "What-in-the-world...?"

"It's a long silly story," Sara says waving it off. "Trust me, you don't wanna know."

Peggy eyes her skeptically. "What did Sam say about all this?"

"Same thing the Sheriff said." Sara twists her lips. "Leave it alone."

Donuts & Coffee

R OCKO TROTS UP TO greet Sara at the shop door. Picking up the cheeseburger scent, he wags his tail, hopeful.

Sara strides by the long workbenches, waving the brown paper bag out in front of her.

Hood down, grinding away, Sam doesn't notice.

"Hey," she yells.

Sam pauses long enough to catch her out of the corner of one eye. Switching off the grinder, he sets down the vice grips and removes the hood. He turns to Sara, smiling with open arms. "Lunch! You're a life-saver."

Sara stops at a clear spot on the metal-clad workbench and drags a tall stool to the edge of the high bench. She opens the sack and pulls out a wad of napkins as Sam wipes his hands on his shirt, grabs a can of Coke out of the ice chest he keeps stocked under the bench, and pulls up another stool.

"It's kinda late for lunch, isn't it?" she teases.

Sam gives his head a shake as she hands him a loaded cheeseburger wrapped in yellow wax paper. "Never too late for Kimo's," he says as he climbs on his stool.

Scooted close, Sara watches Sam wolf down his burger as she picks at his fries.

"How's Peggy doin'?" he asks between bites.

"She's gonna kill herself in that car," Sara says as she tosses a French fry to Rocko.

Eyeing her, he says, "French fries are no good for dogs."

She twists her lips, mildly annoyed. "One French fry isn't going to kill him."

Sam waves it off. "Don't worry about that car. Ralph won't let her have it that long."

"You know how much that thing costs?" Sara asks.

Sam nods as he chews his next-to-last bite of savory cheeseburger. "You want one of those?" he says grinning.

Sara holds up her palms. "Lord, no. The truck works just fine."

Wiping his hands with the napkins, Sam takes a big swig of Coke and starts on what's left of the fries. He gives her a nod. "Whaddabout you—what happened out there?"

Sara's face goes long. After several moments, she leans on her elbows, dropping her head in her hands, rubbing her eyes with her palms, completely drained. "I met Wamaya, the boy's mother."

Listening thoughtfully, Sam gives a slight nod, scooping up ketchup with the last of his fries.

Working her way through her morning, she recounts her dismay and frustration. "You should see what they did to that girl," Sara says. "It's not right."

"Yeah," Sam agrees. "That's pretty bad."

Sara crimps her lips. "I have to do something."

Sam sits up straight and finishes his Coke. "Like what?"

Sara shrugs. "I don't know." She looks him in the eye. "What do you suggest?"

Sam gives her a half smile. "You're as stubborn as they come. You already know what I'd suggest."

Incensed, she hops off the stool and gets in his face. "So, what... I should just leave it alone?"

Sam's eyes sparkle as he meets her gaze. "A little late for that now, don't ya think?"

"Well then, what?"

Sam turns serious. "You believe her?"

"Yes," Sara says, indignantly. "I believe her... I believe that she believes what she's telling me is true."

Sam cocks his head. "And you believe it's true... the bottle was empty."

Sara shrugs. "Hard to know. The woman is an alcoholic."

Sam crimps his lips as he nods. "And the bottle was empty when you found him..."

"I didn't see a bottle. I barely saw anything, a pantleg, maybe a shoe," she says. "It was the Officer, Henry Natomi. He mentioned it after they investigated the scene."

Sam wads up the wrappers and napkins in the brown paper bag and tosses it in a trash can. "And this Henry, he told you what?"

"Not much," she says frowning. "Something about an empty whiskey bottle—that it was under investigation."

"Tell me again, what Ham said," he says turning sideways on his stool.

"I haven't talked to Doc Pratt. Sheriff Bailey told me it wasn't a good idea."

Sam nods. "I can see where George would say that." He rubs his chin, thinking. "Did he mention the Medical Examiner's report?"

Sara shakes her head. "I don't think he has it—that whole jurisdiction thing."

Sam shrugs. "Why don't you drop in on ol' Ham—take him some donuts and coffee, see what he has to say?"

·····•··•····

Rocko trots across the driveway, headed for the truck, eager for a morning jaunt. As Sara opens the driver's door, he leaps in, moves to his spot at shotgun and circles.

Sara climbs in and closes the door. "Ready, Rocko?"

He gives her a grin, his tail wagging as he sits.

Backing out on Spring St., Sara reexamines her motives. What does she hope to prove? What if Wamaya is wrong, or doesn't want to remember, or can't remember? What if Chief Watonami is right? What if the boy drank too much and passed out? She shakes her head as she motors down Beale St. The poor woman, her boy, Bryant was barely a teenager.

Sara parks at an angle in front of the Kingman Bakery, still chewing on all the possibilities. *What if Wamaya is right?* As she enters, her mouth begins watering. It smells heavenly. The aromas of fresh-baked breads and pastries, cakes and cookies carry her away. She isn't here very often; and it's a good thing, her jeans are a little tight these days.

Climbing into the three-quarter-ton Ford, she slides the box of pastries next to the thermos. "Sorry boy," she tells Rocko. "These aren't for you."

Rocko lies down and looks away.

The rich scents of fresh pastries, still warm from the oven, fill the cab as Sara motors up the hill. Past the graveyard on Stockton Hill on her way to the hospital, she tries to imagine what it's like to be an alcoholic. She has

had her share of hangovers, but the misery of constant drunkenness—the cravings, it makes no sense. *What are they trying to escape?*
On the other hand, if one of her boys died... Though, apparently, Wamaya started drinking long before she lost her son.

Pulling into the main parking lot, Sara parks close to the hospital
lobby entrance. "Wait here," she tells Rocko as she gathers the pastry box
and thermos. "I'll be back in a little while. Then we'll go to the park."

Rocko huffs his approval, tail wagging.

Sara marches through the entry and into the lobby area, crossing the
putty-colored vinyl tile on her way to the reception window.

Behind the glass, Margaret Warner looks up from a pile of admittance
forms. She smiles politely, adjusting the nurse's cap pinned on her tight
bun. "Yes?"

Sara lifts the pink pastry box to show her. "I brought these for Doc
Pratt. She opens the box filled with a variety of fresh pastries: sweet
maple sticks, crème-filled chocolate éclairs, cinnamon rolls covered with
gooey icing, and donuts, glazed, or drenched in chocolate, or rolled in
powdered sugar, or covered in sprinkles.

Margaret's eyes light as she slides the glass aside. "Can I have one of
those?"

"Help yourself," Sara says. "Take two." She holds the box out while
Margaret licks her lips and fishes out an éclair.

"Do you want to take another?"

Margaret shakes her head, waving her off. "No. This will do fine.
Thanks."

"Is Doc Pratt in his office?" Sara asks as she closes the box.

With a mouthful of éclair, Margaret nods and points toward the main
corridor.

·····•··•·····

Doctor Hamilton Pratt sits at his cluttered desk in his cluttered office,
underneath a large photo of one of his more successful fishing trips
to Lake Mead. With Walter and Barry standing next to the rawboned
doctor, they hold up their catch: a stringer full of large-mouth bass.
Studying a lab report, Ham frowns when he hears the knock. "It's
open."

Sara peeks her head in. "Hi there, Doctor," she says as she swings through the door with a big pink box and a tall green thermos. Smiling, she sets the box of pastries on the edge of his desk. "I brought you some goodies." She holds up the thermos. "And fresh coffee."

Ham tilts his chair forward and lifts the lid. "What's the occasion, Sara?"

"I was hoping you'd have coffee with me, and a donut or two." She smiles as she sits in a side chair. "You have a few minutes to talk?"

Now in his late fifties, Ham remembers when Sara first came to town, some twenty or so years ago. She's a peach, in more ways than just her looks. As their family physician, he has taken care of Sam and Sara over the years, delivering their two boys, removing Sam's appendix, along with the usual medical complaints. Eyes smiling at the pretty blonde, Ham grins as she plucks a glazed donut out of the box. "For you, I've got all the time in the world." He takes half the donut in one bite. "What can I do for ya?"

Sara unscrews the top of the thermos, fills the stainless-steel lid with steaming Yuban and passes it to Doc Pratt. "Try this. It's a new brand."

Ham accepts the cup gingerly, setting it on a stack of file folders to cool. He pops the last of the donut in his mouth and reaches for a cinnamon roll, smiling. "Fresh donuts hand-delivered by a good-lookin' woman—the best thing that happened to me all morning. What's the occasion?"

Smiling, Sara crosses her legs and interlaces her fingers around her knee. "Sam said I should talk to you," she says, tentatively.

Ham nods as he chews.

"You know, I was the one who discovered that boy's body."

"I heard," he says, sipping his coffee. "Must have been quite a shock—finding him out there like that."

"Well, that's what I wanted to ask you about. The Sheriff said you did a medical exam."

"Due to the circumstances, the tribal police felt they needed me to examine the remains." He leans forward as he takes a bite of a cinnamon roll, then chews a moment. "You know, they don't have a full-time doc on the reservation. I do rounds up there every month or so for chronic cases; and they have a nurse at the school and a two-man emergency medical team, but that's about it. In a case like this, they don't have anybody qualified to do an autopsy or full medical exam."

Sara cocks her head. "But I thought the body was too far gone. I mean, what's the point?"

Mouth full, Ham nods as he swallows another bite. "That's why... The boy's remains were in tough shape. They're covering their asses."

"Covering their asses?"

"If there was a crime, say a homicide, and they failed to properly investigate... dot the i's, cross the t's—you get the picture."

Sara sits up, alarmed. "Homicide? Really?"

"Not as close as I could tell. Like I say, the body was in tough shape, out there in the elements for days. But there weren't any obvious signs of foul play: no stab wounds, or bullet slugs that I could find."

"Sheriff Bailey told me you thought it was alcohol poisoning or exposure."

Ham shrugs. "Best guess, based on the facts. They found an empty whiskey bottle with the body." He takes a swig of coffee and plucks a maple bar out of the box. "But it had some hair on it."

"Hair on it, what does that mean?"

Taking a big bite of the maple bar, he eyes her and leans back. "That body had been out there for days. But it was largely unmolested. No varmint damage, hardly any insects. Very unusual. What tissue remained was an odd consistency."

"Would the alcohol poisoning do that?"

Ham finishes his maple bar and shakes his head. "Not likely."

"Then what?"

"Hard to say—too much decay to know much for sure. I pretty much ruled out homicide, which is what they needed."

"But you can't say for sure it was the alcohol?"

Ham licks the ends of his fingers then grabs for his coffee. "Not really. I gave a copy of the exam report to the Sheriff. It's all there."

Sara watches him drink. "How's the coffee?"

"Darn good," he says grinning.

Cow Ponds

A QUIET TUESDAY AFTERNOON, still as a held breath. Sara sits at her easel, turned away from her canvas, gazing out the window. Thin clouds stretch high above the broken bluffs. Clumps of distant buildings—the high school gym, the grammar school, rooftop parapets of downtown—peek out of the high desert hills like a mirage.

It had been a whirlwind weekend. Timmy had come and gone, out with his friends day and night before rushing back to ASU. At least she saw him for a meal or two. Though now, the emptiness seeps in like the silence at the end of a favorite song. She has never felt more alone.

Listless, Sara attempts to push past her melancholy and get on with it. Staring vacantly out the window is the best she can do. A wisp of a song returns to hang in the air. Tuesday Afternoon—Jack used to play the Moody Blues all the time. With a crooked smile, she remembers how he played that album until she was sick of it. She sits, a touch nostalgic, imagining the melody in her mind, her fondness for the music, comforting. How the tides turn.

Sighing, she dismisses her attempt to paint, disparaging her art as a petty pastime, a frivolous hobby. In her younger days, Sara used to believe art was her true calling. Today, it's hard to muster anything beyond a forced and superficial interest. She tries to look forward to a future with her children as grown men, hoping they will marry someone nice and give her grandchildren to spoil. Doubting Sam has similar concerns, she envies how he manages to stay busy. She gives her head a quick shake to banish her blues. This is no way to spend a day. Standing, she stretches, determined to take a page from Sam's playbook and get busy.

Sara heads down to the kitchen to answer the phone.

"Hey, Sara."

"Hello, Dennis," she says, tickled with surprise. She had forgotten all about him and his runaway buffalo.

"You know, my offer still stands."

Sara gives a quick laugh.

"I thought we had a date," he teases. "I'm beginning to think you don't like me."

"I don't know about a date," she says, half-kiddingly. "Sam may not approve."

"A date in the desert with an old cowpoke like me, how could you resist?"

She laughs. "Good Lord, Dennis. You are such a flirt. What would Rita say?"

"My wife thinks I'm a harmless old blowhard. I'm afraid she knows me too well."

"That doesn't make me feel any safer," she says. "Alone with you, out on the north forty, I'm not so sure."

Dennis chuckles. "Heck, we're goin' buffalo huntin', what's the harm?"

"I can show you where I saw him," she says. "That doesn't mean we're gonna find that buffalo of yours."

··· • • • • • ···

Early Wednesday, a bright yellow dually crew-cab pulls up to Sara's front walk. Jowly and clean-shaven with a pot belly hanging over his hand-tooled leather belt, the big man hops out of his tall Cowboy Cadillac and rounds the hood to open the front passenger door for Sara.

The weather is breezy, as is the conversation, and Sara finds the ride with Dennis Drake entertaining. His leathery face from years in the saddle gives the sixty-something rancher an air of integrity, despite his flirtatious humor. According to Dennis, the Drake family has run the largest cattle ranch in Mohave County since the late 1800s. And his tall tales of life in the cattle business hold her rapt attention to the outskirts of Truxton. Yet, she knows by his long reputation, the man is a powerful figure in the community and not to be taken lightly.

Before they reach the trading post, Dennis turns off 66 onto a rough dirt road. He slows to a stop a few yards in at the chain-link gate. On either side of the locked gate, barbwire fencing runs both directions, parallel to the highway as far as the eye can see. The large sign in the middle of the gate warns against trespassing in faded red letters.

Dennis shifts the Chevy into neutral, stomps the parking brake, dons his sweat-stained Stetson, and opens his door. "Be right back," he says as his scuffed work boots hit the ground.

Sara watches the big man remove the chains and walk the gate out of the way. She's not sure what to expect, but she feels privileged to help this man any way she can.

Dennis climbs in with a grin and rolls the truck through. After securing the gate, he settles in behind the wheel. Shifting the dually into second, he follows a worn pair of tire tracks leading off across the flats.

"You know, this is leased land," he says. "BLM."

"Bureau of Land Management," she says.

"That's right." He nods. "We been running cattle here since before the reservation was established in 1883."

Sara watches the tire ruts wander off across the weedy mesa as the big dually lumbers along. "And you added a buffalo to the herd?"

He shakes his head. "Durn if that bull didn't up and run off the minute he came out of the chute."

She tightens her lips. "Sam said it ticked you off."

"Paid a pretty penny for that big fella."

Sara gives him a sidelong glance. "He also said something about the Hualapai hanging on to him."

Narrowing his eyes, he huffs. "That's what's got my giblets in a twist."

A knotted strip of cottony clouds hangs above the horizon. Below, banded ridges steam south, their travels undetectable to the naked eye. Sara hesitates to ask. "What makes you think they have him?"

Dennis shrugs. "Depends on where you found him."

Raising her eyebrows, Sara mulls it over. "Did Sam tell you? I saw him at the cow pond."

He barks a short laugh. "Which one?" There are a few watering holes out here." With his wrist hung over the steering wheel, he points to a dark swatch of desert a mile or two ahead. "You see that?"

"Uh huh."

"That's one of 'em."

"A cow pond?"

"Yup."

They drive in silence for a few minutes. As they come to a berm of raw dirt, Dennis swings the truck around to the low side, to a rough cut bulldozed out of the earth. An apron of muddy hoofprints leads to a dirty puddle held dormant against the steep side of the berm.

"That isn't it," she says.

"Didn't figure it was." His jowls lift as he scrunches his face. "What did it look like?"

"The berm was bigger. There was more water," she says thoughtfully. "Between a couple small hills."

Dennis nods as he leaves the cow pond in his mirrors, steering the four-wheel-drive dually onto the weatherbeaten trail. "Anything else?"

She ponders his question, trying to recall. "Junipers... and a barbwire fence."

Dennis cuts her a quick glance. "Which side of the fence?"

"I was heading west when I came across the cow pond," she says. "I'm thinkin' the north side."

"Hmph... Could be the reservation."

Dennis veers off the trail, heading out across the raw desert. The big dually lumbers over clumps of weeds and rocks, jostling Sara and Dennis in their seats like sock puppets. He gives her a tight-lipped grin. "Shortcut."

Gripping the armrests, Sara hangs on, her head wobbling like a bobble-head doll. "Shortcut?"

"There should be a fence or two in this direction," he says. "All we gotta do is find a watering hole to go with it."

Sara gives him a skeptical look. "What if it's on the reservation."

"If we spot that buffalo of mine, it'll prove my point."

"That's the biggest thing I've seen on hooves. And the way he ran, I figure he'd have made it back to your holding pen by now." She chuckles. "If he didn't fall in the canyon."

"When I left this morning, the holding pen had a few heifers, but no bull. And you know how them heifers can get without a bull." Dennis leans her direction and winks.

"No bull, huh?" Sara laughs. "Dennis, you're full of bull."

Dennis laughs and lets it ride. Low hills studded with scrub juniper slowly rise out of the mesa. He veers left, cutting through a downed fence line to join up with a dusty set of worn tire tracks heading north-northwest. "There's plenty of fencing to keep our herds separated, but there are also plenty of breaks in that fencing," he says turning serious. "More than you'd usually see. They're sly devils; and those ol' boys won't let us on the reservation to check the brands. They claim we're violating their sovereignty."

Sara sees what Sam meant about ranchers and their livestock. As the dually picks up speed, she keeps her thoughts to herself. Truck tires thump through the rough spots, kicking up a plume of dust. As Dennis slows to cross an arroyo, she wonders if they'll end up spending the entire day out here looking for his rogue buffalo.

Relatively straight but badly eroded, the remnants of a trail rise to meet another barbwire fence line. Its crooked old posts are hacked out of juniper trunks, jutting out of the dirt at odd angles. With a passable cattleguard, taut fencing runs off into the distance on either side. The dually rumbles over the cattleguard, making a toolbox on the back seat jump in place. The trail jogs north, deteriorating into a rock-strewn hill climb. As they crest the low hill, more barbwire exposes itself with a tall berm just the other side.

"That looks familiar," Sara says. "Isn't that reservation land?"

"Over yonder?" Dennis slows the big Chevy, stopping this side of the fence. "Could be." Grabbing a pair of work gloves out of the console, he shuts down the truck and elbows his door open. "Whaddaya say we take a closer look?"

As she climbs out, Sara figures if they get caught on Hualapai land, she's with Dennis, he'll take care of her. She follows him toward the fence, looking over the area, hoping she doesn't see that dang buffalo. "You should've seen it," she says. "That buffalo of yours cleared the fence without breaking stride. I don't see how the Hualapai could hang onto him, even if they wanted to."

Dennis works his hands into his gloves as he approaches the rusty barbwire. "Wait here," he says at the fence. He steps on the middle strand, holding it to the ground with a well-used cowboy boot, using a gloved hand to pull the top strand high. He bends to climb through, careful not to catch his hat or his shirt.

Sara watches from this side of the fence as Dennis clumps up the berm and disappears. "Any buffalo?" she yells.

"Nope," he hollers back. "But he's been here. These 're his tracks."

Sara shifts her weight from foot to foot, increasingly uncomfortable. "Maybe we should go," she yells.

"Be right there, little lady."

The crown of his Stetson bounces above the berm as Dennis reemerges. Breathing hard, he picks his way through the fence. "Not getting' any younger." He gives her a grin, stripping off his gloves as they head to the truck.

Approaching the truck, she shades her eyes with her hand scanning the wide-open panorama. Catching a hint of the Lower Granite Gorge, she figures to come back and tackle that watercolor. She points a finger west along the fence. "We're pretty close to where I found that boy," she says. "He was in an arroyo over that way."

Dennis stops to look, his gaze following the direction of her finger. "That's a durn shame about the kid. I heard he was drunk. A young kid like that—a durn shame."

Sara refrains, hoping to avoid rehashing the whole thing with the rich rancher. "This is your land, right?"

"This side of the fence, it's all mine."

"Can I come out here on my own—if I want to paint?"

"Any time, Sara." He turns and grabs the door handle. "But lemme know ahead-a-time, okay?"

"Thanks," she says as she climbs in. "Will do."

Dennis starts up the truck, shifts into first and cranks the wheel. The truck crawls through a tight about-face. "You wanna be careful out here," he says conversationally.

"I'll be fine." She grins. "I gotta gun."

"That's good and all, but the thing is, this is grazing land—BLM. They run varmint control in these parts."

"Varmint control? What, coyotes?"

"And lions and such—any kinda critters that trouble the beeves."

Sara frowns. "What kind of control are we talkin' here?"

Dennis gives her a sidelong glance. "Baited traps, coyote loads... Watch your step, and watch your dog."

Four Wheelin'

THE LIGHT FADES WHILE shadows of indigo creep across the rugged hills outside Sara's kitchen window. Slipping on her oven mitts, she pulls out a casserole and sets it on a hot plate in the middle of the table.

Sam inhales deeply, losing himself in the enticing aroma of tender meat, rich cheeses, and savory noodles.

Eyes smiling, Sara removes the lid and hands him a serving spoon. She slides out of her mitts and drops into her chair as Sam spoons a big helping onto his plate.

"How did it go today?" Sam asks, meeting her gaze. "Ol' Dennis behave himself?"

Sara grins. "He's a little rough around the edges, but he was the perfect gentleman. I enjoyed his company," She gives him a wink. "And you better mind your p's and q's, he's quite a charmer."

"Did you find his buffalo?"

"I showed him where I saw it," she says as she serves herself. "He saw the hoofprints, but no buffalo."

Sam nods as he swallows a mouthful. "About what you thought, then."

She waves her fork, chewing a bite, waiting to swallow. "That cow pond *is* on reservation land, which is what I thought. But I didn't know it was that close to the border. The Drake Ranch is on the other side of the fence."

"Ol' Dennis…" Sam shrugs. "His family has been ranchin' in these parts darn near forever."

"No kiddin'." She flicks a blonde lock out of her face. "I learned a lot about ranching, today."

He grins. "I'll bet."

She points her fork. "Pass me the salt, please."

Sam hands her the saltshaker. "Since he drove ya, I'm guessing you didn't get a chance to paint."

Mouth full, she shakes her head. She swallows, washing it down with iced tea. "Found a great spot, though—on his side of the fence, darn close to where I was before it all hit the fan. But on the Drake Ranch land, not the reservation."

Helping himself to seconds, Sam digs in.

Sara looks up from her plate. "Dennis said to watch out for varmint traps, something to do with the BLM or Wildlife Services, I'm not sure. He mentioned a coyote load. Do you know what that is?"

Dennis chews vigorously, then nods. "Yeah," he says, eyeing her.

"Well?"

He waves her off with his fork. "You don't want to know," he says as he reaches for his iced tea.

"Whaddaya mean?"

"Not good," he says through a mouthful.

Sara throws up her hand. "How am I going to look out for them, if I don't know what they are?"

"Good point." His features harden in a frown, eyes narrowing as he sets his knife and fork on his plate. "They are supposed to be flagged, but not always; and they are hard to spot. I've heard of people stepping on them. But the bait looks like a little capsule sticking out of the ground."

"What happens if you step on it?"

"It goes off."

"And?"

Looking past her, he pauses for a moment. "It's designed to kill canines: coyotes, foxes, and so on—cats and badgers, too." He pulls his gaze back from outside the kitchen window. "The capsule is filled with cyanide—goes off in their mouth when they bite it. Kills 'em."

"Good Lord." Sara gives a little gasp as she puts her fingers to her lips. "Why would they do such a thing?"

Sam's jaws knot as he gazes out the window. The moment passes and he looks down at his plate, reticent. "Like Dennis told ya, varmints. Protect the livestock."

"I can't believe it." She shakes her head, dismayed. "That's horrible." Letting it sink in, she takes another bite, chewing slowly. "What harm do coyotes or foxes do to cattle?"

Sam shrugs. "I couldn't tell ya. But it's hard on people and pets. If you go back out there, watch where you step and leave Rocko in the truck."

· · · • · · • · · ·

The next morning, after breakfast, Sara loads her painting gear into the truck bed. Feeling horrible, she is torn. The look on Rocko's face when she told him he couldn't go, awful. She justifies it over and over, telling herself she couldn't handle it if Rocko was killed. She is firm on this point. She has to be, she is not a careless person. Still, leaving him behind is sad. A trusted companion, Rocko goes almost everywhere with her, and he loves to go.

Earlier, while packing, Sara thought long and hard about other locations for her painting expedition. But it all came down to the simple facts: she doesn't want to go back to the reservation, begging for permission is beneath her; and she has her heart set on that incredible view of the Lower Granite Gorge.

As she climbs into the cab, she finds strength in her conviction, determined to create a watercolor worthy of the effort.

Dennis left a gate key for her at the main ranch house. He asked that if she sees his wayward buffalo, to let him know right away.

Sara breezes through Hackberry and Valentine without a second glance. The trek to Truxton is getting to be old hat—not exactly what she had in mind when she started this watercolor fandango. How it managed to get out of hand, she's not sure. Tangled up with a corpse, an alcoholic, and a runaway buffalo makes her wonder if there is a secret conspiracy to keep her from painting. She passes by the ranch road turnoff in favor of a cold Seven-Up. The Truxton Trading Post is about a mile up the highway, and she wants to see how Lionel is doing.

· · · • · · • · · ·

Seven Up half gone, Sara climbs back in the big Ford. She backs out to turn south on Route 66. She wasn't actually expecting Lionel to have more news on Bryant or his mom, but she was hoping. Her thoughts wander back to Wamaya—the poor woman. Sara wishes she could do more. Anyway, it's good that Lionel is doing well.

Braking, she slows for the turnoff. The stiffly sprung F250 bounces off the pavement and through the potholes before Sara stops at the gate. She holds a moment, staring across the flats, hazy mountains in the distance, missing Rocko.

Tightening her lips, she kicks open the door, jumps out and strides to the gate. The padlock is heavy duty and stiff from lack of use. Once Sara untangles the shackle from the heavy chain, she finds her determination strengthening, fueled by a hidden resistance on which she can't quite put her finger. This has become more than a peaceful outing for the purpose of exercising her watercolor skills.

She rolls the truck through, steps on the parking brake, pops the shifter into neutral and jerks the lever into four-wheel-drive. Jumping out, she closes and locks the gate, then locks the wheel hubs.

As her three-quarter-ton rumbles along, Sara admires the spring greenery, a rare sight in this barren land. The ranch road is nothing more than a set of badly eroded tire tracks, the trail to the first cow pond barely visible. If she hadn't ridden with Dennis, she wouldn't have a clue.

At the first cow pond, she stops to look over her options. Dennis had gone cross country, but the ranch road wanders off to the northwest. The Lower Granite Gorge lies in that general direction. Feeling adventurous, she shoves it into gear and lets out the clutch.

Sara brakes to a stop as the trail drops off into a deep arroyo. Throwing the gearshift into neutral, she toe-taps the parking brake and hops out for a closer look. She walks up to the edge of the steep bank. The arroyo cuts through the mesa like an angry scar. Its jagged cracks rip into the earth, spidering off toward the reservation. The tire tracks are faint, but they are there. If other vehicles have made it through, so can she. Her four-wheel-drive is more than capable. The only liability is the long wheelbase. She could get the truck hung up in the bottom of this thing and have to hike out. It's not that far of a walk to the trading post, but it would sure be a nuisance. She eyes it carefully, plotting different routes. "Go for it," she says under her breath.

Climbing in, Sara buckles up. She shifts the transfer case into low range four-wheel-drive and eases out the clutch. The big Ford lurches into a crawl as she gives it gas. When the front end noses over, she stares into the deep arroyo. Its sides are so steep it looks straight down. The truck waddles down the bank, tires slipping as it hits loose gravel. At the bottom, Sara heaves a big sigh, unaware she was holding her breath. She pushes in the clutch, letting the truck roll to a stop in the sand. Bending forward, she strains to get a better look at the craggy slope ahead. It looked so much easier up top.

Sara scrutinizes her choices, deciding against her original route. Dumping the clutch, she cranks the wheel hard to the left and steps on the gas. She grits her teeth, sawing the wheel as the truck grudgingly obeys, clawing its way up the steep climb with a roar. As the truck grinds to the top, nothing but blue sky fills her windshield. The trusty truck crawls out of the arroyo, all four wheels on the level. Pleased with herself, she smiles and keeps rolling, tracking the remnants of the faded road. She bumps along, wishing Rocko were here.

The horizon creeps closer as the terrain slopes into the low hills. After chugging along at a snail's pace for a handful of minutes, she comes to a Y in the trail. A badly worn set of tire tracks head toward and away from the reservation. Sara veers toward the reservation, shifts out of low range and picks up speed. This must be the trail they found when Dennis took his shortcut. With the hills, there is higher ground closer to the reservation fence—a better view of Lower Granite Gorge.

Cresting a small rise, Sara spots a downed section of fence. She remembers Dennis saying there are several fences out here—not all of them in good shape. She follows the trail through a dip and tops the next rise. The ghost of a road straightens before she steers through a cattleguard. As the border fence comes into view, the landscape begins to look familiar. She slows as she approaches the reservation fence line, scanning the reservation-side for the cow pond or the Houdini buffalo. What's left of the trail jogs west-northwest to parallel the fence. She stops to gaze across the fence: no cow pond, no buffalo. Engaging the clutch, she steers through the jog, glancing out the passenger window as the truck rumbles along in second gear. Ahead, the striated lips of the Lower Granite Gorge peek through the juniper. Smiling, she senses the perfect spot is on the other side of the rise.

Downed fenceposts lie tangled in slack barbwire as she crests the rise. Starting down the slope, she spots the arroyo. A little different from this angle, but that has to be it. Sara parks near the arroyo and climbs out. Trudging to the edge, she gazes up the deep ravine, shuddering at the sight of tall weeds. The corpse was hidden in those weeds. She holds her ground, letting it sink in: Bryant died there. Wamaya is convinced it wasn't her fault. Sara is not sure what to think. Saddened, she turns away, in no mood to paint.

Rounding the front of the truck, Sara spots an odd patch of color in the weeds. Bright orange—Day Glo orange, now that she looks. She walks over and bends to take a closer look: some sort of paint in a small indentation, as though someone cleaned a brush or a spray-can nozzle. She snaps upright, questions firing off in her skull like flares. Is this from the tribal police? Were they marking a crime scene? What are they not telling her? Did Bryant die of other causes? Doc Pratt said the corpse was too badly decayed to know for sure. Was it a homicide?

Sara gathers herself and marches to the pickup bed. On tiptoes she rummages in her large paint supply bag to retrieve her Polaroid. She marches back to the orange blotch, taking pictures as she works her way around the marker. She half-suspects there are more markers, but she is not sticking around to find out. Done, she walks to the truck, tosses the photos and the camera on the seat and climbs in, determined to get answers for Wamaya's sake.

Through The Looking Glass

O N THE OUTSKIRTS OF Kingman, her stomach rumbles, reminding Sara she missed lunch. Her little ice chest with a hardboiled egg and a spinach salad sits in the bed with her painting gear, untouched. Ignoring her hunger, she heads downtown. Sara pulls into a spot in front of the Court House, gathers the Polaroids off the seat, and climbs out. With a purposeful stride, she hustles up the walk and into the Sheriff's Office.

By the time Janet shows her into Sheriff Bailey's office, Sara begins to wonder. Maybe she should leave it alone.

Sheriff Bailey comes out from behind his mammoth desk to greet her with a condescending smile. "Hello, Sara. I wasn't expecting to see you around these parts for a while."

Smiling politely, she extends her hand. "Me, either. Do you have a minute?"

"For you, any time," Bailey says as he shows her to a side chair. He returns to his seat and leans forward to fold his hands on his desk. "What can I do for ya?"

Sara reaches into her purse, extracts the Polaroids, and hands him the photos.

Bailey takes the photos and shuffles through them, studying them one by one. "What am I lookin' at?"

"I don't know, Sheriff. I was hoping you could tell *me*."

He shuffles through them again and looks up. "Where'd ya take these?"

"I was on the Drake Ranch, out by the reservation."

"This have anything to do with that body you found?"

Sara gives him a sharp look. "I went out there to paint. I didn't go on Hualapai land... as far as I know.

"Hmph," he says as he takes another look at the pictures. "I thought you were done with all that."

"It just happened to be close to where the body was found, I didn't go looking for it," she replies. "Could that be a boundary marker of some kind—part of the tribal police investigation?"

The Sheriff leans back in his high-back leather chair, frowning. "It looks like a marker, all right. But it ain't no boundary marker. Looks more like one of them coyote getters went off."

"Is that what Dennis Drake called a coyote load?"

Sheriff Bailey pulls in his double chin and nods. "Probably. They are all over out there—varmint control. They call 'em a couple things: cyanide device or cyanide bomb. Wildlife Services uses them."

"And the Day Glo orange... Is to keep people from stepping on it?

"No. You don't see that unless it has been activated. You see any dead critters?"

"You mean, it already went off?"

Tilting his head up, the Sheriff tugs on a neck wattle. "Yeah, something set it off. That orange stuff usually gets all over the critter's face when it inhales the poison. Should've been a dead animal right around there, somewhere."

"Not that I saw." Sara shakes her said. "But I didn't look that close. I was..."

Bailey rocks forward, holding up the pictures. "You said this was close to where you found that corpse?"

Rubbing her chin, Sara wonders how much she should say. She waits a beat, then another. "You remember the place... the weeds in the wash, where the body was?"

The Sheriff nods.

"I could see those weeds from the spot where I found this."

The Sheriff's head twitches as he looks past the wall. Pressing his lips into a tight scar, he turns back to Sara, picks up the pictures and waves them in front of her. "Can I keep these?"

Sara extends a hand. "Give me one or two and you can keep the rest. Is that okay?"

He spreads the pictures like a poker hand, plucks out two of the Polaroids, and hands them over.

She tucks the pictures into her purse. "What are you going to do with the rest?"

"Don't know yet," he says. "If we went back out there, could you show me where you took them?"

"When?"

"Don't know yet," he says standing. "I'll call ya."

·········

On her way to the truck, Sara replays the exchange. It's what the Sheriff didn't say. Maybe she should show the pictures to Officer Natomi. Though strictly speaking, the spent cyanide device is on Drake's ranchland. Or so it appears. Besides, She's not up for another trip to Peach Springs. She will tell Dennis Drake that she didn't see his buffalo when she returns the gate key; maybe she should ask him about it. The darn thing was on his ranch. The idea of that thing going off in an animal's face—it's barbaric, evil.

Sara motors down 4th St. to the light at Andy Devine. Doc Pratt—what was it he said? Something wrong with the consistency of the tissue. She crosses to the east-bound lane when the light turns green, heading up the hill. On Stockton Hill, her stomach reminds her she skipped lunch. When she swings into the hospital, that hardboiled egg is on her mind. She parks, grabs her purse, and jumps out, the egg forgotten.

Sara smiles and waves at Margaret on her way through the lobby. At Doc Pratt's office door, she knocks lightly.

"Come in."

Sara lets herself in and closes the door. "Doctor Pratt," she says, smiling. "I have a couple more questions. Do you have minute?"

Grinning widely, Ham waves his arm toward the only empty chair. "The donut lady. Hello, Sara. Sit down."

"Oops! I forgot the donuts," she says jokingly as she sits.

"Your pretty face is plenty," he says. "What do you want to know?"

Perched on the edge of her seat, she digs through her purse and pulls out the Polaroid snapshots. She looks Doc Pratt in the eye as she hands them over. "I took these close to the site where I found the body."

Ham bunches his chin as he looks over the photos. "Is that what I think it is?"

"Sheriff Bailey told me it is a cyanide device."

Clicking his teeth, Ham gives a little nod. "How far from where you found the corpse?"

Sara thinks for a minute, recalling the spot, looking back at the weeds. "About fifty yards."

Ham looks at her, then looks at the pictures as he works his jaws. "This is a spent cartridge... Did you find the dead animal?"

Sara shakes her head. "The Sheriff asked me the same thing."

Ham drops the photos on his desk as he stands. "Wait here a minute." He moves around his desk and exits into the hall.

Sara watches him head down the hall through the partly open door. She hasn't let herself speculate too much on the Sheriff's reaction, but this... Painfully curious, she half dreads Doc Pratt's return.

Ham walks in and closes the door, holding a brown file folder high in one hand. Noticing the look on her face, he says, "Forgive me. I didn't mean to startle you. It could be nothing. I just want to double check." He crosses to his desk, drops into his chair, and opens the folder.

Sara leans in for a better view. "That's Bryant's medical report?"

Ham gives her a quick grin as he lifts out a large glassine envelope. "A copy," he says. "The Tribal Police have the original." He slides a thin stack of photos out of the envelope and spreads them on his desk. Reaching in the pencil drawer, he retrieves a large magnifying glass. Bent over the photos, he squints one eye to peer through the glass, making strange noises in the back of his throat.

Looking up, he sets down the magnifying glass and slowly leans back. "At the time, I couldn't definitely attribute it to anything—the level of decay, the amount of time out in the elements," he says turning serious. "But the odd tissue consistency, and the remains unmolested after that long..." He lays out his hand, palm up.

Sara's eyes widen. "What?"

Ham rubs his hands worriedly. "It's hard to tell... But it's a possibility which should be considered."

Busted

INDIGNANT, SAM RAISES AN eyebrow. "What?"

"He wouldn't tell me." Sara moves to the table with her iced tea and her salad. "But based on his reaction, I'd say he found a connection."

Sam looks her in the eyes. "What're ya thinkin'?"

"What if..." Sara crosses her legs and sips her tea, then turns her head to gaze out the kitchen window. "What if Bryant stepped on that cyanide bomb?"

"I don't know that much about them," Sam says. "I guess it could kill him, but I don't know." Sam gives her a look. "What if he did? How would that change anything? You said they found him with an empty whiskey bottle. It's tragic, but the boy is dead."

Sara turns to meet his gaze. "It would mean that Wamaya is right."

....

"Here's to you Mrs. Robinson..." While Sam snores in his recliner, Sara half-heartedly watches *The Graduate*. Worried to distraction, she loses track of whatever the heck Dustin Hoffman is doing. It's right there, top of mind. Like an itchy scab, she can't leave it alone. *What if Wamaya is right?*

Sara pries her tired bones off the couch, stumbles to the TV, bends down and turns it off. "Come on, Daddy. Movie's over. Let's go to bed."

Sam grunts, tumbles out of the recliner, and sleepwalks to bed.

In her pajamas with her teeth brushed, Sara hits the sack. Already snoring, Sam sounds like one of those newfangled jumbo jets on takeoff. At his feet, Rocko adds to the ruckus. She shakes her head. Between Sam and Rocko, it's a wonder the roof doesn't blow off. Done listening to Sam, she rolls him on his side, away from her. When they were first married, she thought she would get used to his snoring. After this many years, it seems unlikely.

Turning her pillow, she squirms, trying to get comfortable, her thoughts bouncing around in her head like ping pong balls. The way Sheriff Bailey asked to keep the pictures, the way Doc Pratt side-stepped her questions makes her suspicious. She wonders if the tribal police know about the cyanide device. Maybe they found it first. Maybe that's why they wanted Doc Pratt to do the medical exam. But what difference would *that* make?

·····•·····

With the morning light shining through her kitchen curtains, Sara leans against the counter working on her second cup of Yuban. She didn't sleep worth a darn and the coffee isn't helping much. Before Sam left to start his route, he mentioned lunch and something about whipping a dead mule. The dead-mule remark didn't help her mood. Deprived of sleep, it's hard not to be cranky.

Sara swirls the dregs, resolving to call the Sheriff after this cup. She would have called an hour ago if she knew what she wanted to say. Again, she thinks it through, step by step, allowing for any possible diversions Sheriff Bailey might throw at her. Sighing, she pours herself another cup. *This has got to work.*

Now that she thinks about it, maybe she should go see Wamaya first. But what is she going to tell her? She doesn't know anything for sure. *Not yet.*

Sara picks up the handset and dials. "Hi Janet. Is the Sheriff in? ...Thanks."

Waiting on hold, she takes another sip.

"Hi Sheriff, it's Sara... Yes, I know... I'm going back to the Drake Ranch today, if you want me to show you the spot where I took those pictures... No... I'm going to paint... I see."

Perplexed, Sara hangs up. That didn't go at all like she planned. Why would the Sheriff be so adamant about staying away? To heck with that. She can go paint on the ranch anytime she wants, Dennis said so. Not that she wants to go anywhere near where Rocko found the body... Besides, she can detour around the spot. Her favored view of Lower Granite Gorge awaits.

Sara frowns at the phone, takes a swig of coffee, and picks up the handset.

"Hello, is Mr. Drake there? ...Yes, tell him it's Sara Wayland." She hears a TV in the background—sounds like the news. "Oh... he's out... Well, I returned a gate key yesterday. Would it be all right for me to borrow it today? Oh... I see."

Suspiciously eyeing the phone, Sara hangs up. *Coincidence?* She doesn't think so. Yesterday, it was no problem picking up the key. Dennis said any time. He wasn't there when she picked up the key, yesterday. All of a sudden, he's out somewhere and she has to wait? Maybe it's nothing. Maybe he has the key with him. Though she can't help wondering if he has been talking with Sheriff Bailey.

·····•·····

Rocko watches as Sara loads the last of her gear into the back of the pickup.

She gives Rocko the eye. "You can go, but you have to stay in the truck. Okay?"

Wagging enthusiastically, Rocko grins.

Opening her door, she tells him "Let's go."

Rocko leaps onto the seat, scooting to his spot at shotgun, one happy dog.

Her head thick, Sara looks around, trying to remember. Sam has the step van today. The shop and the house are locked up. Her gun is in the glove box, fully loaded. She plans on being home in time for lunch with Sam. And the way she feels—probably a nap.

·····•·····

It's almost 11:00 by the time Sara pulls into the Hualapai Police Station in Peach Springs. Sara figures to do it by the book, take them head-on. As she parks, she asks Rocko, "What are they going to do, make me go home?"

Turning his head, Rocko gives her a dubious look.

She fills his water dish in the footwell and rolls her window down a couple inches for air. "Wait here," she tells him.

Still sluggish from lack of sleep, she struggles out of the cab, the caffeine not cutting the mustard. She gathers herself, cranking up her courage as she enters the police station. She has the pictures in her purse but doesn't plan on showing them. Walking to the reception desk, she pastes on a polite smile for the withered Hualapai woman holding down the fort.

"Is Officer Natomi in this morning?" Sara asks.

The old woman eyes her like a chicken eyeing a cricket. "He's here. Whaddaya need?"

Sara struggles to be pleasant. "I'd like to ask him something."

Picking up the handset, the old woman punches a button, her eyes fixed on Sara. "Henry. That white woman is asking for ya, again. Get out here." She hangs up without taking her eyes off Sara. "He'll be right out."

Sara paces in small circles, gazing at the floor while she waits, doing her best to ignore the unpleasant old woman.

From a side door in the back wall of the modest reception area, Officer Natomi strides out business-like, a quizzical look on his dark features, his too-tight navy blue and grey uniform crisp. As the old woman watches, Natomi pulls up in front of Sara. "What can I do for you, Mrs. Wayland?"

The old woman shuffles papers, pretending not to listen.

Sara pins the woman with a quick glare before focusing on Officer Natomi. "Hi, Henry. The Chief suggested I check in with you before I go out to paint."

Officer Natomi looks at her askance as he hooks his thumbs in his gun belt. "Chief Watonami wanted you to check in?"

"That's what he said." Switching gears, Sara says, "Did you find out more about what happened with Bryant?"

Frowning, the officer gives his head a quick shake. "The case is closed."

Sara demurs. "Wasn't there a new medical report?"

Perturbed, Natomi turtles his head, doubling his chin. "I don't know what you're talking about. The case is closed."

"Oh…" Sara inspects the nails of her right hand. "So, alcohol poisoning is the official cause of death?"

Officer Natomi's hackles come up as his lips press into a thin line. "The case is closed. I can't talk about it. You need to leave it alone." He clamps his arms over his chest. "In fact, I think you should leave."

Sara steps around Natomi to the reception desk, leans a hand on the desk and locks eyes with the old woman. "I want to see Chief Watonami."

Startled, the old woman freezes, her wide eyes shining.

Sara leans in closer. "Now, please," she says in a threatening tone.

Her withered hand snatches the receiver as the old woman punches a button. Lifting the phone to her ear, she blurts, "Mrs. Wayland needs to see you." She hangs up, nods at Sara, then stands. "I'll take you back."

Sara follows the spry old bird into a short hallway to the second door on the right. The old woman raps softly on the unfinished door.

Through the bare wood, Sara hears the Chief. When the Hualapai woman opens the door, Sara pushes through, then snaps it shut, leaving the old woman spluttering in the hall.

The Chief slumps at his desk, disputatious, his dark chin raised, his brows lowered. His black eyes shine, his gaze fierce.

Sara moves to sit across from him, meeting the Chief's eyes with a fierce look of her own. "Your Officer Natomi is being rude. I hope you can do better."

Chief Watonami tilts his head. "I thought we were done."

Sara lowers her eyes. "I'm here based on your advice."

"How so?"

"You suggested I check in with you before I go on the reservation to paint."

"But you didn't bother to check in with me before you saw Bryant Watachka's mother, did you?"

A frisson of guilt burns, turning Sara's face beet red. She looks at her hands, and in a small voice says, "No."

"And now you come here..." The Chief laces his fingers behind his head and leans back in his chair. "...and you want me to let you paint your pictures on our land."

Twisting her fingers, she looks up to meet his gaze. "I'm sorry about Wamaya. I should have asked first. But I was afraid you would say no."

"And you were right," he says smugly. "I would have said no."

Her eyes blaze. "Why? What are you afraid of? All I did... I felt sorry for her and wanted to see if there was anything I could do."

The Chief sits up, dropping his fists on his desktop as he bunches his chin. "That's why," he says gruffly. "We don't need your help. We've had about all the help we can stand from you white folks."

Sara folds her arms across her chest. "White, black, red, or brown, Wamaya is a woman and a mother—a mother who lost her only child. She needs help. Whether you think so or not."

The Chief shakes his head, his chin wobbling. "It's none of your business. We take care of our own."

"You blamed Wamaya for her son's death. That's how you take care of your own?"

"None of your business."

"What if it wasn't alcohol that killed Bryant? Who would you blame then?"

The Chief levels a hostile glare. "Do you want to join her?"

"What are you talking about?" Sara says knitting her brow. "Is this some sort of threat?"

"You are on the Hualapai Nation reservation, sovereign land." He wags a fat finger. "You are breaking the law…"

"What law?" Sara demands.

The Chief rises to his feet. "Trespassing. And resisting arrest."

Sara stands to leave as the Chief grabs her arm, spins her around, and roughly cuffs her.

"Stop! You can't do this!"

The Chief pushes her into the chair, rounds to the phone and calls for Natomi.

· · · • · · • · · ·

Officer Natomi marches Sara, hands cuffed behind her back, to a small holding cell in the back of the building.

"Henry," Sara says. "What about my phone call."

Stone-faced, Natomi looks straight ahead. "I'll check with the Chief," he grumbles as he unlocks the cell door and removes her cuffs.

"I have rights," Sara protests as Natomi shoves her in and bolts the door. Gripping the window bars, she says, "I'm entitled to a phone call." Panicky, she turns to see two rickety cots and a filthy slop bucket. The stench is overpowering. A heavyset Hualapai woman lies on one of the cots, facing the wall. Moving to the edge of the other cot, Sara thinks she recognizes the woman. Startled, she looks closer. "Wamaya?"

Lunch Date

A T NOON, WHEN SAM parks the step van in front of the shop, he doesn't think much about it, but the truck isn't in its usual spot. Sara could have gone to the store, or a hundred other things, and he's sure she'll be back for lunch. When he has in-town routes like today, he always tries to make it home for lunch. And it's more than just a routine, he's so busy with work, he misses her, feeling like they never get to spend enough time together. And, with Timmy off to college, he is short-handed. Somehow, he never seems to have enough time in a day.

Sam sits alone at the kitchen table at half past, beginning to worry a little. Sara is a rock, as dependable as the rising sun. She would let him know—call him, leave him a note—if she was going to miss lunch. He pushes up from the table, taking the stairs two at a time to her studio. As he opens the door, he sees her paintbox and easel are gone. Puzzling. He doesn't remember her mentioning a field trip at breakfast. Obviously, he missed it. Or she changed her mind. Or...

Downstairs, at the kitchen counter, Sam picks up the phone and dials.

"Hi, Peggy. Have you heard from Sara this morning?"

"Hey, Sam. I haven't heard from her since the other day. Why?"

"Nothing much. It's just that we had lunch plans, and she hasn't showed."

"I'll let you know if I hear from her," Peggy says.

"Thanks."

As Sam hangs up, he wonders if she went out to paint on Drake's Ranch. Maybe she forgot about lunch. He dials the phone as he puts the handset to his ear.

"Yeah, hi. This is Sam Wayland. Who's this?"

"Hi, Sam. It's Rita."

"Oh, hi Rita. Didn't recognize your voice. Is Dennis there?"

"Sorry, Sam. He's out right now."

"I'm trying to track down Sara. Do you know, did she pick up a gate key this morning?"

"Not that I know of," Rita says. "Do you want me to leave a message?"

"No. That's okay. Thanks."

Sam hangs up and looks through the phone, lost in thought. Maybe Sara went somewhere else to paint. Maybe she was planning on lunch but forgot about the time. But it is nearly 1:00 and she is rarely if ever late, certainly not *this* late. Sam has been meaning to put a CB radio in that truck. She has the base unit on her desk, and he has a mobile unit in the step van—convenient when he's around town or on a service call, though, if she is out painting in the hills, she would be out of range anyway.

Thinking it through, Sam crimps his lips as he gazes out the kitchen window. Yesterday, the whole thing with the coyote load had her cranked up. Sara was still fuming at the dinner table, convinced that Doc Pratt and Sheriff Bailey were holding out on her. But if Sara went out to the Drake Ranch, she would need the gate key. Yet, she took Rocko and her painting stuff with her. Sam slowly shakes his head. *Doesn't make sense.*

········

Perched on the end of the cot, Sara looks around the grungy little cell, exasperated, her nose wrinkled against the smell. She glances at Wamaya every few seconds. The Hualapai woman hasn't stirred since Sara was locked up. She didn't move when Sara called her name. More than a little worried, Sara isn't totally sure that the woman is Wamaya. She's not even sure if the woman is breathing.

Sara leans forward, gently shaking the woman's leg. "Wamaya?"

Jerking her leg, the woman grunts.

Sara jumps back, startled. "Wamaya?"

Wamaya rolls toward her, squinting through one eye, raising her head off the cot, before letting it drop with a groan.

"Are you okay?" Sara asks.

A deep moan escapes Wamaya's throat as she rolls to face the wall.

Sara stands and shuffles between the cots. Leaning over Wamaya, she lays her hand lightly on Wamaya's shoulder. The alcohol fumes rising off the obese woman make Sara's eyes water and she quickly backs away.

The poor woman is dead drunk, nearly comatose. Sara wonders how long Wamaya has been incarcerated like this—inhuman. Can't leave her like this. Wamaya needs help.

Sara lunges to the cell door, grabbing the window bars, shaking the door. "Henry!" she yells. "Henry, hurry!"

········

Sam lifts the handset and dials.

"Mohave County Sheriff's Office."

"Hey Janet, is George in?"

"Hi Sam. Hold on, I'll get him."

Sam leans a hip against the kitchen counter, worry grumbling in his empty stomach.

"Sam," the Sheriff says. "What can I do ya for."

"Hey George. Have you heard from Sara today? She didn't stop by there, did she?"

A long silence ensues.

"Nope," the Sheriff says in clipped tones. "Haven't seen hide nor hair."

Tensing, Sam waits a beat. George's tone hits him as odd. The man is usually affable to the point of effusive, never short. Something is not right. "But she was by there yesterday, is that right?"

"Yeah, she dropped in for a minute," George says with his good-ol'-boy nature restored. "Had some photos she wanted me to look at."

Sam's eyes narrow. "Of the coyote load?"

"Well," George says. "I don't know about that—could be. Hard to tell."

"Did she tell ya? She was out on the north end of Drake's Ranch, looking for that buffalo of his."

"She didn't mention a buffalo."

Hanging up, Sam wonders where she could be—off painting somewhere, but where? She has her heart set on that watercolor project. And the way she described the Lower Granite Gorge... But out there and back by lunch is a stretch, if she's working on a painting. The reservation? Tightening his lips, Sam picks up the handset and dials "0."

"Yes, operator... Do you have a number for the Hualapai Visitor Center in Peach Springs? ...How 'bout the Police Station?"

·····•··•·····

Frustrated, on the verge of tears, Sara plops on the cot, nearly hoarse from yelling. *Good Lord, what's the matter with these people?* It is obvious they can hear her. Lifting her head out of her hands, she glances at Wamaya, worry gathering like a storm. She is pretty sure they took everything when she was arrested—her purse, her keys, her wallet—but she pats her pockets in case they missed anything. She must *do* something, Wamaya is in trouble, Rocko is locked in the truck, her gun is in the glove box. Sam is probably wondering where the heck she is.

Sara scans the crappy little cell, searching for a way out. The place looks impenetrable: walls clad in sheet metal; the only window is in the door, and it is barred; the concrete floor has a crusty drain in the middle, the ceiling is metal with a caged bulb—no way out. Rubbing her hands on the canvas webbing, Sara glances at the worn out Army Surplus cot. She shifts her weight from side to side, sneering at its wobbly frame. Catching a second wind, she lifts off the cot, grabs the end, and drags it a foot or so to the door. She tips it over and kicks at the legs until the wooden frame folds up and falls apart. Picking up one of the legs, she starts banging it against the bars, screaming, "Help!"

·····•··•·····

The boxy step van wallows up Route 66 on its way to Peach Springs. At full throttle, the little diesel engine sounds ready to explode, its echo roaring in the empty step van. Sam concentrates on the road, letting off steam by keeping his foot in it and sawing at the wheel. By the time he hits Hackberry, the temperature gauge rises near red, and he backs off. A walk-in delivery truck, the step van wasn't made for long-hauls on the open road. Not that Peach Springs is a long haul, only an hour or so from Kingman, but it wasn't made to go ninety, either.

Climbing out of Crozier Canyon, Sam bristles. The idea of Sara, locked in the Hualapai jail makes him want to punch somebody a couple times, bloody a nose or two, teach these durn fools a lesson. They can't treat his wife this way. Trespassing... *Really?* A trumped-up charge. Though resisting arrest, he has to give her credit. He guesses those boys didn't know who they were up against. In sight of the Truxton Trading Post, he hopes she's all right.

As Sam pulls into the Police Station, he spots their F250. *Rocko...* He parks next to the truck, jumps out of the step van and rounds to the driver's side. Rocko's face fills the driver's side window as he barks. Sam unlocks and opens the door. "Good to see you, too," Sam says as he rubs Rocko's ears. Sam steps back to let Rocko out. "You need a break?" He watches as Rocko gallops to the nearest bush and lifts his leg. "Okay, boy," he says. "You're with me."

Sam digs Sara's pistol out of the glove box, stuffs it in the back of his pants, and locks up the truck. With Rocko at heel, Sam marches into the Police Station and zeros in on the shriveled old woman. He stops in front of her desk. Rocko sits. Doing his best to keep from yelling, Sam carefully eyes the old crone. "I'm here for my wife, Sara Wayland," he says evenly.

········•····

Without a word, Sara follows Sam and Rocko out to the parking lot. She can't believe they are leaving Wamaya in there. It's a hellhole, not fit for human habitation. It's not that Sam didn't try, but...

Sam stops between the step van and the truck, pulls her pistol out of his waistband and hands it over.

Sara opens the door for Rocko and sets the pistol on the dash. She turns to Sam, ready to apologize for causing a ruckus in there. But before she can say anything, he wraps her up in his arms, hugging her tight as he nuzzles her neck.

"Please don't ever do that again," he says softly. "You scared the crap outta me."

Sara lets go, melting in his arms, letting the moment wash it all away. *What a day...*

When Sam finally turns her loose, he grins and wrinkles his nose. "You smell funny. I'll see you at the house."

She gathers herself, watching him round the front of the step van, rack back the door, and climb in. Sara waves as he backs around, then suspiciously sniffs her sleeve. With Rocko grinning at shotgun, she climbs into the truck and stows her pistol. She wheels the truck out onto Diamond

Springs Road and follows the big white box of a step van out to the highway.

Breathing a deep sigh, Sara crosses the reservation border, relieved to be leaving the Hualapai Nation. Sam said they would go see Robert Green, their attorney, once they were back in town. She conjures up an image of the Chief. If she had shown Chief Watonami pictures of the cyanide device, what then? Would he get off Wamaya's back?

Sara barely notices the trading post as she motors through Truxton. If only Wamaya hadn't been so out of it... Would Wamaya have believed her? She thinks so. Would she quit drinking, or maybe slow down? She hopes so. After losing her son, the poor woman needs to give herself a fighting chance.

In the step van, Sam winds through the curves of Crozier Canyon with Sara close behind.

Watching the back end of the step van pitch and sway, Sara lets her mind wander, though not very far. Natomi seemed to draw a blank when she mentioned a new medical report. Doc Pratt acted like he was going to do something. Did he change his mind or have the tribal police not yet received it?

As they pass through Valentine, the late day sun glares through the windshield. Sara glances at her speed. Following Sam, it seems like it is taking forever. *Why is no one doing anything?*

Showtime

B ACK IN KINGMAN, ROUTE 66 widens to four lanes, adopting the 'Andy Devine' alias as it hits town. As they motor through Hilltop, the Smoke House bar and grill slides by on the left, then the Denny's on the right, all glass and plastic. Showing its age, the El Trovatore motel and restaurant squat next to the highway. The railroad tracks hug the canyon on the other side of the bluff as Andy Devine curves and dives downhill. Sara follows Sam, veering off onto Beale St. It has been a long drive, and a longer day. Rocko is hungry. She's hungry too, and tired, and needs a long shower. Unsure of the time, she hopes Bob Green is still in his office. As she follows the step van into the parking lot, she hopes she is not too stinky. Parking next to Sam, she tells Rocko to wait, then climbs out.

Sam waits next to the step van. As she walks up, he says, "I don't want to sue those yoyos, but I would like to get our money back. For both fines, I had to give 'em $750.00. It's highway robbery."

Sara grabs his arm and steers him toward Bob's office. In a small strip center on the low side of the street, the storefront office of Robert B. Green, Attorney at Law, sits between a hair salon and a Farmers Insurance agency.

As they enter, Celia, Bob's gal Friday, pops out of her chair and rounds the reception desk. "Sam, Sara, hello. I assume you want to see Bob?" She briskly leads them into the conference room and winks. "You're in luck, he's here." She waves an arm toward the little conference table. "Have a seat. I'll go get him."

Her blue eyes round, Sara says, "I'm sorry I threw a fit back at the police station."

Sam waves it off, shaking his head. "I was about ready to throw a humdinger, myself."

Her eyes sparkle, her grin mischievous. "By the way, what were you thinking when you took my pistol in there?"

Sam shrugs it off. "Better to have a gun..."

"Yeah, I know... I believe you've mentioned that a time or two before," Sara says, kiddingly. "But if you had drawn down on those tribal police, we both would have gone to prison."

Sam cocks his head, giving her a look. "One way or another, I was taking you home with me."

Her grin widens to a tender smile as she reaches for his hand. "I knew there was a reason I loved you."

Taking her hand, he smiles. "I'll love you even more once you get that jailhouse funk washed off."

She grimaces. "Is it that bad?"

He smirks. "It ain't good, sweetheart."

Looking away, Sara shakes her head. "It stunk so bad, you wouldn't believe it. Like a sewer pond mixed with booze—horrible." Her thoughts turn to Wamaya, stuck in that tiny cell, sick from too much whiskey. Startled, she looks up to see Bob Green enter. Nearing the end of the day, he appears more harried than normal. His disheveled suit matches his flabby physique. The crooked tie and wrinkled dress shirt are weak attempts at professional attire.

A gold Cross pen and a yellow legal pad in hand, Bob gives a weak smile. "Hi, guys," Bob says as he sits across from Sam. "What brings you in today?"

Sam looks him straight in the eyes. "Sara was arrested."

Bob Green raises his eyebrows as he sits up. "Holy crap! Sara? Arrested? When was this?"

Sam proceeds to relate the whole scene at the Hualapai Police Station while Bob scribbles on his legal pad.

"Trespassing," Bob mumbles. "Resisting arrest..."

Sam nods toward Sara. "I paid a lot of money to get her out. I want it back." His eyes narrow as he glares at Bob. "It's outrageous. These people think they can do anything they want out there. It ain't right."

Sara waits for her chance. When Sam finally winds down, she gives him a look. Turning to Bob, she says, "What Sam didn't tell you is, the woman who lost her son is an alcoholic, and Chief Watonami is persecuting her. There has to be a way to stop him. The poor woman is not responsible for her son's death, I'm sure of it."

Bob Green gazes openly at Sara before glancing at Sam. "Have they charged this woman?"

She shakes her head. "I don't know... They must've charged her with something. We were in the same cell."

Bob nods sagely as he makes a note. "Probably drunk and disorderly. Unless, in the case of her son's death, they're charging her with manslaughter or reckless endangerment."

Sara waits a moment, unsure how much she wants to tell him, uncertain how much Bob can accomplish with the tribal police.

Sam speaks up, "Bob, whaddaya think?"

Creasing his brow, Bob taps his pen on his legal pad, scrutinizing his notes. Quickly glancing at Sam, then Sara, he returns his gaze to his pad. "I'm not sure what to tell you. Since it's the tribal police and on the reservation, I'd say the money for the fines is unrecoverable, unless you want to make a federal case out of it." He glances up at Sam.

Sam gives him a snide look, shrugs, and turns to Sara.

Bob glances at Sara as he twiddles his pen. "My best advice," he says with a serious look. "I don't think you can do much for the woman. As long as she is a Hualapai living on the reservation, she is subject to tribal law. I'd leave it alone."

···•••••···

Gusting wind kicks up the dust at the top of Spring St. Swirling clouds of grit blow across the barren hills, the vacant lots, and down the streets, filling the sky with a dirty haze and the promise of a tough day in the high desert.

Breakfast dishes are done. Rocko and Sam are well fed; and Sam is off to run his Bullhead City route. Having her second cup, Sara gazes out the kitchen window, her thoughts somewhere else, her mind, circling the wagons. Wamaya, Bryant, and a spent cyanide cartridge—there must be something she can do. Certainly, Chief Watonami must have seen the new medical report by now.

Rinsing her cup in the sink, she talks to Rocko. "If you want to go, you can, but you'll just have to wait in the truck."

Sara swings through the bedroom, grabbing her purse and checking her face in the mirror. Rocko waits by the downstairs door, ready to go. With

Rocko loaded, Sara tosses her purse on the bench seat and starts the engine. Rolling down Spring St., she sets her sights on the Kingman Bakery. A dozen of their best pastries and she is on her way up the hill. At the hospital turn-in, she questions if this is a good idea.

Sara strides across the lobby toward the reception window, a pink box of donuts and pastries balanced on one hand. Smiling at Margaret behind the window, Sara holds out the box. "I brought you a treat," she says as she opens the lid.

Margaret slides back the glass to better see the selections. The aroma of sugary pastries wafts through the window. She plucks a warm glazed donut off the top, licking her lips. "Thanks, Sara."

Sara closes the lid. "Is Doc Pratt in his office?"

With a mouthful of donut, Margaret holds up a finger. "He should be coming out of surgery any time, if you want to wait."

Sara winks. "I don't want the donuts to get stale. Is it okay if I wait in his office?"

Margaret consults the schedule book. "He doesn't have any appointments." She glances up at Sara. "It should be fine."

Sara lets herself into the dark office and flicks the switch. The buzzing fluorescents reveal Doc Pratt's cluttered workspace in sharp relief. Haphazard stacks of paperwork are piled high on both ends of his Steelcase desk. In the far corner, the top of a small worktable sits buried under archive boxes. Behind his deck, sheaves of paper stick out between medical journals and hardcover texts crammed together in a floor-to-ceiling bookshelf. Hoping her medical records aren't in there, she glances around for a spot to park the bakery box. Clearing off a chair, she ends up keeping the box in her lap, wondering how long this little vigil is going to take.

More than an hour later, Sara fidgets in the hard chair, grease spots showing on the box of pastries. Against her better judgement she ate a glazed donut and a cinnamon roll to kill time. At this rate she will end up eating all the pastries before Doc Pratt shows. She opens the box to examine the next candidate. Frustrated, Sara closes the pink box and sets it in the middle of his desk as she stands. He must have run into complications.

·········

Sara arrives home close to lunch with no interest in food, drained from the sugar high. Plodding up the stairs, she turns through the formal dining room into the kitchen.

Stuck in the truck most of the morning, Rocko makes a beeline for his food and water dishes, happy to be home.

Sara sheds her purse on the kitchen table and reloads the Coffeematic. Dropping into a chair, she waits for her newfangled automatic coffee percolator, rehashing events of the last couple days.

Thank the Lord for Sam. Walking into the tribal police station armed, ready to rescue her, whatever the cost. She smiles lovingly as warmth floods her skin. To have someone who loves you no matter what... How could she be so lucky?

Bob Green wasn't much help with Wamaya, but she suspected as much. Wamaya needs to know about the cyanide device. The coyote load sticks in Sara's craw like a tangled mess of barbwire. How cruel. It's bad enough killing animals, but if Bryant died because of it... How can such a thing be legal? And for Wamaya to torture herself over her son's death... There must be a way to relieve her misery.

Carrying a fresh mug of Yuban, Sara saunters down the stairs, across the rec room, and into the office. On her desk, a stack of receipts waits for journal entry. Setting her coffee to the side, she craves another donut and is thankful she left them behind. At forty-four, it is harder than ever to keep her figure. She whisks through the receipts, wondering when Doc Pratt will get out of surgery. Closing the ledger, she gazes at the phone, thinking it through. She trots upstairs to retrieve her purse, determined to take care of Wamaya. At the kitchen counter, she digs for Chief Watonami's card and dials the tribal police station.

"Hello," she says stiffly. "Chief Watonami, please."

"Who's calling?"

Sara pretends not to recognize the old Hualapai woman on the other end. "This is Sara Wayland. He's gonna want to talk to me."

"Hold on."

The wait seems to drag on, irritatingly slow. A hundred things to say race through her mind like a runaway locomotive.

"This is Watonami."

Caught off-guard, she splutters, "Chief Watonami?"

"Yes," he says impatiently. "What do you want?"

"My attorney says I can speak with Wamaya. Put her on."

"She's been released," the Chief says as he starts to hang up.

"Wait," she blurts, searching for what to say.

"What is it?"

"I asked Officer Natomi about this. He didn't seem to know," she says, softening her tone. "Have you seen an updated medical exam report from Dr. Pratt for Bryant Watachka?"

Abruptly, the Chief's silence fills the phone for several moments.

"Chief?"

"Yes..."

"Well?"

At length, he replies with a low and measured tone. "You know I can arrest you for interfering with an investigation..." A long pause drags out in tense silence. "What makes you think there's an updated report?"

"I'm not sure," she says hesitantly. "But if there isn't, there should be. Did anyone report the cyanide device?"

"Where are you going with this?" the Chief says gruffly.

"Bryant's death—it may not have been alcohol poisoning. I can show you."

The Cover-Up

A LITTLE AFTER 3:00 p.m., Sara mills around inside the Truxton Trading Post, looking at the cold cases and aisles of snacks and candy, killing time as she sips her Seven Up. After the small talk ran down, Lionel retired to the room at the back of the store, leaving Sara on her own. Her plan is simple enough: show the Chief her Polaroids, let him take it from there. She glances at her watch. He's late. She could leave now, if she wanted. Why did she offer? Nervous at the prospect of facing the surly chief, she bolsters her courage, telling herself that he can't arrest her off the reservation. She hopes like heck it's true. At least Rocko is safe at home.

Meandering past their cigarette machine, Sara glances out the front window. She catches the Chief's silver Jeep raising a cloud of dust as it rolls into the trading post. Her heart thumps, nerves tingling—the prospect of jail rattling her cage. Now that she thinks about it, she should have talked to Doc Pratt first. *This is a mistake.*

Sara pushes through the front door and stops, battling her misgivings. As the police Jeep parks, she waits, eyeing the dark cab. When the engine shuts off, she walks toward the driver's side.

Chief Watonami cranks down the window and gives her a deadpan look, his dark features camouflaged by the shadowy cab. "Okay. Show me."

Sara rests her purse on the door and fishes out her photos. Handing them to the Chief, she stands back, watching his face.

Watonami studies each Polaroid for a moment, then looks her in the eyes. "What are these?"

Sara steps up, looks at a photo and points. "Sheriff Bailey said it looks like a cyanide device went off."

Shuffling to the next photo, Watonami shrugs.

Sara points. "Same thing, different angle."

Watonami meets her gaze. "So what?"

Tilting her head, Sara looks him in the eyes. "I took these pictures next to the arroyo where I found Bryant." Watching his face sour, she taps the Polaroid with a pastel pink nail. "Look Chief. See the Day-Glo stuff?"

"Yeah," he nods. "The orange marker."

"The Sheriff said there should be a dead animal carcass to go with it."

Watonami scrunches his lips. "Depends. Carcasses don't last out here."

"How long was Bryant's body out in the elements?" she asks.

"What difference does that make?" he says, frowning.

"What did the medical report say, a week, maybe longer? There shouldn't have been much left, right?"

Watonami pulls in his double chin, studying the photo. "Where is this? It can't be on Hualapai land. We are not subject to the BLM or Wildlife Services. We don't allow the use of varmint control devices on tribal lands. With the exception of Hualapai tribal members, there is no fishing, hunting or trapping on the reservation without permission."

Sara crimps her lips. "It's on the Drake Ranch, right next to the reservation, within a stone's throw of where I found Bryant's body."

The Chief returns her pictures and starts the Jeep. He cocks his head out the window. "Follow me."

·····•·•····

The highway rises into the hills, scrub juniper gather ranks on their flanks. At the edge of the horizon, mountains hide in the haze. For Sara, it is eyes on the road. On Route 66, she crosses the border onto Hualapai land, her resolve weakening. She follows within a few car lengths of the Chief's Jeep, questioning her motives. Sam said it, *Why are you so hung up on this?*

From the very beginning, everyone told her to leave it alone. And yet, here she is, following the tribal police chief onto the reservation, the chief who arrested her and threw her in jail on a trumped-up trespassing charge. Her impulse started off as an offer to help a woman in trouble, help a fellow human being. She begins to wonder if she is doing this for the right reasons; or doing it just to get even, prove this arrogant cop wrong. Regardless, she intends to see it through one way or another. It's a matter of principle now. And to think, it started out as a day trip to paint a watercolor.

Peach Springs waits for her a few miles up the road. Whatever the Chief has in mind, she intends to see Wamaya. Sara slows as the road gradually curves, keeping the Jeep in sight. When his brake lights flare, she pumps her brake pedal. He signals, turning left off the pavement and onto the dirt. She rolls up her window as the Jeep kicks up dust. Hard to see much and she doesn't recognize the turnoff until her big Ford rumbles over the cattleguard. As the road disintegrates, she wonders how far she should go. Is the Chief taking her to the arroyo to set her up, or...? Maybe she is just being paranoid. He *is* an officer of the law. He can't get her out in the middle of nowhere and do whatever he darn well pleases. She glances at her glove box. ...*A gun when you need it.* One thing for sure, she's not going back to jail.

The rough dirt road dwindles to a cattle track, more ruts, more dust. Downshifting, Sara manhandles the wheel, keeping the heavy truck on the Jeep's tail. The cow pond looms ahead on the right. It makes her think of Dennis Drake and his not-so-subtle accusations about Hualapai rustling his livestock. She couldn't believe it at the time, but with the way she has been treated, her opinion has shifted. Normally a trusting person, she refuses to be naïve. Watching the Jeep slow for a washout, she brakes and drops into a lower gear. She shakes her head. Men will fight over the darndest things—a buffalo, for heaven's sake. Giving the Jeep a little slack, she lets the truck trundle around the berm. She scans the area around the cow pond as her F250 lumbers through potholes and bounces over tufts of scrub brush. As she suspected, no buffalo.

With the dust flying and the windows rolled up, the end of their little jaunt takes on a gloomy blur. Without A/C, late afternoon heat builds up in the stuffy cab. Sweat beads her forehead, her chest and armpits damp. When the Jeep stops at the top of the arroyo, Sara pulls alongside and parks. Before the dust settles, she leans across the seat and grabs her pistol out of the glove box. She hesitates, and instead of wedging the gun in her waistband at the small of her back, she stuffs the gun in her purse. For an instant, she hovers motionless, a hair's breadth above the seat, contemplating the Chief's reaction when she shows him the spent cyanide device. She shoulders her purse as she tugs on the door handle.

Outside, Sara trudges around the Jeep's backside to find the Chief standing at the edge of the arroyo, back to her, hand on his hips, arms akimbo. Her heart thumps hard, her face reddening as she walks toward him with her hand in her purse.

The Chief turns at the sound of her footsteps, his heavy features creased by too many years on the job. He points at her purse. "Do you have the photos?"

Sara stops next to him at the top of the bank. Pulling the Polaroids from her purse, she lets her eyes wander down the arroyo. A rough footpath descends the bank, the sandy bottom has been thoroughly trampled, along with the weedy area where the body was found. The extraction, the investigation, a dead body, identity to be determined: how could a person do a job like that? "Here," she says, handing the Chief the photos.

Chief Watonami slowly nods as he inspects the photos. Looking up, he sweeps an arm toward the site. "Show me where you took these."

Using the footpath, Sara works her way down the steep bank, pausing for a moment at the strip of trampled weeds, imagining what it must have been like for Bryant.

Sara turns to catch the Chief huffing along the trail a few yards back. "This way." Winding her way down the arroyo, she is on the lookout. From this angle, none of it looks familiar. The steep banks gradually drop away as the sandy bottom jogs to the left. The arroyo narrows, cutting downhill, carving a jagged scar into the barren slope. As Sara tromps through the jog, twisted loops of barbwire lie tangled around crooked fenceposts along the arroyo rim. Climbing the bank, she is close. Her pulse quickens as she picks her way through the downed barbwire. Glancing back, no Chief. "Are you coming?" she calls out.

Watonami stops to catch his breath. "I'm coming," he hollers back.

The faint trail leads off in both directions along the fence line. Sara heads for the spot where she was parked, dragging her feet, not wanting to lose the Chief. Turning, she walks backward. Hands cupped around her mouth, she calls out, "Where are you?"

A helmet of blue-black hair, thick and straight, bobs into view as the Chief grunts his way up the steep bank of the arroyo. Panting, he stops at the top of the bank and raises a hand. "Right here."

Sara waits. "I was parked over there," she says pointing the way.

Watonami trudges alongside Sara, too winded to say another word.

Looking for the spot, Sara slows, bending to inspect the ground for her tire tracks. Oddly, the dirt trail shows signs of recent traffic: two, maybe three sets of tire tracks. When she was here last, it was obvious the fence line road, rutted and washed out, hadn't seen use in years.

Sara searches along the fresh tire tracks, hunting and pecking around until she finds the area where she parked. Scanning full circle, she checks her reference points: the arroyo from this angle, the downed fence, the hill to the east, the rim of Lower Granite Gorge to the west. This is it.

Sara catches the Chief watching. Stopped dead, he looks like he's questioning her sanity. The crazy white woman, she gets it. "I stopped here," she says, "...when I saw the arroyo."

Hands on hips, Watonami nods, looking around. "This is not Hualapai land."

Giving him a hard look, she says. "I came out here to paint, not to trespass."

Watonami lifts his lips in a snarl. "That's all well and good, Mrs. Wayland. Now show me why you dragged me out here."

Sara takes a couple steps to where she figures the front of the truck stood. Glancing at a patch of fresh dirt next to the tire ruts, she sees a few dead weeds and fill marks from a shovel. A frisson of fright lights her up with recognition. This is the spot! It has to be! The indentation, the Day-Glo orange spatter, the spent cartridge, all gone. "It was right here."

Watonami walks closer, scrunching his chin as he fails to see what she is talking about. "This is where you thought you saw the cyanide bomb?"

Sara points at the spot, waving her finger in small circles. "I swear, it was right here. There was that orange stuff and a small hole in the ground where the thing went off. This is where I took the pictures."

Watonami stares at the disturbed ground, then looks back at the arroyo. "Well, it's not here now."

"But you see where it was, right? Look at the pictures."

Chief Watonami pulls the photos out of a shirt pocket, hands them to Sara, then turns and trudges off.

She calls after him, "Someone has been here! They covered it up!"

Lack Of Evidence

SARA SQUINTS INTO THE sun as she wheels the F250 down the hill into downtown Kingman. After quitting time, the traffic on Andy Devine heading to Hilltop thickens, though traffic going her direction is light. Antsy, she pushes a yellow light at the bottom of the hill. Questions swarm her thoughts like blowflies on roadkill—her anxiousness building on the return trip from the arroyo. The most troubling questions revolve around who would do such a thing, and why. She lost track of all the possible permutations she dreamed up on the way back, though it still seems reasonable to call the Sheriff. After all, if it is on the Drake Ranch, it is in his jurisdiction. She motors through the 4th St. light, heading straight home, deciding to call the Sheriff as soon as she arrives. This late in the day, Sheriff Bailey may have left.

Rocko greets her at the downstairs door, eager to see her. When she stoops to pet him, her troubles evaporate in the moment. If only people were as friendly, as loyal, as forgiving. She bends to hug him. "I missed you, too."

Sara crosses to her office, sets her purse on the desk, picks up the phone and dials.

"Mohave County Sheriff's Office, Deputy Adams speaking."

"This is Sara Wayland. Is Sheriff Bailey in?"

"Let me check to see if he's still here."

Sara clicks her nails on the handset while she waits.

"Sara, what can I do for ya?" the Sheriff says with a twang.

"Someone has messed with the evidence," she says in a firm voice.

"What evidence?"

Annoyed, she fiddles with the telephone cord. "You know, that cyanide device that went off—the pictures I showed you."

"Oh, that," the Sheriff says jovially. "Yeah, no need to worry about that."

Stunned, Sara goes silent. *He's blowing it off!* Of all the possibilities she considered, this wasn't one of them. "What about the boy, Bryant?"

"What about him?"

"Aren't you going to investigate?"

"Investigate what?" the Sheriff says gruffly. "The Hualapai boy died on the reservation, drank himself to death, from what I understand."

"What if he didn't drink himself to death? What if he stepped on a cyanide bomb?"

"Well...," he says, condescendingly. "That's not for me to say—not really my jurisdiction. I'm sure the tribal police have it under control."

Seething, she feels her blood surge. "What about my photos? I want them back."

"Well, Sara," he says indignantly. "How was I supposed to know? I tossed 'em."

Sara pulls the phone away from her face, struggling not to lose it, giving herself a moment to simmer down. Right now, she wants to reach through the phone and strangle the Sheriff. Does he care so little that he won't lift a finger? She slams the handset onto the base, hanging up without another word. Her frustration erupts in a scream, her face red, her hands balled into fists. She grabs her purse, rushes out of the office and stomps up the stairs.

Sara drops her purse on the kitchen table, crosses to the counter and turns on the Coffeematic. Supremely peeved, she takes a seat at the table, trying to cool down as she waits for the coffee to percolate.

Rocko sits next to her chair and gently places a paw on her thigh. He hates it when she gets upset.

When she sees the look on Rocko's face, her rage falls to pieces. She can't help but smile. Times like these, she couldn't love him more. Rubbing his head, she gives a silly laugh thinking, *Rocko is more help than that clown of a Sheriff.*

······•·····

On the back patio, waiting for the moon to rise, Sara admires the stars shining in the western sky. Drink in hand, she muses. What did Van Gough see when he looked at the night sky through his asylum window? Inspiration for *The Starry Night*? Was his vision true and bright, or laced with an intensity known only in his world? She wishes she could see through the eyes of the great painters, let her brushstrokes trace theirs. She takes a sip of her Salty Dog, convinced she needs more practice, wondering if she'll live long enough to capture the Lower Granite Gorge in watercolor.

In his chair, Sam sips his Seven & Seven then swirls the ice. "You didn't say much at dinner," Sam says as he rubs Rocko's head. "Everything okay?"

Sara huffs, then sips her drink and stares off through the stars. "As they say, rode hard and put away wet."

"Hmm," Sams says. "That good, huh?"

She nods. "Let's just say it was a long day… and weirdly strange."

"Painting?"

"I went back out to the reservation." Her hard tone betrays her.

"At least you didn't wind up in jail," he says, jokingly.

"I met the Chief out at Truxton. I thought he would investigate further once he saw the cyanide device."

Sam swirls his drink. "And?"

"What a joke!" She gives a cynical laugh. "I can't believe I was so naïve."

Sam gives a crooked smirk. "I can't believe you went back out there."

"Yeah," she grumps. "And I'm not done yet."

· · · · • · • · · · ·

After Sam is on his way and the breakfast dishes are done, Sara pours herself a second cup of Yuban. She leans on the kitchen counter, sipping her coffee. Gazing out the window past the wash to the highway, she lets her thoughts merge with traffic. She couldn't have imagined this bizarre concatenation of events if she had tried. What started off as a simple exercise to paint a watercolor, mutated into a set of menacing circumstances. She has a good mind to just walk away—leave it alone, like everyone suggested. However, when she thinks of Wamaya, she simply can't.

Sara sets her half-empty cup on the counter and picks up the phone.

"Hi Margaret," she says. "Is Doc Pratt in his office this morning?"

"No surgeries scheduled," Margaret replies. "He should be in his office all morning."

Sara grins. "Do I need to bring donuts?"

"Well, he certainly enjoyed the ones you left for him."

· · · · • · • · · · ·

On the way to Hilltop with a half-dozen donuts in a white paper bag on the seat, Sara rehearses what she wants to say in her head. Rocko keeps his eyes glued to her, sensing her determination. Wheeling the big Ford through the hospital parking lot, she gives herself a quick peptalk, reminding herself that she has every right to know what happened to Bryant. She turns to Rocko. "I need to know if I'm going to do Wamaya any good." Rocko seems to agree.

Sara stops at the reception window just long enough to let Margaret pluck a chocolate-covered donut out of the bag. Hustling to Doc Pratt's office door, she knocks lightly and lets herself in when she hears his voice.

She smiles and holds up the sack of donuts when he looks up. "Your donut girl returns."

"Keep this up and I'll be fat in no time," he says, grinning.

A rawboned rail of a man, he could stand to put on a little weight, and she laughs. Placing the sack of donuts in front of him, Sara eases herself down in the only empty chair. Sitting primly, she retrieves the Polaroids from her purse. "You remember these?" she says as she lays them next to the bag.

Ham picks up the photos, looks them over and nods. Setting them down, he fishes a donut out of the bag. "Yeah, I remember," he says as he takes a bite of a glazed donut.

Sara waits patiently while he chews.

Picking up the photos, he studies them while he munches. He sets the photos to the side and reaches for another donut.

"Did I miss something?" she asks. "I had the impression you were going to update the medical report."

Ham nods thoughtfully as he chews. As he swallows, he pulls a wad of napkins out of the bag and wipes his hands. "I wanted to go over it with the Sheriff before I did anything."

Sara looks at him askance. "I already spoke with Sheriff Bailey. An explanation isn't the same as a solution. Do you realize that the boy's mother, Wamaya, is being blamed for her boy's death? This will haunt her the rest of her life. If there is any possibility that the boy's death is due to the cyanide device, you can't just let it slide."

Ham's face turns to stone as he opens a desk drawer and pulls out a file folder. Rifling through the contents, he removes a glassine envelope, pulls out the postmortem photos, and spreads them across his desk for Sara's inspection.

As Sara leans in to look, he pulls his magnifying glass from his pencil drawer and hands it to her. She examines the photos more closely. "What am I looking for?"

"Right hand and right side of the forehead," he says.

"Those tiny dots?"

"Does that look like the same color to you?" he asks.

"I don't know... I can barely see it. Maybe... It's kinda faded." She looks up at him. "Do you think that's the same orange—the Day-Glo orange from the bomb?"

Clasping his hands on the desk, he says, "Could be, given the amount of time and the condition of the tissue."

Cocking her head, she looks at him long and hard. "And the Sheriff is the only one who knows?"

Ham crimps his lips, leans back, and crosses his arms. "I bet Drake knows."

Errand Boy

O N Stockton Hill Rd., Sara passes the Mohave Savings and Loan building. Its modern architecture and big-city exterior stand out like an Arabian in a herd of burros. She hasn't given it much thought, but she doesn't like the trend. The City of Kingman is growing.

When she rumbles by Dunton motors, she is still chewing on it. Without the Chief's okay, she doesn't dare step foot on the reservation. And she doesn't figure she can wait on Doc Pratt. When it came to informing the tribal police, he wouldn't say one way or another. Though when she thinks about it, it doesn't matter. Someone has to tell Wamaya. And if the rest of these yahoos won't do anything...

Sara whips the big truck into the driveway, hops out, and storms into the downstairs office with Rocko on her heels. Glancing at the time, she drops her purse on the desktop, picks up the phone, and dials 0 as Rocko takes up station on his horse blanket.

"Yes, operator... Do you have a number for the Truxton Trading Post?" Sara grabs a pad and pen and jots down the number. "Can you connect me, please?"

Sara drops into her chair, leans her elbows on the desk and taps her toe. "Hello. Lionel? It's Sara."

"Mrs. Wayland? Hi. Yeah, it's me."

Lionel's voice sounds faint, and she questions if she has a bad connection. "Are you expecting Bryant's mom anytime soon?"

A staticky silence ensues as Lionel goes quiet. "Wamaya Watachka?"

"That's right, Wamaya. When is she due in next?"

"She usually cashes her check around the fifth of the month," he says. "Why?"

"Shoot," Sara says. "We can't wait that long. Do you have a car?"

"I have a motorcycle, a Honda 125."

"Street legal?"

"Uh huh."

"Do you have a driver's license?"

"Yes, ma'am."

"I need you to do me a big favor," she says. "I'll pay you."

Lionel's voice lights up. "Okay."

"I need you to go get Wamaya."

"Okay."

"Can you bring her to the trading post?"

"I, uh... don't think she will fit on my Honda."

"I didn't see one when I was out there. Does she have a car? Could she follow you?"

"Yeah. An old pickup, I think... But what if she doesn't want to?"

"Tell her I have something important I need to talk to her about."

"You could go see her," he says.

"I can't go on the reservation. They'll arrest me," Sara pauses, letting it sink in for Lionel. "If you can get her to the trading post, I could meet you guys there."

·····•······

A little after one, Sara barrels up the highway through Crozier Canyon. She had to promise Sam that she wasn't going on the reservation, and to take her pistol, as though she needed reminding. Her nerves are on edge, though Rocko appears unaffected, napping in his spot at shotgun. A non-stop stream of scenarios barrels through her thoughts. What if Wamaya doesn't want to come, isn't home, or worse, is back in jail?

As Route 66 tops out onto the plateau, Sara pushes her speed to seventy, hoping Lionel won't get into trouble. Sam said he would be in the shop and to call from the trading post and let him know she was all right. He thought she was crazy, but she has to give it a try.

The big Ford roars past the Truxton sign, the coffee shop & motel. She hits the brakes hard as she veers off the highway onto the dirt. Bouncing across the shoulder, she slides to a stop at the front of the trading post. "Wait," she tells Rocko as she hops down.

Sara strides through the door, looking for Lionel and Wamaya. "Lionel?" No answer. Working her way to the counter, she calls out, "Lionel!"

Still no answer. She glances toward the back. "Lionel. Are you here?" She marches to the back of the store, around the last tall cold case to knock on a door marked private. "Lionel?" Nothing. She knocks again before trying the knob. Locked.

"Can I help you?"

A voice from behind the register startles Sara. Flustered, she walks out of the back. "Yes." She almost doesn't recognize the woman as she approaches the counter. Older than she remembers, the Apache woman gives her a little wave. "Cora?"

"Hello, Sara," Cora says with a wizened smile. "Good to see you. Lionel said you were on your way."

"Oh hi, Cora," Sara says, smiling politely. "Did Lionel tell you why?"

Cora slowly shakes her head. "Not really—something about a job he's doing for you."

Sara broadens her smile as she sets her purse on the counter next to the register. "Do you know Wamaya Watachka?"

"Not personally," Cora says as she opens the register. "I know who she is. I heard about her boy." Cora glances up to meet her gaze. "I heard you found him."

"Yeah." Sara glances away, wanting to change the subject. "Do you know if there are AA meetings in Peach Springs?"

Cora slides a tally sheet under the cash drawer and closes the register. "Not that I know of."

"I know they have them in Kingman," she says. "I was just curious if they have them out here?"

Cora shakes her head. "You're thinking about taking Wamaya Watachka?"

"If I can convince her to go," Sara says. "Do you think it's a good idea?"

Cora shrugs as she steps out from behind the register. "It's worth a try." She leans her forearms on the glass counter and looks Sara directly in the eyes. "But I wouldn't get my hopes up too high."

Nodding, Sara looks down, examining the cans of Copenhagen and Skoal in the glass case. She looks at Cora. "How long ago did Lionel leave?"

"He's been gone almost an hour. What's he supposed to be doing for you?"

"He's supposed to bring Wamaya here, if he can."

Cora purses her lips. "Told me he would only be gone a few minutes. He's supposed to be minding the store. He better get his young hide back here. I got better things to do."

Sara pushes away from the counter. "I think I could go for an ice cream." She turns for the old freezer box near the front door. "You have drumsticks, don't cha?"

Cora points. "Over there."

Sara saunters to the frozen foods freezer on the other side of the cigarette machine. Sorting through a box of drumstick cones, she picks the one with the least damaged wrapper. Her back to Cora, she peels the drumstick, catching the peanut pieces and chocolate crust with her tongue. She stares out the front window at the highway, eating her cone.

Sara hears him before she sees him.

The whiny Honda putters down Route 66, leaving the reservation. Head down, his thick black hair blown back, Lionel squints into the wind. He slows as he leaves the pavement, rattling across the dirt shoulder.

Antenna up, Sara doesn't see anyone on the motorcycle with Lionel. There's no pickup following him either. Holding her hand under her melting drumstick, she opens the door with her shoulder.

Lionel extends both legs, toes up, as he coasts to a stop. Shutting off the engine, he climbs off the little Honda and drops the kickstand. He grins as he walks up to her. "I'm sorry. I couldn't get her to come. She was too drunk."

··•••••••··

Sara idles across the dirt to stop at the highway. Foot on the clutch, she looks up the road. She considers heading for Peach Springs and throwing Wamaya in the truck. She calculates the odds of getting in and out before anyone knows it. Not good. Not that she couldn't get away with it. But if she got caught... She can't do Wamaya any good in jail. She drops her head, staring through the steering wheel. Her eyes well as she thinks of the poor woman. To lose a son like that... She looks up, tears in her eyes as she shakes her head. *It's not right.*

Rocko gets up, pads to her side, and gives her a little kiss on the cheek.

Sighing, Sara turns on her blinker, eases out the clutch, and heads for home.

The Lazy Double-D

S ARA CHALKS IT UP to another weird one, and the day is not over yet. It's only the middle of the afternoon. One thing, for sure: she is not getting any painting done. Somehow, she needs to unravel this rat's nest. She gave Lionel ten bucks before she left, and he promised to call her if and when Wamaya shows up at the trading post. But the way things are going, the fifth of next month seems like a long way off.

Out on the flats, heading into Kingman, it comes to her in a flash—Dennis Drake. Doc Pratt said it. Sheriff Bailey must have told Dennis. The device was on his ranch; the BLM land he leases that butts up to the reservation.

The Drake Ranch Road turnoff is just before the Kingman Airport. Slowing for the right-hander, Sara flicks the turn signal and downshifts. She whips the wheel, turning off the highway onto the smooth dirt road. Rumbling through the cattleguard, she gazes across the wide plain to the Cerbat Mountains rising in the distance. Tops of its tall trees barely visible, the ranch compound is about a third of the way, another five miles or so.

Wide and recently graded, Drake Ranch Road bends like a hockey stick, a straight shot to the main gate with a short chute to the ranch grounds. She slows to take the tight curve, crossing through the main gate. Its steel-pipe barricades are racked back for business and wide enough for two lanes of semi haulers. On the tall gateposts, the massive sign arches high overhead. Fashioned out of steel plate and wrought iron it displays the brand: a pair of capital Ds leaning back at an angle, the Lazy Double-D.

Rolling up the main drive, she passes two sets of corrals and a large roping arena. The original ranch house stands out back: high-pitched gables, their clay tile shingles shading thick adobe walls. Stables and an enormous barn sit off to the side. Behind them, looms a giant metal shed. A heavy-duty stake truck, a road grader, and a bulldozer sit haphazardly in front of its gaping double doors. Inside, a Cessna Skymaster and a little two-man Bell helicopter perch in the shade between a scattering of dirt bikes and three-wheeler ATCs.

The main ranch house stands alone, the centerpiece, surrounded by tall cottonwoods and giant oaks, a ten-thousand square foot refuge of stone and timber and glass. Sara jogs right, parking in front of the split-rail fence around the shady front lawn and next to Dennis' yellow one-ton dually. She recalls Dennis bragging about his stable of fancy cars: a baby blue El Dorado convertible for his wife, Rita; a neon-red Plymouth Hemi 'Cuda for his youngest son, Richard. Dennis said the silver Mark III Lincoln Continental and a brand-new Jaguar XKE coupe in British racing green were his personal vehicles. Sam said he doubts Dennis ever drives them—said he has never seen him in anything but his yellow Cowboy Cadillac. At least she knows he is home.

Sara fills a water dish in the footwell for Rocko, grabs her purse, and climbs out of the truck. With the afternoon sun at her back, she walks up the wide flagstone path and mounts the steps to the timber and lodgepole veranda. Walking the length, she marvels at the opulence of the cattle baron's castle. She vaguely remembers hearing about the new ranch house construction a couple years back. A stone's throw east of the old family homestead, its stacked stone and hand-peeled lodgepoles rise through the trees, fit for a modern rancher. At the hand-carved entry door, she rings the doorbell.

As the massive door opens, Dennis fills the doorway. His belly bulges over his rodeo buckle in a too-tight red-plaid shirt with mother-of-pearl snaps. His pressed Wranglers bunch up across the arch of his sharp-toed riding boots. "There she is. And what a beauty. If I were Sam, I wouldn't let you wander around alone," he says, grinning.

Squinting one eye, Sara cocks her head and grins up at the big man. "Flattery will get you everywhere," she teases. She looks in her purse, rummages around, and pulls out her two Polaroids. She shoves them at Dennis. "Have you seen this?"

Dennis takes the photos as he steps out of the doorway. "Whaddaya got there, little lady?"

"You remember when I borrowed your key?"

"Sure do," he says, giving the Polaroids a quick glance. "Did ya paint somethin' nice for me?"

Sara grimaces. "I never got around to it." She points at the photos in his hand. "But I found that."

Dennis slowly nods as he examines the pictures. "Ol' George showed me some just like these." He looks down at her, his eyes narrowing. "You didn't see my buffalo though, did ya?"

She shakes her head. "Sorry." She steps closer, pointing at the remnants of the cyanide bomb in the photo. "Sheriff Bailey called it a coyote getter. He said it looks like it went off."

He scrunches his chin, nodding. "Looks about right... This what brought you out here?"

"Yup." Sara bites her lower lip. "I found it on your land, not too far from where I found the corpse of that young Hualapai boy, Bryant Watachka."

"Hmph." Dennis purses his lips as he studies the photos. "What's one got to do with the other?"

She moves to his side to point out the Day-Glo spatter on the ground around the spent device. "You see that orange stuff?"

"Yup." He eyes the top Polaroid, then gives her a stern look. "That's what Wildlife Services use to mark their coyote loads. When a varmint bites it or pulls on it, it explodes in their face and marks them at the same time."

Sara meets his gaze. "I dropped by Doc Pratt's this morning. He showed me postmortem photos." She taps the top photo with a pale pink nail. "That orange stuff was on the dead boy's hand and face."

Giving her a sidelong glance, Dennis mulls it over. "I see where you're goin' with this and I'm sorry the boy is dead, but there's nothin' I can do for ya."

Holding his gaze, Sara shakes her head. "It's on your land."

Dennis narrows his eyes. "Technically, that's not true. That land belongs to the US government. I lease the grazing rights." Dennis hands back the Polaroids. "Those grazing rights come with varmint control. You may not like it, but it's a US Wildlife Services varmint control program under the BLM. We lose a lot of livestock to varmints every year."

"Those cyanide devices also kill pets and people."

"The Wildlife boys do their best to make sure those things are flagged with warning signs, so that kinda horsepucky don't happen."

Sara sneers. "My dog can't read."

Dennis shifts to lean on one leg, tapping his toe. "Look, little lady, if anyone was harmed by one of those coyote loads, he'd have to work at it."

He opens his hand, palm up. "He'd have to ignore the no trespassing signs and go over a barbwire fence. He'd have to ignore the warning flag on the durn thing, get down on his hands and knees and pull on the cartridge until it went off. It ain't that easy to do." He shrugs. "Some gotta win, some gotta lose."

Sara glares at him, recalling the downed sections of fence. And how this ostentatious cattle baron, Mr. Dennis Drake, had pointed them out. No wonder the Sheriff blew her off. *Are ranchers' livestock more valuable than human life? Why should you have to choose? All life is precious, including the lives of the so-called 'varmints.'* In her mind's eye, she sees the vast plateau stretching horizon to horizon. There's room for everyone. She wonders if his wife, Rita knows about the cyanide bombs. She clenches her jaws, looking him directly in the eyes. "I see."

Sara drops the Polaroids in her purse, turns for her truck, and strides off the veranda. Without a backward glance, she hits the gas, leaving Mr. Drake and his extravagant ranch house in a cloud of dust.

·····•··•·····

Long shadows cascade through the rugged hills as the daylight drains away. A smattering of porch lights blinks to life through Sara's kitchen window as neighbors settle in for the evening.

Drained from the day, Sara slumps at the kitchen table, waiting on Sam and take-out tacos. It wasn't hard to convince him that she didn't want to cook. Mexican food to-go from El Mohave is always a good idea.

When the screen door bounces off the frame, she snaps awake in the dark kitchen, unaware she had dozed off. Sam hits the kitchen lights, arms full of dinner. She grins at the scent of warm Mexican food as Sam sets bags of take-out on the table. She scoots her chair back, but before she can get up, Sam hustles to the silverware drawer.

"Sit tight," he says, smiling. "I'm running the chuck wagon tonight."

Sam distributes knives, forks, spoons, and extra napkins. Pulling a sixpack of Tecate out of the fridge, he airlifts it to the center of the table and straddles a chair.

Sara yawns, stretches, and gives him a sleepy grin. "I knew there was a reason I married you."

Sam digs a clamshell of enchiladas out of a paper bag, his eyes twinkling with a smile. "Someone's gotta ride herd on you."

"Good work there, cowboy." She lifts out a Styrofoam container full of tacos, rice and refried beans, and tosses the bag to the side. "Pass me the salsa."

Sam scoots a small cup of salsa her direction, then rips a Tecate out of the sixpack. "Head 'em up. Move 'em out," he says, handing her a cold cerveza.

Slurping beer and crunching tacos, she feels better, her dismal day fading into obscurity.

"Rough day?" he asks around a mouthful of tamale.

She nods noncommittally as she chews. "I'd tell you about it," she says, swallowing. "But it was so crappy, I don't know where to start."

They plow their way through the savory dishes, picking their favorites, stuffing their faces, and washing it all down with sweating cans of flavorful lager beer.

Done first, Sam leans his chair back on two legs, patting his full belly with both hands. "Why don't you start with this morning. You can fill in the rest from there."

Sara pushes the to-go box out of the way to lean on the table. Twisting her beer can, she turns glum. She turtles her neck, looking into his eyes. "I'm worried about that woman." Turning away, she fusses with the Styrofoam container.

Sam scrunches his chin and folds his arms across his chest, waiting her out. After several silent moments, he says, "I know, babe. Is there something I can do?"

Sara tightens her lips as she shakes her head. Taking a big swig, she finishes her beer and opens another. "Doc Pratt showed me the postmortem pictures this morning." Her face clouds up. "That's how my day started."

Sam barely bobs his head. "What did the pictures show?"

Sara shrugs. "If you look close—I had to use a magnifying glass—it looks like there are tiny dots of that orange stuff on one hand and part of his forehead."

"At least you're on the right track," Sam says, scratching his neck.

"It's far from conclusive." Sara drinks a swallow of Tecate. "If I didn't know what Wamaya told me about her near-empty whiskey bottle, I would have my doubts."

"But you believe her," Sam says.

Sara shrugs and takes another swig. "More than I believe the rest of these yahoos."

"Which yahoos are we talkin' about here?"

"Take your pick." She throws up her hands. "Sheriff Bailey, Doc Pratt, the Hualapai Police Chief, Dennis Drake—I don't understand it."

Sam barks a short laugh. "Modern-day cowboys and Indians." Leaning forward, he sets his hands on the table. "Leave the chief out of it for a sec. You're right up against it. We're talkin' about the good ol' boy network, old fashioned cronyism right here in Kingman, Arizona. Dennis Drake pretty much owns Mohave County. He and his family have had running disputes with the Hualapai, from minor tiffs to all-out war, for near a century. And I'm sure the tribe has no love for the Drake family. Bailey and Doc Pratt, they're just protecting their interests."

Sara sits up and takes notice. "I'm trying to help the dead boy's mother. You can't imagine what she's going through."

Sam crimps his lips. "Watonami threw you in jail for trespassing. Imagine what he'd try with ol' Dennis if he was convinced a Hualapai boy was killed on Drake's ranch by a varmint load. Manslaughter? Murder? It could get ugly in a hurry."

Sara chews her bottom lip. "I see what you mean... but it doesn't have to be that way."

Sam smirks. "Now who's being naïve?"

Emergency Rescue

AFTER HER MORNING ROUTINE and the day's ledger entries, Sara tries to stay busy around the house, resurrecting half-done projects. Staying busy makes it easier to block images of a cyanide bomb exploding in a boy's face. Still, they haunt her. And what about other children, family dogs, coyotes, mountain lions, and kit foxes? Heartbreaking when no one seems to care. She transfers damp pillowcases from the washer to the dryer. This is what it has come to—discouraging. And busywork around the house is only making it worse.

Sara shuts the dryer door, twists the knob for cottons, and leaves the laundry room. In her bedroom closet she kicks out of the flipflops and pulls on jeans and thick socks, then stuffs her feet into her hiking boots. "Rocko. Here, boy."

Rocko leads the way up the rough grade behind Gold St. Tongue hanging, he trots ahead. Nose to the ground, he zigzags, checking both sides of the long-abandoned dirt road. He loves their excursions in the hills behind the house. On the hunt, he'll likely scare up a chipmunk, maybe a snake, or a jackrabbit.

Sara hikes up the rocky slope, puffing hard by the time she crests the first ridge. She stops to catch her breath, her gaze sweeping 360°. Barren slabs of rock protrude from the rugged hills in every direction. The view from the nose of the ridge is breathtaking: endless sky overhead, reddish-black escarpments of broken lava line the horizon like old molars of ancient monsters turned to stone. High desert air, fresh and dry, space that goes on forever, it all works to clear her mind—a sense of perspective. In the greater scheme of things, this land was here long before people and will be here long after her fellow humans are gone. Sad in a way, but purifying. Regardless of what others do or say, when it all comes to pass, there is only one question to be answered. Did she harm, or did she help? For Sara, there is only one satisfactory answer.

Maybe she can't fight the powers that be when it comes to the cyanide bombs, but she refuses to abandon Wamaya to the wolves.

"Come on, Rocko," Sara says, turning down the hill for home.

·······

Sara races up Route 66 in the dark, the Ford V8 roaring in the cab like a scalded bear. 4:00 am, eyes wide with caffeinated adrenalin, she can't believe she's doing this. It's not as though it is some noble venture, well-planned in advance. She simply couldn't sleep. Tossing and turning, up and down until around 3:00, she finally struggled out of bed, knowing that if she was ever going to get a decent night's sleep again, she had to do something about Wamaya, even if it was wrong.

Before Sam rolled over and went back to sleep, she told him to watch Rocko, and that if she wasn't home by noon to come bail her out. She took his grunt as full acknowledgement.

On the flats outside of Truxton, Burma Shave signs jump into the high-beams like hitchhikers trying to bum a ride. Where this hairbrained scheme of hers comes from, Sara isn't quite sure. Nearly to the reservation border, she tries to shore up her plan to rescue Wamaya. Her brilliant idea, her epiphany, came to her in a moment of sheer exhaustion. She figures timing is everything. This early, everyone including the cops will be in bed. Also, if Wamaya has been on a drinking binge, she should be sleeping it off about now. This is Sara's best chance, and it is scaring the crap out of her.

When the highway sign reads, "Entering Hualapai Indian Reservation," a shudder runs up her spine. *What am I doing?* Slowing to the speed limit, she inhales and holds her breath. Exhaustion turns on her, grandiose ideas of a rescue mission tumbling to dust. Taking her foot off the gas, she pushes in the clutch and coasts. Before she pulls off the road, it hits her hard. What is she going to do? Go home? Do nothing? What if it were her, drowning her sorrows, one of her sons dead? *There but for the grace of God...* Downshifting, she drops the clutch and gives it gas.

On the outskirts of Peach Springs, sharp-cut faces of solid rock glare in the headlights, black gashes hide deep ravines in the early a.m. darkness. As Route 66 curves through the ghostly hills, shadowy canopies of ancient oaks and cottonwoods loom over the highway, their spindly limbs ready to pounce. From an era long dead, abandoned buildings of stacked stone and weathered lumber squat along the side of the road—silent, troll-like sentinels, their empty windows agape.

Slowing, Sara veers into the left turn lane, downshifting to swing onto Diamond Springs. As she motors up the low hill, her truck is the only vehicle on the road. Maybe it's her, but the main street through Peach Springs looks different in the dark, less friendly, more sinister, unpredictable.

Sara drives into the heart of the Hualapai village, watching her mirrors and the road ahead as she tiptoes past the tribal police station. The police station sits back off the street, hunkered down in the dark. No lights. She is probably safe, for now. Wamaya's place is not much farther.

Killing the headlights, she pulls up next to Wamaya's trailer. She shuts off the engine, takes a deep breath and looks around, checking to see if her arrival has been noticed. Sara exits the truck as quietly as she can and picks her way through the dark to the rotting wooden steps and Wamaya's trailer door. Knocking lightly, she waits. The neighboring trailers are all dark. There's a slight nip in the air, and time seems to standstill as a universe of stars shimmer overhead. No answer. She knocks again, louder. Shifting, from one foot to the other, she fidgets, ready to turn around and go home before she gets caught.

Sara tries the knob on impulse. It's unlocked. Cracking the door, she peers inside. It's blacker than tar, impossible to see anything. "Wamaya?" she softly calls. Nothing. She waits, listening hard. Still nothing. Not good. Opening the door another smidge, she raps her knuckles on the thin metal skin and calls out, "Wamaya. Are you home?" She waits, the door open part way, wondering what to do as a foul stench escapes. If the cops come along, see her with the door open, would they shoot?

Sara quietly pulls the door shut and backs down the rickety steps. Rounding to the passenger side, she digs in the glove box for a flashlight and her pistol. She stuffs the pistol into her waistband at the small of her back, grabs the flashlight and heads for the door. She taps the butt of the flashlight against the door and waits, growing more antsy by the second. On the Hualapai reservation, down the street from the police station, in the wee hours of the morning, this is the last place she wants to be. She carefully turns the knob and eases the door open part way, letting the smell of fresh garbage and sour whiskey discharge into the air. "Wamaya?"

she calls. "Is anyone home?" Crinkling her nose, she shields the flashlight lens with her hand as she turns it on. Dim light filters through her fingers as she scans the little living room/kitchen combo: worn out carpet, the nap ground down to grimy bald spots; warped paneling of fake wood bows from the walls; filthy kitchen counters are strewn with trash, the sink piled with dirty dishes. Shadows shift as she takes a step inside. Is that a pile of blankets between the yard-sale coffee table and the ratty old couch? Looking closer, no. That's black hair and a hand. She moves closer, bending for a better look. Wamaya lies face-down, tangled in a wad of bedding. Sara holds still, listening. Wamaya is breathing, thank the Lord. She gently shakes Wamaya's shoulder. "Wamaya, wake up?"

Wamaya grunts, swats at a fly, and rolls up on her side. "Where am I?"

Sara shines the muted flashlight on her dark doughy face.

Wamaya squints, throwing a hand up to block the weak light. "Who are you?"

"It's Sara," she half whispers. "Sara Wayland."

Wamaya squirms away from her to grab the arm of the couch. "Wut chu doin' here?" She pulls herself up to flop on the couch, whiskey fumes spewing from her pores.

Sara watches dumbstruck. How could anyone live like this? "I, uh…" She gathers herself, thinking it through. "I came to tell you something important."

"You that crazy white woman." Wamaya closes her eyes and swats at the light. "Get away from me."

Next to the coffee table, Sara bends down on one knee. "No, really. This is important. It's about your boy. It's about Bryant."

One eye open, Wamaya glares at her. "Wur's my bottle?" She twists her head, looking around. "You stole my whiskey." Moaning, she squeezes her eyes shut. "Bryant stole my whiskey."

Sara bites her lower lip. Staring at Wamaya, she contemplates her next move. The woman is incoherent. Trying to tell her anything is a waste of time.

Moving to the couch, Sara leans over Wamaya and puts a hand on her shoulder. "Do you want your whiskey?"

Wamaya slowly nods, her lids drooping as drool leaks from the corner of her mouth. Holding out a hand, she works her fingers. "Gimme my bottle."

Glancing around, Sara spots a whiskey bottle on the floor at the foot of the couch. On its side, nearly empty, missing its cap, the bottle contains a thin finger of coppery liquid partially hidden behind the Old Grand Dad label. She snatches it up and uses the flashlight around the end of the couch to find the cap. Screwing on the cap, she swirls what's left of the whiskey, trying not to think of Bryant.

Sara moves to sit at Wamaya's side, showing her the whiskey bottle just out of reach. "Do you want this?"

"Gimme that." Wamaya struggles up to sit cockeyed, reaching for the whiskey with both hands.

Grabbing her hand, Sara holds the bottle out and away. "Come on. Let's go." Pulling Wamaya to her feet, Sara stumbles, dropping her flashlight. She rights herself, retrieving her flashlight, steadying Wamaya while keeping the whiskey out of reach. Steering Wamaya toward her sandals, Sara holds her up while she fumbles into rotten rubber flipflops. She guides her out the door, bracing her as Wamaya wobbles down the steps and around to the passenger-side of the tall truck. Setting the whiskey bottle on the hood, Sara opens the door for her and gently pushes her up and onto the seat. She closes the door, grabs the bottle, rounds to the driver's side and climbs in. Handing Wamaya the whiskey bottle, Sara starts the engine and backs onto the road. She catches a glance of the obese young woman slumped against the door, passed out.

Idling through town, Sara upshifts, lugging the engine to keep the noise down. She steps on the clutch and coasts by the dormant police station. The empty street winds through the dark, past the school and through the patchy neighborhood. She keeps to the posted speed. The fiery blue glow of dawn outlines the mountains to the east. Turning onto Route 66, she eases through the gears, letting the truck pick up speed. She grits her teeth, checking her mirrors for the tribal police every few seconds, holding it to 65 until she leaves the reservation. When she tops 75, she backs off, suddenly cognizant that she has a Hualapai woman passed out drunk and an open container on the seat. If she was pulled over, how could she explain it? The Arizona Highway Patrol are not known for their sense of humor.

Weaving downhill and out the bottom of Crozier Canyon, Sara breathes a sigh of relief, gaining comfort as they move farther from the reservation. Too stressed, she hasn't been able to do anything but react until now. Wamaya's heavy snore starts her thinking. She didn't have a specific plan for bringing her back to Kingman. Once off the reservation, she was half-hoping to stop in Truxton, tell Wamaya about the cyanide device, and play it by ear.

Crashing from the adrenaline, Sara fights exhaustion, the highway tugging at her consciousness. The miles tick off in a blur of white lines; and the monotony of Wamaya's snoring, the roar of the V8, and the rumble of the big offroad tires, drop her into a head-nodding stupor. When a front tire grabs the edge of the pavement, her head snaps up, startling her awake. She gasps and jerks the wheel, veering across the highway into the oncoming lane. Whipping the truck back into her lane, she slows, pulls onto the gravelly shoulder and skids to a stop. She looks out at the empty highway, shaking all over.

Stomping the parking brake, Sara leaves the engine running and climbs out. She walks around to the front of the truck, taking deep breaths with her hands on her hips, pacing back and forth in the headlights' glare. As a big-rig semi storms up the grade, she grits her teeth, realizing how close she came. She could have killed them both.

Sara kicks at the gravel with the toe of her boot, irritated with herself for getting involved in this mess. Grimly determined to see it through, she knows there is no turning back now.

Nobody's Fault

GOLDEN FLEECE HUGS THE Hualapai Mountains east of town as Wamaya saws logs slumped on the seat. The early a.m. traffic on Hilltop is light as Sara motors down Andy Devine. Numb from the neck up, burnt out and bleary-eyed, she discards a couple half-baked ideas. Crossing to Beale St., she drives by the A&W drive-in, closer to home, slowing for the turn onto Metcalfe. She pulls into the driveway, parks next to the step van and quits.

Sara leaves Wamaya undisturbed and trudges into the house. Rocko greets her with a woof and a wagging tail. "Hello, boy," she says, bending to rub his neck. She pounds up the stairs with Rocko on her heels. Sam won't be up yet, and she's not sure what to tell him when he is. Coffee first, then she'll wake him.

After downing her first cup, Sara refills, then fills a cup for Sam and heads for the bedroom.

Sam raises his head, half asleep as Sara sits on the bed. "I thought I heard you come in," he says, propping himself up on one elbow. "How did it go?"

She hands him a cup of coffee. "I need your help."

"Thanks," he says taking a sip. "Whaddaya need?"

Reluctance creeps into her voice. "I have the boy's mother in the truck."

Sam lowers his eyebrows with a stern look. "Why?"

She looks down at her hands, turning her cup. "I'm not sure."

Sam takes another sip, eyeing her. "What does *she* think about all this?"

Sara shrugs. "I have no idea. She was falling-down drunk when I picked her up. She's sleeping it off in the truck."

"Good one." He says with a smirk. "What are you gonna do now?"

Coming up blank, Sara bunches her chin and gazes at the radiant sunrise outside her window, letting the moment pass. "I don't know. I thought, maybe..."

"Hmm." Sam takes a slug of coffee, slowly nodding as he gives it a think. "Let me get this straight. You found this drunk woman and you brought her home."

"Something like that."

"Where did you find her?"

"She was passed out in her trailer."

Sam maneuvers his legs past her to sit up. "You were on the reservation..."

She nods meekly.

"And you, what... kidnapped her?"

Frowning, she vigorously shakes her head. "It wasn't like that."

Sam pulls in his chin, giving her a look. "Then how was it?"

"I went to tell her about the cyanide device—what Doc Pratt showed me. I figured if she knew, she might not be so hard on herself. And when I got there, she was too drunk. I don't know what I was thinking. I couldn't' just leave her there like that."

"Yup," he says. "I see what you mean." He finishes his coffee and sets the cup on his nightstand. "Now what?"

Sara turns to him, smiling. "That's where I need your help."

"Right," he says, twisting his lips into a half-grin. He leans his elbows on his thighs and interlocks his fingers. "And this woman is an alcoholic..."

"Yes, I think so," Sara says. "What do you think she'll do when she wakes up?"

Sam stands, yawns, and stretches. "I guess we'll find out," he says as he heads for the bathroom.

Sara slugs down the rest of her coffee, her stomach burning, her head aching as the sunrise blazes through the bedroom window. A heck of a day, so far. And it has only just begun.

· · · · · · · · · ·

Showered, shaved, hair combed, and dressed for work, Sam sits at the office desk, phone in hand. When Sara checked the truck a few minutes ago, the

Hualapai woman was still sleeping. He is not sure how long that will last. Dialing the hospital, he asks for Doc Pratt.

"Ham it's Sam Wayland. You're up early this morning."

"I like to get an early start—schedule all my surgeries for first thing."

"Do you have a minute?"

"Sure thing," Ham says. "What do you need?"

"Did Sara talk to you about this Hualapai woman?"

"The mother of the dead boy?"

"That's right."

"That dead boy, what a tragedy," Ham says.

"Did she tell you the mother is an alcoholic?"

"She might have mentioned it. I don't recollect."

"What do you do for an alcoholic?"

"Get 'em to stop drinking," Ham quips.

Sam smirks. "That's it?"

"I'm kiddin' with ya," Ham says. "Weaning them off the booze is not easy. It can have serious complications. The sad part is most of the time it doesn't do much good. Unless they really want to quit, it's a waste of time."

"How can you tell if they are an alcoholic?"

"Whether or not they crave it," Ham replies. "As well as how much and how often."

"How long does it take to wean them off it?"

"Again, it depends on how much and how often."

Sam pauses, sorting it out before he says anything. "Sara brought her home. The woman is out in the truck, passed out. Sara wants to help her. Is there anything we can do?"

"Except for rounds, I'm pretty much open the rest of the morning," Ham says. "Why don't you bring her in. I'll take a look at her."

· · · • • • • · · · ·

Eyes burning, blonde hair a stringy mess, Sara sits next to Sam in the Emergency Room waiting area, too exhausted to worry anymore. Wamaya was a handful, but they managed to deliver her to Doc Pratt. He has been in an exam room with her for several minutes. If it wasn't for Sam, they never would have made it. Up since three this morning, she leans her elbows on her knees, dropping her head into her hands, doing her best to tough it out. If she could explain it to Wamaya... if Wamaya was halfway coherent... if... She can't think, her mind a painful blank.

Sam lays a hand on her neck, gently kneading the knots with strong fingers. "How 'bout some java?"

She groans, working her neck. "Not sure coffee will do much good."

"Hey," he says with a sympathetic grin. "It's straight out of the vending machine. You'll love it."

Head down, she grunts. "Don't stop rubbing."

Kneading her shoulders with both hands, Sam spots Ham coming out of the exam room.

Sara slumps when Sam stops. "Hey. Keep rubbing."

As Doc Pratt walks up, Sara sits tall watching expectantly. "Is Wamaya okay?"

Doc Pratt looks down his nose, his eyes shifting from Sara to Sam and back. "She's not in good shape," he replies. "Any idea how long she has been drinking like this?"

Sam furrows his brow, glancing at Ham, then Sara.

"She has an account at the Truxton Trading Post," Sara says. "She cashes her check there, then buys whiskey. They might know."

Doc Pratt shrugs. "We won't know the extent of liver damage until we get the blood test results."

"What does she think about all this?" Sam asks.

Doc Pratt sneers. "Non-communicative, belligerent. I'm not sure how much of this she'll put up with."

"What will it take to dry her out?" Sam asks.

"Four, maybe five days minimum," Doc Pratt says. "But we can't admit her involuntarily."

Sara looks to Sam as he crimps his lips and rubs his chin.

Sam gives Ham a hard look. "What's that gonna cost, ya figure?"

Doc Pratt shakes his head. "There are government assistance programs. Between the Arizona Department of Health and the Bureau of Indian Affairs, she's pretty-well covered."

Sara and Sam nod in unison.

"If she needs anything, just let me know," Sam says.

Sara's eyes fill as she grabs Sam's arm with both hands and hugs him tight. She turns to Doc Pratt. "Can I see her now?"

"She's awake," Doc Pratt says. "We gave her a light sedative, so she may be a little groggy."

"Groggy would be an improvement," Sara says as she climbs to her feet.

Doc Pratt motions, leading the way while Sara and Sam follow him into the exam room.

Walking in, Sara catches a glimpse of the young woman. Mouth open, jaw slack, Wamaya lies partially reclined in a narrow Emergency Room bed: her black hair, thick as a helmet, her pie face round and puffy, her eyes half-closed, her wide torso a lumpy mound under the hospital blanket.

When Doc Pratt stops at the foot of the bed, Sara moves to the bedrail. She turns to Doc Pratt and Sam. "Would you gentlemen excuse us, please?"

Sara turns her gaze to Wamaya, waiting as the exam room door closes behind the men. "How are you feeling?"

Groaning, Wamaya slowly rolls her head from side to side. "Need my bottle," she mumbles.

"Do you remember me?" Sara asks.

Wamaya stares through half-lidded eyes. Beneath the drugged haze, she is wary, scared like a little child. "Why are you doin' this to me?"

"You need help."

Wamaya glances around the room, bleary-eyed. "Why am I in prison?"

Sara tightens her lips, her heart sinking. "It's not prison. It's a hospital. They will help you feel better," she says, trying to reassure her.

"I want my bottle." Wamaya pouts. "I want to go home."

As Sara looks her over, a grim reality sets in. What's in store for this young woman? A woman who has lost her son, herself, everything. What kind of life will she have? Turbulent emotions wash through Sara: wells of pity, knots of doubt. Is the poor woman beyond help?

Sara reaches over the bedrail and takes Wamaya's hand. "You won't find what you need in that bottle."

"You crazy," Wamaya grunts. "Leave me alone."

"What happens when you run out of whiskey?"

"Get some more," Wamaya grumbles.

Sara slowly shakes her head, on the verge of tears. "Are you *trying* to kill yourself?"

Wamaya shrugs, bunching her face in an ugly frown. "What's it to you?"

Sara turns her gaze to the ceiling, blinking back the tears. After the worst of the hurt passes, she turns to face her: a young mother, lost and alone, whose son is gone, ripped out of her life forever. "I don't know if you are ready to hear this," Sara says. "But I hope so."

Closing her eyes tight, Wamaya grunts and turns her head away.

Leaning over, Sara lightly brushes her fingers over Wamaya's forehead, rearranging strands of hair. "It's not your fault," she says quietly.

Wamaya throws her head back and forth against the pillow, eyes shut tight, tears leaking from the corners. "No," she wails.

"Shh." Sara's tears fall. "It's going to be all right." As the words come out of her mouth, she wonders how. Taking a deep breath, she steadies herself. "You were right. Chief Watonami is wrong. It's not your fault."

Wamaya opens her eyes to look at Sara. Choking back a sob, she begins to calm.

"Are you okay?" Sara waits for her nod before reaching around to her purse and digging out the Polaroids. "I want to show you something." Sara holds them where Wamaya can see.

Wamaya squints, reaching out to pull the photos closer. After studying them for a moment, she gives Sara a quizzical look.

"It was most likely an accident," Sara says. She points at the top picture. "I'm sorry to have to show you this. These things are used to kill varmints." She pauses, afraid to go on, worried how Wamaya will take it. "Bryant could have set it off by mistake."

Wamaya gasps, drops the photos and covers her mouth with her hands, her eyes flying wide. She stares at Sara in horror.

Sara shakes her head, trying to hold back the tears. "I'm so sorry..." Leaning over the bedrail, she gives her a hug, holding her while she cries. If somehow, she could take away the pain... Her thoughts turn inward. What if she lost Jack or Timmy or Sam? They used to go rabbit hunting in the hills around Kingman when the boys were younger, they could have stepped on one of those things. What if Rocko found one of those cyanide bombs? She can't imagine. *Lord, no.* How can she think Wamaya will be all right, ever?

Standing back, Sara watches Wamaya's face for any sign of hope. Grim determination tightens her jaw. She will see it through—help Wamaya conquer her demons, no matter what. Light as a feather, she places a hand on Wamaya's shoulder. "You were right. It's not your fault. The Chief is wrong. Don't listen to him. Bryant didn't die of alcohol poisoning. He wouldn't want you to die from alcohol, either. Please stay in the hospital until you are better. I'll be here for you, all the way."

Citizen Complaint

AFTER BREAKFAST ON THE third morning, Rocko lies on the cool mulch pile in the shade of a leafy cottonwood, keeping one eye open. Sara kneels in her anemic flower garden, stabbing at the caliche hardpan with a hand spade. She wipes her sweaty brow with her sleeve, wondering why she bothers. How long has she tried to grow flowers? Way back when, at her urging, Sam carved three terraced beds out of the steep slope along the northeast side of the house. She remembers how he spent three weekends jackhammering and hauling away the foot-thick caliche. The top-soil Sam hauled in helped, at first. Sara did the rest: planting, nurturing. But the soil is so poor.

The flowerbeds were dug in a couple years after she had Timmy. Both the boys were eager to help when they were too little to be much help. When they were big enough to be a real help, they lost interest. Sitting back on her heels, she sighs at the pathetic crop of stunted plants: iris bulbs with a few stubby leaves, a spindly rose bush that hasn't bloomed in years, woody clumps of lavender. She has been weeding and watering and fertilizing faithfully. This late in the Spring they should be going great guns. She smiles wistfully at Rocko as she climbs to her feet, thinking she should stick to painting.

Wamaya comes to mind as Sara stows her garden tools in the shed. She has been at the hospital with Wamaya every afternoon, sitting bedside. Gut wrenching. Wamaya thrashed and moaned, shaking, sweating, complaining about headaches and nausea. Doc Pratt says, since Wamaya is a long-time heavy drinker, the symptoms are likely to get worse over the next day or two. He expects her agitation to increase despite the Valium; fever, seizures and vomiting are possible, along with hallucinations—delirium tremens. Sara will head out to the hospital after lunch.

What a mess. How she managed to get roped into all this, Sara is still not sure. Her biggest concern is what Wamaya will do once she dries out. What kind of future awaits her? More welfare whiskey from the Truxton Trading Post? An empty trailer on the reservation? After the way Chief Watonami has treated her, how can she go back? But where else does she have to go? Sara hopes like heck she can convince her to attend the local AA meetings. That way, Wamaya would at least have a chance.

··········

After a few arduous hours at Wamaya's bedside, Sara leaves the hospital frazzled. Watching the poor woman suffer through withdrawals, she swears she never wants another drink. She speeds down Stockton Hill Rd., needing to calm down, get herself under control before their appointment. On Andy Devine, barreling down the hill, she thanks the Lord Sam will be there with her.

Swerving to the right, Sara heads down Beale St. She slows to turn into the little strip center. Parking next to the step van, she climbs out of the big F250 and strides purposefully into the office of Robert B. Green, Attorney at Law.

Seated at the front desk, Celia smiles and waves her through. "They're in Bob's office."

Bob looks up when she enters.

Sara closes the door on her way in, then takes the chair next to Sam.

"Hi, babe," Sam says as he turns and smiles.

"We were just discussing Wamaya's situation," Bob says with sympathetic eyes. "How is she doing?"

Sara grimaces. "About as well as can be expected."

Bob hangs his head. "That's tough."

"You have no idea." Sara slowly shakes her head. "She may never be free of this." She looks up, locking eyes with the attorney. "But that's why we're here."

Returning her gaze, Bob crimps his lips. "Right."

Sam leans to catch Sara's eye. "We were just discussing the possibilities of a wrongful death suit."

"A civil suit?" she asks.

Bob nods. "In such a case, Ms. Watachka could be compensated for her loss."

"I see," she says. Her eyes turn hard as marbles as she sneers. "What do ya figure her son's life is worth?"

Sam lays a hand on her forearm. "Easy there, babe. We're just talking."

Bob throws up his hands, shaking his head. "I'm not sure who we're gonna sue, or if she has a case."

Sara smirks. "Her son is dead, seems like a wrongful death to me."

"I understand how you feel," Bob says, palms out. "But Wrongful Death is a legal term. And a suit for Wrongful Death must meet specific criteria for any chance of success."

"What kind of criteria are we talkin' about here?" Sam asks.

"To win, you gotta prove someone caused her boy's death." Bob turns to Sara. "Who does she plan on suing?"

Sam glances at Sara.

Sara mulls it over. She knows what that glance meant. She and Sam have to live here. Kingman is their home. "The device that probably killed Bryant was a cyanide bomb, used for varmint control," she says. "It was on the Drake Ranch, near the reservation."

Bob pushes back in his chair, interlocking his fingers as he glances at Sam. "This woman wants to sue the Drake Ranch—Dennis Drake?"

"Is that a problem?" Sara snaps.

Frowning, Bob shakes his head. "I guess not... As long as she's sure."

"As sure as we can be," she replies.

"Due to a conflict of interest, I'll have to bow out. I've done some legal work for Mr. Drake in the past. But I can refer you to another attorney."

Sam leans sideways, propping an elbow on the arm of the chair. "What if it was accidental?"

"You still have to show negligence," Bob says. "Burden of proof for negligence is a high bar—tough to prove."

Looking at her hands, Sara chews her lower lip.

"This cyanide bomb," Bob says eyeing Sara. "You think Mr. Drake—that his use of it was negligent, and that it was responsible for the boy's death?"

"I don't know," she says. "That's why we're here."

Bob nods as he steeples his fingers. "To show negligence, she'll have to prove specific elements: Duty—that Mr. Drake owed a duty of care to the decedent. That he breached that duty. And by breaching that duty, he caused the decedent's death. Then there's damages."

"Damages." Sara bunches her brow. "What do you mean?"

"She'll have to show how she was damaged by her son's death—how much she should be compensated." Bob leans forward, resting his forearms on his desk. "This is going to sound cruel. But the economics of this case are not good. The boy was a teenager, from what I understand, still in school. He probably wasn't providing any income to the household. Any financial loss will be hard to prove."

Sara slams a fist on his desk. "You mean to sit there and tell me the boy's life was worth nothing?" She pins him with a fiery glare. "How dare you!"

Bob rears back, throwing his palms up in surrender. "Hey. I'm not saying any such thing. I've got kids of my own. I feel for the mother here. But in the eyes of the law, it's a cold hard fact."

"If she wins..." Sara ponders in the moment. "Does Dennis have to quit using those varmint control devices?"

Bob shrugs. "Not likely."

"What about the BLM?" she asks.

"I'm not following you," Bob says.

"Dennis Drake told me he leased the land from the BLM, and they provide varmint control through the US Wildlife Services as part of the deal."

Bob smirks. "Ya ever heard the old saw 'you can't fight city hall'?"

Sara and Sam glance at each other.

"Try multiplying that by a thousand," Bob says. "Suing any part of the US Government is a long and expensive exercise in futility."

"To sue 'em," Sam says. "How much we talkin' here?"

"More than you got," Bob says. He turns on Sara. "Have you talked to Mr. Drake or anyone at the BLM about this?"

"Dear Lord, what a mess." Sara grabs her forehead, looking Bob in the eyes. "I saw Dennis, took the photos out to the ranch and showed him," she says. "He blew it off, but I didn't say anything about a lawsuit."

"And the BLM?" Bob asks.

Sara shakes her head. "I wouldn't know where to start."

Bob gives her a sympathetic look. "My advice," he says. "Before you hire an attorney, you should talk to them. I'll dig up a name and number for ya."

"Do you really think they will stop using them, if I call?" Sara says sarcastically.

"Heck you can go on over there," Bob says. "It's on Hualapai Mountain Road, on the right. You can file a citizen complaint for free and see what happens."

·····•••····

A golden glow fills the kitchen with a cozy warmth. Filtered through lacey curtains, sunlight angles over the counter, across the floor, and over the kitchen table—the antique walnut hutch alight with a lustrous shine.

Sam finishes his eggs, sits back from the breakfast table, and sips his coffee.

Sara sips her coffee and admires her husband, his eyes sparkling in the morning light. They have spent most of their lives together, yet she never tires of the journey. She loves watching him when he's not noticing. Capturing moments like these are what she hopes to remember most.

He catches her, and she lights him up with a smile. "I'm heading up to the BLM in a little bit."

Sam can't stop grinning. She always looks great in the morning. In fact, durn near anytime. He knew the minute he first saw her; she was the girl for him. After all these years and raising two boys, he admires her more than ever—not just her beauty, but her sweetness and strength of character in the face of what most folks would consider overwhelming odds. She is the kindest person he has ever known. He lifts his coffee in a toast. "Give 'em hell."

"I'll go see Wamaya after that."

Sam nods and sets down his mug.

"I need to ask you something before you leave," she says.

"Shoot."

"I need to get Wamaya into a program. I looked around. Alcoholics Anonymous has meetings in Kingman, but there's nothing for her on the reservation. What if she moved into one of the spare bedrooms? She could help around the house, and I could make sure she is going to AA."

Sam smiles as he gets up from the table. "Up to you, Mom. I'm behind ya, all the way."

· · · • • · • · · ·

The mid-morning sky gleams like a marble, a hard blue. On Andy Devine, Sara holds steady as the truck chugs up through the cut to Hilltop. Rocko watches traffic from his spot at shotgun. Bearing to the right, Sara turns on Hualapai Mountain Rd. Ahead, the mountain range fills the horizon, a jagged jaw of misty peaks shrouded by a low band of outlaw clouds. Intrigued, she envisions the scene as a watercolor: foothills of burnt sienna, mountains in a mist of thin white over burnt umber and primary blue. Touches of deep violet and ivory black to bring depth to the mountain faces. For the clouds and sky, bright white over a light azure with hints of turquoise. She hasn't had time to paint lately, but she can still dream.

Blue skies out of mind, Sara turns into the entry drive for the squat stucco box that serves as The Bureau of Land Management, Kingman Field Office. If she were going anywhere else, she would be in a wonderful mood. She's not big on confrontations, tries her best not to instigate them. But hey, if it happens, she won't back down.

Parked in the third slot from the entrance, Sara hops out, leashes up Rocko, grabs her purse off the seat, and locks up the F250. Signage on the glass doors gives days and hours of operation and forbids firearms, but there is nothing about pets. Opening the door for Rocko, she follows him in. She leads Rocko to the empty reception desk and sits in one of two side chairs. "Down," she tells him. As Sara scans the small reception area, Rocko lies down next to the chair, his head touching her calf. The nameplate on the desk reads "Mrs. Torbert." She looks at Rocko, then crosses her thighs and sighs, figuring to give the woman two more minutes.

The large oak door to the back opens outward with a whoosh as a lanky woman in an ill-fitting print dress walks through. Dark hair in a messy bun, she looks to be in her early thirties, though the thick horn-rim glasses and lack of makeup add a few years. Mrs. Torbert glances at Rocko and gives Sara a tight smile as she sits. "I hope you haven't been waiting long. How can I help you?"

"I want to file a complaint," Sara says brusquely.

"I see..." Judy Torbert lowers her chin, giving Sara the eye over the top of her glasses. "You realize there are no pets allowed."

"I didn't see the sign," Sara says with a smirk. "At least I left my pistol in the truck."

Judy pauses, weighing her options against a path of least resistance. She faces an older woman in her mid-forties: trim for her age, expensive turquoise jewelry, flaxen hair the color of golden wheat well past her shoulders, ice-blue eyes flashing daggers. The woman is obviously upset. A rich rancher's wife? An armpiece? If so, she doesn't recognize her. "I'm sorry," she says. "But your dog..."

"Rocko stays. He's a service dog and it's perfectly legal for him to be here," Sara says, clipping her words. "I checked. My dog stays."

Judy raises her eyebrows and slowly nods with trepidation. "I see..." She straightens a stack of papers and slides it into her top drawer. "Okay... You want to file a complaint."

Annoyed, Sara nods. "That's right." She whips her purse onto the desktop, digs out the Polaroids, and tosses them in front of the squirming Mrs. Torbert. "I want you people to stop this. You're killing people, along with everything else."

"Excuse me?" Judy says, rearing back.

Sara leans over the desk, poking at the photos with a pastel pink talon. "Take a gander at these. You'll see what I mean."

Judy picks up the photos, holding one in each hand, glancing between the two. "What are these supposed to be?"

Red-faced, Sara snaps, "*That*, is a cyanide bomb—your cyanide bomb."

"I don't know what you're talking about. We don't work with varmint control from this office." Judy shuffles and restudies the photos. "I don't see anything."

"That's because it exploded," Sara says. "In all likelihood, it killed a thirteen-year-old boy—exploded in his face."

Skeptical, Judy cocks her head as she lays the photos on her desk. "I'm sorry. I don't see it. But you're welcome to file a complaint."

Cyanide Bomb

TURNING ONTO STOCKTON HILL Rd., Sara sits tall, both hands gripping the wheel, her fury burning down to smoking embers. She can't get over it. What an obstinate woman. She sneers—typical bureaucrat. She glances at the wad of blank complaint forms shoved in her purse, thinking her pistol would have worked better.

Downshifting, Sara turns into the hospital main parking lot. People can be so exasperating. She glances at sweet Rocko's smiling face as she grabs his leash. "You get to go with me," she tells him. At least *he's* happy.

Forcing a polite smile, Sara waves at Margaret behind the admittance window.

Margaret stands and motions her over.

With Rocko in tow, Sara veers to the window.

"You know you can't bring pets in here," Margaret says, quietly.

Sara smiles amiably. "Rocko goes everywhere. You know, like a seeing-eye dog."

"Okay, this time." Margaret waves her off, smiling.

Rocko trots next to Sara as she strides down the wide corridor. She ducks through the doorway to the "C" Ward for indigents. Pushing aside the privacy curtain, she finds Wamaya's bed empty. At the nurses' station, she discovers Wamaya was last seen walking the corridor. She rechecks Wamaya's bed, just in case. No Wamaya.

Sara could wait, but... Wamaya must be around here somewhere. Squatting next to him, she gets a kiss from Rocko as she rubs his ears. She reaches up to the bed, grabs a corner of a blanket and holds it out for Rocko. "Wamaya," she tells him as he eagerly sniffs the blanket. "Let's find her."

Rocko gives a small bark and paws the tile.

"Go." Sara stands and lets Rocko lead her out and down the main corridor to the last doorway on the right. She enters the dayroom behind

Rocko, glancing around: half-a-dozen laminate tables with hard-plastic chairs, a small color TV high in the corner, hanging from a bracket, the sound off, the screen showing daytime TV. Three patients at separate tables absently watch the show in silence. No Wamaya.

Rocko trots across the room, dragging Sara to a sliding glass door. Outside are metal chairs on a small, covered patio. Back turned, Wamaya sits in one of them.

Wamaya turns her head as Sara and Rocko join her.

Sara takes the chair next to Wamaya, noticing her eyes seem clearer, if sad. The view across the foothills and into the Cerbat Mountains is spacious and peaceful. Sara breathes a tentative sigh as Rocko lies down for a head pat. "Good Boy."

After a few quiet moments, Sara turns to face Wamaya. "Looks like you're doing better."

Her dark face stoic, Wamaya bunches her chin. "Yeah." She gives a little nod. "Better..."

"That's good," Sara says encouragingly. "That's better than Doc Pratt expected. You're doing great."

Wamaya drops her gaze to her lap, twisting her fingers.

Sara raises an eyebrow. "Did you have a chance to look over that information I left?"

"AA," she says, her round face expressionless.

"I think it could help," Sara says.

Wamaya looks off to the Cerbats, her face closed.

Take it slow, Sara tells herself. They can talk about AA and a place to stay tomorrow or the next day. Looking away, she switches gears, considering whether she should mention the accident. No point in reopening deep wounds.

·········

Shadows grow long as the sun sinks behind a rugged ridge. Dusky light descends on Spring Street and the Wayland home, the downstairs windows in deep shade. In her office, with Rocko on his horse blanket, Sara struggles with the three-page, carbonless complaint form—in particular, a block of blank lines under the heading 'Description.'

Sara tries to imagine who will be reading this darn thing. She would like to yell at them, shout it to the hills, scold them, get their attention anyway she can. And while she might feel better temporarily, screaming at them is not going to help. She knows this. She also knows the evidence against the BLM is too sketchy. According to Bob, no reputable attorney would take the case on a contingency basis. Sara is forced to agree; it is not clear who is at fault. A freak accident? Hardly matters, she and Sam could never afford the cost of such a lawsuit. Yet these cyanide bombs are indiscriminately killing animals and people. It's criminal, or at least it should be. It just needs to stop. If Sara could get the right people at the BLM to see that... Which comes down to who will be reading this darn thing.

Twiddling her pen between thumb and forefinger, Sara stares at all the blanks, procrastinating. She shifts her gaze to the ceiling. Maybe Sam will have some good suggestions.

·····•·····

After dinner, Sara mixes a Salty Dog and heads for the back patio. She holds the screen door for Rocko, then eases into her chair next to Sam.

She smiles as he offers his glass in a toast. As their glasses clink, she asks, "What are we toasting?"

Lifting his drink, he gives her a crooked smile. "Well, Mom, looks like we made it through another day."

Sara tilts her head back with a half laugh. "I hope your day went better than mine."

Sam takes a swig of his Tanqueray and tonic and glances her way. "That good, huh?"

Wordless, Sara sips her drink, shifting her gaze to the night sky.

"Well, at least ya aren't in jail," he says, leaning back with a grin.

Sara sets down her drink, twisting up in the chair to face Sam. "I gotta get these people to stop."

"Who, the BLM?"

"Yes. These BLM people... I don't even know who, but someone there can stop this. These devices are so dangerous... It's barbaric."

"What did they say?"

"They gave me a three-page form to file a complaint," she says, exasperated. "Will it do any good? Darned if I know."

Sam swirls the ice around in his gin and looks up to meet her gaze. "You want me to take a look at it?"

·····•··•·····

Looking both ways, Sara pulls out of the BLM parking lot. Mrs. Torbert accepted the complaint without any drama, letting Sara know to check back on its status in a week or two. Sara was happy to get out of there. The hospital is next.

Sara chews her lower lip, dissatisfied. The BLM seems like a big waste of time. She has been spending too many days this way—running around like a lost child. It's not her. She refuses to live like this. It was tough enough with the boys. When they reinstated the draft for Vietnam, Jack was eligible. She couldn't sleep more than a few hours a night. It wasn't until his high lottery number saved him that she could breathe again. She and Sam set up a college deferment for Timmy, but by that time the draft was abolished. *Thank the Lord.*

Sara runs the truck across the tracks to the stop sign at Andy Devine. Her thoughts turn to Wamaya. Life can be hard, probably more so on the reservation. The barren desert and rugged mountains of Mohave County are a tough place to raise a child. It's a hard and cruel truth, some don't make it. But you can't give up like that. Drinking, drugs, they only make your troubles worse.

Jogging onto Fairgrounds Blvd., she sweeps around the Circle K, through an older, poorer area of Hilltop. Drinking socially, Sara doesn't see anything wrong with that, but to drown yourself in whiskey...

Mulling it over, she hangs a left on Davis Ave., keeping her speed at 25 until she reaches Stockton Hill Rd. You'd think at some point a person would pull their head out of the sand, take a good look at the real world, and do something about their troubles. She has seen it before. People can lick their bad habits, turn things around and get on with it.

Sara cranks the wheel, steering the big Ford into the hospital parking lot. Truth is, she would rather be off somewhere out in the hills with Rocko, working on a watercolor. Her art, her painting calls to her. Will she ever perfect her technique? It is something to hope for, something to look forward to.

With Rocko leashed and on heel, she pushes through the double doors, entering the hospital lobby, wondering how Wamaya is doing today. Sara is a little nervous about suggesting that Wamaya stay with them. She doesn't know her all that well, just that she's in trouble. What if AA doesn't work for her? Maybe Sara should stay out of it, let her go back to the reservation, leave her alone.

After checking her bed, Sara finds Wamaya in the dayroom slumped in a plastic chair—her arms folded as she stares out at the Cerbats. The second day in a row that Wamaya is up out of bed. Taking a seat next to her, Sara figures it is a good sign. She quietly waits a couple moments to see if the young woman will respond to her presence.

Wamaya sits still as a stone.

Finally, Sara asks, "Wamaya, how are you doing?"

"Wanna go home," Wamaya mumbles as she stares at the mountains.

Sara turns her gaze to the Cerbats, chiding herself. She knew this would come up. She suspected Wamaya would want to dive right back into a bottle. "I understand." She lets time stream out, the silence between them deepening. Sara wonders if anyone on the reservation has missed her. "You can go home whenever you like."

Wamaya holds the mountains in her empty gaze as though hypnotized.

Sara sits patiently, letting time unwind, waiting her out. After several long moments, she intervenes. "The only thing I would say... Before you go home." Sara glances at Wamaya's blank face and turns away. "I want to make sure you understand what happened to your son, Bryant." Sara glances back for a reaction. Nothing. She begins to wonder if it is still too soon. She puts on an upbeat air. "Why don't you come stay with us—just 'til you feel better?"

Wamaya frowns, snapping her head to give Sara a hard look. "Why?" she blurts.

Caught off guard, Sara flinches. "I thought if you wanted to try AA, you could stay here in town, with us."

Wamaya turns back to the mountains, staring off past the horizon.

Wishing she knew what to say, Sara watches the clouds float above the Cerbats, a puffy crown of silvery-white darkening the mountains with shadows of rust and coal. If she could find a way to reach her... She glances down at Rocko as she rubs his head. Empty moments slow. She feels sluggish as though hungover. But she only had one drink before bed, it can't be a hangover. Is Wamaya rubbing off? Has Sara's empathy for the poor woman betrayed her? She never feels like this. She turns to Rocko, smiles, then turns back to Wamaya. "You haven't formally met Rocko yet," she tells her. "He likes you."

On cue, Rocko pops up and swaggers past Sara to stand close to Wamaya. Grinning, he wags his tail inviting the morose young woman to stroke his soft coat.

Hesitating, Wamaya looks blankly at the friendly yellow lab in front of her. She tentatively reaches for Rocko's head, giving him a quick pat. Bryant wanted a dog, but she said no. Maybe if she had let him have a dog, he wouldn't have taken off across the desert by himself—with her bottle. She furtively looks at the connection, afraid to look closer. Maybe the Chief is right. In a way, she is responsible.

Rocko gives her fingers a little kiss as she starts to pull away. Something breaks and Wamaya leans forward, bursting into tears as she hugs Rocko.

Sara gasps, reaching out to comfort Wamaya.

Holding Rocko's head to her cheek, Wamaya sobs, burying her face in his fur. Rocko twists to lick her tears away. Gradually, Wamaya's sobs subside to blubbering hiccups.

Regaining her composure, Sara backs off, letting Wamaya cry it out. She finds it a tiny bit ironic: if Wamaya wasn't an alcoholic, she would probably offer her a drink about now. Torn, she wonders what she should do. After everything Wamaya has gone through, she can't simply walk away, let the poor woman drink herself into oblivion. Yet, Wamaya doesn't seem to want her help. Sara sits, simmering, her lid rattling with the escaping steam. She has come this far. She can't turn back now. Turning to Wamaya, she keeps her gaze steady, determined to make it work. "Please listen to me. I'm going to explain... I hope it gets through, so I'm going to tell you straight out. Do you know what a cyanide device is?"

The Dream

MUTED MORNING LIGHT FILTERS through her studio curtains. Sara cleans her brush and drops it, tail first, into her brush jar, then caps a tube of Titanium White and sets it in the paintbox. Standing, she stretches her shoulders and neck. She closes her eyes and groans as she thinks of Sam's neck rubs. Hands on her hips, she moseys to the window. She pushes a curtain aside, daydreaming of time alone with Sam. They keep missing each other lately. With a boarder, it's not likely to improve soon.

Two days ago, Sara was worried that Wamaya wouldn't stay with them or attend AA. A few hours from now, Wamaya will be released from the hospital into Sara's care. Sara has the guest room and guest bath all set up. She bought her a few things; she hopes they fit. But her overriding worry is having a recovering alcoholic in the house. When she had Sam lock up all their booze in a shop locker, he told her she was overreacting, but she stood firm—no drinking in the house. The truth is, she has never had to care for anyone with a drinking problem. Despite Doc Pratt's coaching, she doesn't know what to expect.

Sara glances over her shoulder at her new start, a mostly blank canvas waiting on her easel. Lack of time, lack of determination, lack of inspiration, they're ganging up on her—dreary demons, invisible, stealing her soul. Painting without passion, is it possible? She wonders, is misery a form of passion? This must be her blue period.

Turning her gaze out the window, she lets the view lift her spirits: modest houses here and there, nestled in the high desert hills, scrub and tumbleweeds whipped to a frenzy in the gusty spring wind, a wide sky, endless blue, spattered with wispy clouds. This is her home, where she raised a family, made life-long friends—she loves this place, her little city of Kingman, comfortable, peaceful, as though she was always meant to be here.

Sara glances at her hands, her thoughts running to the afternoon ahead. Shrugging it off, she decides there is no need to worry. One way or another, it is bound to work out. Lifting her eyes, she admires the view, wistful yet contented.

·····•·••··

A little after 3:00, Sara wheels Wamaya out of the hospital entrance and onto the loading apron. She helps Wamaya as she huffs her way out of the wheelchair. Rocko wags his tail and barks, following Wamaya to the truck. Sara scurries to open the passenger door, her nerves betraying her. Wamaya didn't say more than three words during the release process—little more than grunts. Sara wants to hurry her home before she changes her mind.

Sara climbs into the driver's seat. Rocko stretches out on the bench seat, his head in Wamaya's lap. Wamaya slumps next to the door at shotgun, rubbing Rocko's ears. Every time she stops rubbing, he nudges her hand with his nose. His antics make Wamaya smile, and it quickly becomes a game. By the time Sara pulls the F250 into their driveway, Wamaya has a small case of the giggles.

Elated, Sara hops out of the pickup and trots around to open Wamaya's door. When she pulls the door wide, Rocko grins at her from Wamaya's lap, making her smile. "Okay, you two. Let's go."

Rocko bounds over Wamaya to run around Sara in circles while she gives Wamaya a hand down. Wamaya steadies herself with the door, then bends to give Rocko a pat. Sara tries to suppress her enthusiasm. She has never seen Wamaya like this. Of all the scenarios she had for this homecoming, this wasn't one of them. She loops an arm loosely around Wamaya's shoulders. "This way," she says, pointing to the downstairs door.

Inside, with Rocko on her heels, Wamaya follows Sara up the stairs through the main floor to the top floor and into the guestroom.

Sara sweeps an arm toward the clothes laid out on the twin bed. "I hope these fit." She smiles. "If not, we can take them back."

Wamaya shuffles toward the bed, nodding in amazement. She picks up the dress and holds it up to the light, eyes watering. Meekly holding the dress against her chest, she turns to Sara for approval.

Sara rubs her chin as she nods. "Looks like it'll fit... Looks nice."

Rocko rubs against Sara's legs, then Wamaya's legs, wagging his tail—almost a nuisance. Noticing Wamaya's weak smile, Sara stops herself from calling him off. He rarely behaves this way and never with strangers, only Timmy and Sam and her. Whatever his instincts are telling him, they're right.

Smiling at Wamaya, she says, "You can try it on, if you like, or take a nap, or whatever you want." Sara points to the hall. "The bathroom is just across the way. Dinner will be ready in a few hours." She smiles. "I'll leave you two alone." Bowing out, she leaves the door open wide enough for Rocko. Bouncing down the stairs, she hasn't felt this good in days.

·········

Sara keeps dinner simple. Sam flips burgers on the grill as she fires up a batch of tater tots in her iron skillet. Wolfing down the homecooked meal like it's her last, Wamaya doesn't say much. Sara can't help but notice the occasional tremors in her hands and her sad eyes—always looking down. Sara's mood sinks, realizing Wamaya's recovery won't happen overnight. When it comes to her son Bryant, Wamaya remains mute. Heartbreaking. The cyanide device explanation hasn't helped. Was it a mistake to tell her? Was Sara just rubbing salt into the wound?

After the dinner dishes, Sara trots up the stairs to check on her houseguest. When she peeks through the gap in the door, the soft yellow glow of a nightlight shows Wamaya asleep on top of the covers with an arm around her dog.

Rocko picks up his head, eyeing Sara, letting her know he'll take good care of the young Hualapai woman. Watching her leave, Rocko lays his head next to Wamaya's chest and sighs.

Her sweet dog's warmth is unexpected. Backing away, Sara wipes at the corner of an eye. She has always taken Rocko's heart of gold more or less at face value. From the time he was a pup, he has been right there for her and Timmy—by her side since Timmy left for ASU. This is a side of Rocko she hasn't seen: a depth of caring, of nurturing; working miracles with Wamaya she couldn't have imagined. Her loyal companion all this time and she never knew.

Dozing, Rocko listens to the young Hualapai woman snore. When she whimpers, he gives her a kiss on the chin and her gentle snoring resumes.

Deeply connecting, he calms her, there for her to lean on. Rocko takes comfort, knowing that he's there to help—that she needs his help more than she knows. Her guardian angel, he'll stay by her side for as long as she needs.

·····•·•····

Outside the kitchen, stiff winds blow clouds of dust around like skittish quail. Across the street, a dust devil bears down hard, swirling dirt and debris into the sky. Window screens rattle as the whirlwind whips by the house to twist through the yard.

At the kitchen table, after breakfast, nursing a fresh cup of coffee, Sara enjoys her quiet time. Sam left on his vending route a few minutes ago and she has yet to hear a peep out of Wamaya. She wanted to take Wamaya on a walk behind the house this morning; but with the wind kicking up, it would be miserable. The wind reminds her of how harsh the barren terrain of Mohave County can be. Windy days are wicked—the one thing she truly dislikes about Kingman. Relentless, unforgiving, are the biting winds a soulless warning? She wonders if the BLM and their cyanide bombs are simply a reflection of that careless cruelty.

Wamaya has her first AA meeting this evening. Sara figures it ought to be interesting. In looking into AA, it sounded reasonable. She hopes it works.

Sara turns her head at the sound of footsteps on the stairs. Wamaya must be up. Popping out of her chair, Sara moves to the stove and slides a skillet onto a front burner as Rocko trots in.

Shuffling, head down, Wamaya follows, her hair a tangled mess, her frumpy dress, slept in.

"Good morning," Sara says cheerfully.

Without a word, Wamaya avoids eye contact and fumbles into a chair on the far side of the table. She interlaces her fingers, setting her hands on the table in front of her, staring at them as though afraid to look away.

After Sara hands out his morning chew bone, Rocko rounds the table, parks next to Wamaya's chair, and works his bone. He scoots up to lean a shoulder against Wamaya's leg as he chews.

Absently, Wamaya reaches down to stroke his head.

Sara takes the chair across from her. Leaning in, she works to catch Wamaya's eye. "Are you hungry?"

Wamaya shakes her head. Covering her eyes with her hands, she weeps.

"Are you okay?" Sara asks. "What's wrong?"

Wamaya wails into her hands.

Rocko drops his chew bone, stands up, and nudges her calf with his nose.

Gasping between sobs, Wamaya winds down as Sara worries. "Do you want to go back to the hospital?"

Wamaya goes quiet. Dropping her hands from her puffy face, she reaches for Rocko, bending to hug him. Ever so softly, she says, "I had a dream."

Sara lays a comforting hand on her shoulder. "It's just a nightmare. Doc Pratt says they'll pass. Just give it time."

Wamaya looks up sorrowfully. "Not that kind of a dream."

Sara withdraws to sit straight. "I don't understand. What kind of a dream?"

"It was Bryant," she says, her eyes filled with pain.

Stunned, Sara parts her lips but words fail her.

"He came to me," Wamaya says. "He told me he loves me." Blinking rapidly, she holds up, pausing for a moment, trying to keep it together.

Sara's eyes widen as a misty image of Wamaya's boy forms in her mind. Shining, he smiles.

Rocko lays his front paws on Wamaya's knees as he drops his head in her lap.

"He thanked me for being his Mom." She rubs Rocko's head with both hands, trying not to break down. Turning to face Sara, she says. "He said everything's okay. He runs with the coyotes now."

·····•·•·····

Kingman sits in the dark. Dim stars and porchlights. Gusting wind stirs the haze, damping out the night.

In the pickup with Wamaya and Rocko, Sara is electrified. Heading toward downtown on Spring St., she pushes in the clutch, her head spinning as she brakes for the stop sign at Grandview. Across the street, bordering the public pool, ancient cypress bristle in the wind, trembling in the darkness like giant feather dusters. Sara recalls when her eldest, Jack, huffed and puffed his way through fifty laps of the front crawl for his Boy Scout mile-swim badge. Winded, he clung to the coping when he touched for the last time, pretending it was no big deal. She was so proud of him.

A softer sense of pride wells up for Wamaya. This is their first AA meeting. Sara has a feeling it will go well. With Rocko by her side, Wamaya will be fine.

Sara cuts across Grandview, the big V8 rumbling as she hunts a parking space in front of the Junior High. She remembers, before the Junior High was built, when the boys were little, this land used to be a graveyard. As a young sprout, Jack used to test his courage by walking through the graveyard while his friends went the long way around. Tonight would be a good night for spooks, as dark as it is.

Cranking the wheel, Sara whips into an angled space facing the other way. She checks her note for the room number, kills the engine and grabs the door handle. Rocko pops up ready to go when the dome light flickers to life. Sara glances at Wamaya. "Here we are," she says cheerfully as she clips the leash onto Rocko's harness.

Wamaya gives her a worried look. "It's okay if he comes, too?"

Rocko barks his approval and Sara ruffles his ears. "Rocko can come, too. Here." She reaches around Rocko to hand Wamaya the lease. "He wants to go. You take good care of him. I want you to bring him back to me after your meeting."

Wamaya's eyes grow round. "You are not going to the meeting?"

Sara gives her a tender smile. "You don't need me."

Bullpucky

E XASPERATED, SARA HANGS UP the phone. When the first week passed with no word, she was not all that surprised. She has called the BLM to check on the complaint status every day since. That was eight days ago. They are stonewalling her, she knows it. The question is what to do about it.

Frowning, head down, she tromps up the stairs. Turning into the kitchen, Sara softens.

Leftover newspaper covers half the kitchen table. Wamaya sits at the table with Sara's good sliver neatly sorted, polishing an heirloom: a sterling gravy boat that belonged to her great grandmother. Wamaya hums softly, Rocko lying at her feet as she diligently works the polishing cloth into the creases.

Moving to the counter, Sara snatches her mug out of the sink and grabs the Coffeematic. She pours her mug half full and takes a sip. Turning to face Wamaya, she leans against the counter. "Thank you," she says, smiling gratefully. She holds up her mug. "Want some coffee?"

"Not right now, thanks," Wamaya replies, rubbing carefully.

When Wamaya asked if there was something she could do, Sara was not sure if she was serious. That was a week ago and Sara is already running out of projects. She doesn't want to overreact, but she couldn't be more pleased. If only the BLM was half as diligent.

Sam shrugged when Sara cornered him about the BLM's lack of responsiveness, claimed he didn't know anyone at the BLM office, suggested giving Dennis Drake a call. *"If anyone can get them off the dime, ol' Dennis can,"* he said. Based on her last encounter with the steadfast cattle baron, ol' Dennis is not likely to be part of the solution. She has waited long enough. Time to pay the BLM another visit.

·····•·•····

Going up through the cut to Hilltop, Sara gives the big truck gas. The roar of the V8 invigorates her spirit. Screwing up her courage, she makes a pact with herself, determined to get the BLM moving forward. If that frump Torbert thinks she can give her the runaround, she has another thing coming.

Taking the corner hard, she leans into the throttle, charging up Hualapai Mountain Rd. The mountains loom in the near distance, rising into the sky, beacons of solid rock, begging for her artistic attention. She refuses, pushing their majestic view aside, hanging on to her outrage like a life raft in a Force 9 Gale.

Sara cranks the wheel, whipping the F250 into the BLM parking lot. Parking in the space closest to the entry, she kills the engine. She leans, reaching for the glove box, punching the release. When the glove box door flops open, she grabs her .375 Magnum. Sitting up, she turns her holstered pistol in her hand, admiring its weight, the feel of the grip in her hand. Tempting. She leans forward to fit the holstered gun in her waistband at the small of her back. As she reaches for the door handle, she pulls up short. Feeling ridiculous, she pulls the pistol from her waistband, restoring it to its rightful place in the glove box. She has no intention of shooting anybody, no matter how much they might deserve it.

·····•·•····

Dusky shadows drive away the light of day. Burnt embers of a dead sunset vanish in the evening gloom. It's dinnertime at the Wayland house and Sam is on his way.

Wamaya carefully lays out the silverware while Sara retrieves a casserole from the oven. Removing the Pyrex lid, Sara transports the steaming food to the hotplate in the center of the table, filling the kitchen with a mouthwatering aroma of tender beef, and cream cheese with Texas spices blended in a melted cheddar crust.

Sam walks in, rubbing his hands together on his way to his chair. Sara's Texas Cream Cheese casserole, like all her casseroles, is a work of culinary art—better than her painting, the way he sees it. *Dang!* He hadn't realized he was this hungry. "Hello, ladies," he says, staring at the cheesy crust. "How we doin' this evening?"

Wamaya gives a small nod as she finishes up.

"I hope you're hungry," Sara teases.

Sam straddles the chair and whips his napkin into his lap. "Smells like heaven. Let's eat."

Sara sits across from Sam, spearing the casserole with a serving spoon.

Rocko walks around the table to lie next to Wamaya as she timidly takes her seat.

Sam spoons a helping onto his plate, meeting Sara's gaze. "How was your day?"

Sara takes the spoon and helps herself. "Well," she says, passing the spoon to Wamaya. "You didn't hav'ta bail me out." She winks with a mischievous grin.

"Heck of a deal," Sam says between bites. "Tell me about it."

"Maybe later," Sara says.

"It's a date," he says with a grin. Sam smiles at Wamaya. "How's the grub?"

Mouth full, Wamaya nods her head. When Rocko barks, her eyes light with a smile.

Sara chews a bite, watching Wamaya take a big swig from her grape Nehi.

Wamaya sets down her soda. "I have a job interview," she blurts. Glancing from Sam to Sara and back, she waits.

Deferring to Sara, Sam gives his wife a quick glance.

Sara swallows hard, her wheels grinding to a halt. "A job... That's great... Where?"

"The market," Wamaya says, timidly.

"In Peach Springs?" Sara asks.

Wamaya nods.

Sara glances at Sam for support. She is not sure whether to be happy for Wamaya's initiative or worried about her destination. Wamaya has been doing great, sober ever since Sara shanghaied her. Rocko won't leave her side. He makes her forget for a little while—makes her happy. Now this. Letting her thoughts churn, she turns to Wamaya. "You want to go back to the reservation?"

Wamaya nods more slowly. "I don't want to be like Jasper."

"Bryant's father?"

She gives Sara a sorrowful look. "He didn't come to the ceremony."

"Bryant's funeral?"

Wamaya nods, her lips pouty.

Time slows to a stall. Not knowing what to say, Sara whispers low, "I'm so sorry."

The kitchen stills like a held breath. "I can't stay here anymore," Wamaya says quietly.

"Why not?" Sara says, taken aback.

"I won't be no white man's clown."

Turning to Sam, Sara raises her eyebrows.

"I see," Sara says.

Wamaya averts her eyes to her plate. "Need to go back where I belong."

Trying to come to grips, Sara gathers herself. "When is your interview?"

"Day after tomorrow."

"What time do you need to be there?"

"He said I could come in anytime in the morning," Wamaya says. "I can take the Greyhound to Peach Springs tomorrow."

"Morning, day after tomorrow... I can take you to your interview—Rocko and I can take you if you like."

Wamaya reaches down to rub Rocko's head, then smiles and raises her eyes to meet Sara's. "Thank you."

·········

After dinner, Rocko leads the way to Wamaya's room. He hops up on his side of the twin bed and lies down, waiting for Wamaya.

Wamaya follows him up the stairs and into the guestroom, closing the door behind her. Lying down on her side of the bed, Wamaya pulls a large, hardbound volume, borrowed from Sara's collection. This is the third book in the Oz series, Ozma of Oz. She reads every chance she gets, escaping into the wonderful Land of Oz, oblivious. She takes extra care not to damage the pages or break the spine, it's an heirloom and precious. Pulling Rocko closer, she snuggles under the covers, enthralled with the Nome King. Deep down, she hides in the dark. Going back to the reservation... But she doesn't have to think about it now. She has Rocko.

·········

On the back patio, Sam balances a virgin Coke-on-the-rocks as he drops into his chair.

The screen door bangs behind her as Sara joins him in the starlight. She sits and holds up her lemonade to toast. "Salud."

"What are we toasting," he asks, kiddingly. "The end of the Wayland prohibition?"

"That, too," Sara says wistfully. "I hope she does all right. I hope she has been sober long enough…"

Sam crimps his lips, his thoughts meandering into the quiet desert night. "She'll have to face it sometime."

"She wasn't doing much of a job of it before," Sara says. "I just wish she'd take more time. Rocko really turned her around—there for her every step of the way. How is she going to get along without him?"

"You could let her take him home."

Sara clenches her jaws. "Not a chance. I don't mind him taking care of her while she's here, but I love that dog, and he's not going anywhere."

Sam shrugs. "Timbo might not be too happy with that, either." He turns to face her. "I think we have a date, so spill it."

Sara scoots down in her chair, resting her head against the back, gazing at the starry sky. Swirling her glass, she takes a sip of fresh-squeezed lemonade. "You might get a call."

Sam lets it lie, giving her room to breathe. "Like you said, at least I didn't have to bail you out of jail," he says with a smile. "You didn't pull a gun on 'em, did ya?"

Sara scoffs. "I probably should have. Might've done more good."

Sam jiggles the ice, holding it up to peer through the Coke, wishing he had something a little stronger. "I'm guessin' it didn't go the way you hoped."

"I was there darn near all day." Sara huffs. "Took me an hour to get past the receptionist. And at least that long to convince the office manager to let me see the director. What a joke. Do you know this guy, Simon Dalton?"

"Doesn't ring a bell," Sam replies.

"Did you know…" She glances his direction. "…this Dalton character told me that the BLM only provides varmint control by request. The person leasing the land, the rancher, must ask for it in writing. Can you believe it?"

Sam cocks his head. "I'll be darned."

"What's more," Sara says. "Mr. Dalton claims that the rancher has to ask them to stop."

"Your ol' buddy, Dennis Drake," Sam says.

"And get this, Dalton sat right there and said he'd reviewed my complaint two weeks ago, and that the BLM will take no further action." Sara shakes her head in indignation. "Pure bullpucky. They didn't even have the guts to tell me."

Sam presses his lips together. "What about ol' Dennis?"

Toe-To-Toe

F LAT AND STRAIGHT, ROUTE 66 stretches ahead to disappear into the Music Mountains. Huge metal hangars rise into view, the Kingman Airport coming up on the right. The Drake Ranch Road lies just ahead. Sara didn't bother to call. Whatever she has to say to Dennis Drake, she wants to say it to his face. She figures to catch him off guard. Not that it will do any good, but she intends to give it a go.

Hitting the turn indicator, Sara downshifts for the turnoff, feeling a bit lonely without Rocko. Though leaving him with Wamaya is the right thing, for now. Pumping the brakes, she gently pats a copy of the BLM complaint on the seat. She wants to see Dennis's reaction when he reads it. Though knowing how things work with the BLM, Dennis has probably seen it by now.

On the other side of the cattleguard, her offroad tires kick up the dust. The wide road is unusually smooth for dirt, no washboard, no ruts, no potholes. The Drake Ranch Road heads off across the biggest spread in Mohave County, a grand old cattle ranch with a storied history. From here, the prairie runs flatter than a flapjack, spreading to the distant Cerbats.

Sam told her to watch herself. Of course, he's right. Kingman is home. These people are their friends and neighbors. She doesn't want things to get ugly or out-of-hand. Dennis Drake has a lot of clout. The Drake Ranch runs cattle on thousands of acres, big business for the Kingman area. He could make their lives miserable without hardly trying. But she knows, overall, he's a decent man. She hopes the game ol' cowpoke still has a soft spot for her.

Approaching the main gate, she slows for the bend. She downshifts, rolling under the torch-cut sign high above, 'Lazy Double-D' burnt out of the plate steel like a brand. As she rumbles up the main drive, the size and scope of his operation impresses Sara with all its corrals, outbuildings, heavy equipment, and rich-boy toys. This idea of hers could get tricky, approaching the big man on his home turf. She reminds herself to keep it cordial.

The rustic modern mansion basks in the shade of the mature trees. The yellow Chevy dually sits sideways under a massive oak. Pushing in the clutch, Sara pulls into the parking area for the main ranch house, stopping nose-in to the split-rail fence. She turns off the ignition and sits for a moment to think it through. Picking up the copy of the complaint, she skims it. She did her homework. The facts are there, but are they compelling enough to change things? For Sara, it is inhumane. She has a hard time understanding how people allow such indiscriminate cruelty. However, she understands that a cattleman needs to protect his livestock. There *has* to be a better way.

Sara jumps when the cattle baron's knuckles rap on her window. Giving him a startled smile, she cranks her window down. "Hey, Dennis."

Dennis Drake stands tall, outfitted for business: alligator boots with cutting toes and riding heels, polished to a high sheen. His hands are stuffed into spotless, sharp-creased Wranglers. A dove-gray Premiere Stetson hugs his head like he was born wearing it. Mother-of-pearl snaps gleam on his western-cut, black silk shirt. The single scarlet rose luxuriantly embroidered above each breast pocket would be brash on anyone else. The big man gives her a goatish grin. "Wasn't expecting to see you around here. But a pretty lady like you is always welcome. I gotta head out to a meetin' in a few. What can I do fer ya?"

Sara gives him the once over. "You sure look spiffy there, Dennis." She winks. "This meeting of yours—business, is it?" she says teasingly.

Dennis looks away, chuckling. "Nice of you to say," he says, meeting her eyes. "What's on your mind?"

Sara glances at the complaint copy in her hand before offering it to Dennis. "You've probably seen this, but I wanted to see you about it."

Dennis takes the complaint, nodding while he scans it. "Yeah... I seen it," he sneers. He lifts his eyes to hers and tries to hand back the complaint.

Sara holds up a palm. "That's your copy. You keep it."

"I don't need a copy." He barks, "This why you're here? You drove all the way out here, to my ranch, uninvited, to hand me this piece of bull crap?" Dennis grunts as he turns away.

Sara hops out of her truck. "Dennis, wait. I didn't come here to start a fight."

Dennis stalks off to his dually. "Gotta meetin'."

Sara trots up to his truck as he climbs in. Smiling, she knocks on his window when he closes the door in her face.

He pins her with a steely gaze as his window hums down. "Make it snappy."

Moving closer, Sara places a hand on his window frame. "It doesn't have to be this way. All I'm lookin' to do is get your help with the BLM. You're the head honcho around these parts. You run the show. They'll listen to you."

"I'm not following ya here, little lady." Dennis huffs. "I don't care *what* you do with the BLM."

"You can request that they stop," she says urgently.

"Stop what, varmint control?" Dennis clouds up.

"The cyanide bombs—they'll stop, if you ask them."

He twists his face into a scowl. "Why-the-heck would I do that?"

"Those cyanide bombs are inhumane," she protests.

"Ya don't get it," he blurts. "I gotta cattle business to run. I got no use fer varmints. As far as inhumane, you take that up the BLM." His features pinch, turning ruddy. "I don't give a hot horse apple what you do. Just don't do it 'round here." Rolling up the window, he turns and starts the engine.

Sara steps back as he reverses out and turns the big yellow truck around. He spins the rear tires, leaving her squinting and puffing in a cloud of dust.

·········

After dinner on the back patio, Sam swirls the ice in his coke. "Guess who I ran into today?

Sara gazes across the bluff. On Route 66 a semi grunts its way through the Highway 93 intersection. Just the other side of the bluff, the A&W sign shines like a beacon. About now, a frosty mug of root beer would be a better deal than her Seven Up. "No idea," she replies.

"I was filling the cigarette machine at the Elks Club around quittin' time. Ol' Dennis Drake was holding forth at the bar—had quite a crowd.

Looked like he was buyin'. When I closed up the machine, he waved me over and bought me a beer. You know what he told me?"

Sara gives a crooked grin. "Lemme guess."

"Ol' Dennis told me that my pretty wife was as hardheaded as a mule."

"Sounds about right."

"You know what I told him?" A sly smile crosses his face.

She twists her lips. "After how many beers?"

Sam smirks and shakes his head. "I told Mr. Drake that my gorgeous wife has a mind of her own, and she's not afraid to speak it." Sam grins at the telling. "He said he couldn't disagree with me there. But he didn't offer to buy me another beer—especially after I asked him if he ever found his buffalo."

Sara lights up, she can't stop smiling. She comes out of her chair and drops into Sam's lap, throwing her arms around his neck, pecking little kisses all over his face. Pulling back to look into his eyes, she says, "I'm glad you think so."

Sam winks and toasts her with his Coke. "Long as I don't have to keep bailing you outta jail."

"Speaking of which..." She gives him an impish grin. "I'm taking Wamaya to her interview tomorrow... on the reservation."

Sam shakes his head. "You don't give up, do ya?"

"That's why you love me."

Turning serious, he says, "Look, if you do end up in jail and you can't reach me, call Bob. In fact, call Bob before you go. Let him know you might need some help. I'm likely to be out most of the day."

Sara rolls her eyes and gives him another kiss. "Don't worry. I'll take my gun."

The Interview

O N THE FAR SIDE of Valentine, Route 66 winds through Crozier Canyon. The weekday morning traffic is light. Sara glances at Wamaya as she drives. Bright sunlight slants through the passenger window, highlighting Wamaya's raven hair with shiny strands of silver. Leaning against the truck door with Rocko's head in her lap, Wamaya hasn't said much since they left Kingman nearly an hour ago. In fact, Wamaya hasn't said much since breakfast. Of course, sobriety has changed her, she may be a little too timid and quiet now, but at least she has her wits about her. At times she is so sad, though with Rocko's help, those episodes have become less frequent. However, this is different. Sara is not sure if it has to do with her return to the reservation or saying goodbye to Rocko.

Across the flats and up the long grade through Truxton and a mile or so, Sara spots the reservation border sign. She hasn't thought much about Chief Watonami or his bogus charges. She expects it will be different this time, if she runs into him at all. It would have helped if the evidence of the cyanide bomb hadn't been erased. But to some degree he must know she is serious. It is probably best to steer clear of him, if she can.

Through the trees into Peach Springs, the big truck slows to a trot, five m.p.h. below the limit. Sara fully extends her antennae, on the lookout for the tribal police. Ahead on the left, next to the Post Office, the market hides behind a line of mature oak at the intersection of 66 and Diamond Springs Rd. As she slows for the turn-in, Sara tenses, her nerves aflutter, the sensation strange, as though a premonition. What if Wamaya gets the job? No son, nobody around, no Rocko... What will she do on her own?

Overfull dumpsters crowd the short drive between buildings before the narrow asphalt dumps into the rear parking lot. Mostly empty, the lot has plenty of spaces. Sara pulls across the lot from the entrance and parks. Giving Wamaya a smile, she says, "You're gonna do great. Ready?"

Smiling, Rocko sits up as Wamaya opens her door.

Sara calls to her as she climbs out. "I'll wait for you," she says to Wamaya's back.

Wamaya waves a hand as she trudges toward the double-door entry.

Sara leaves the truck door cracked, slouches down in the seat, and props one foot on the dash, prepared for the long haul. Rocko turns around to lay his head on Sara's thigh. Sara absently rubs his ears, glancing in her mirrors every few moments. The air is a touch cooler and moister than Kingman, refreshingly so. She admires the big oaks, green and leafy in her mirrors. Despite the waiting, it's a pleasant morning. Smiling, it reminds her of her son Jack's favorite saying: *"Wherever you go, there you are."*

A dented pickup swings in to park in front of the double doors and Sara loses sight of the entrance. Peering between buildings, she sees the police Jeep turn off 66 and onto Diamond Springs. A moment of panic passes, and she breathes a sigh when the silver Jeep wanders up the cut between the hills.

Sara loses track, time dribbling out like a leaky water fountain. She is sure Wamaya will be strolling across the lot at any moment. She has a feeling that Wamaya will get the job. It's worrying, but she'll ford that stream when she comes to it.

When Wamaya pushes through the doors and trots across the lot, Sara's concerns are confirmed. She smiles as Wamaya opens the truck door and climbs in. Rocko bounds to her side, tail wagging.

Wamaya's dark round face splits into a wide grin as she hugs Rocko. "I got the job," she says breathlessly.

"Congratulations! I knew you would." Sara's eyes light. "Tell me about it."

As Rocko licks her face, Wamaya gives a nod toward Diamond Springs Rd. "Can you take me to the trailer? I'll tell you on the way."

Sara starts the truck, backs out and steers for the street. Pulling out on Diamond Springs, she heads up the incline through the hills. "When do you start?"

"Mr. Tomlinson wants me to start this afternoon, at 1:00."

"Is it full-time?"

"Afternoons, evenings, and weekends—forty hours a week."

"Wow." Sara guides the truck through the curve as the road crests between the hills. "What will you be doing?"

"He's going to show me how to bag groceries," she says shyly. "He says if I do a good job, I can work up to checker, work behind the register." She can't help smiling.

Older houses hide between mature oaks and cottonwoods on the left, a barren bluff rising on the right. Concerned, Sara asks, "How much do they pay?"

"They pay seventy-five cents, to start. But if I get the checker job, it's two-fifty an hour." Wamaya beams as she rubs Rocko's neck.

"Seventy-five cents an hour..." Sara crinkles her nose. "Can you live on that?"

"With my government check, I'll have enough," Wamaya says. "But I need a job. Without Bryant, my monthly check will be smaller."

Sara glances toward the police station as they pass. The silver Jeep is parked facing out, near the end of the main building. Through the intersection at Hualapai Way, the houses grow smaller and closer together—perimeter walls of block or stone give way to intermittent chain-link fencing or weedy vacant lots. The street narrows curving to the subdivision outskirts. Single-wide trailers on lots deep and narrow replace low-end housing. As she turns on Canyon View, Wamaya's rusting pickup sits facing the street. "Here we are," she says as she pulls into the rocky drive.

Wamaya turns to Rocko, burying her face in his neck with a hug. She holds him, quietly murmuring for several moments. When she looks up, her eyes meet Sara's gaze. "I don't know why you did what you did—why you bothered with me, at all." Her eyes fill as a grateful smile brightens her face. "You're a crazy white woman."

Sara chuckles fondly. "After everything you've been through, it's the least I could do." She catches a flash out of the corners of her eyes. Checking her mirrors, she jumps. The silver police Jeep turns into the drive and crawls over the rocks, emergency lights blinking red. She glances at Wamaya, then the glove box, then her mirrors, flashing between furious and terrified, determined not to go back to jail.

Henry Natomi exits the Jeep on the passenger side while Chief Watonami hops out, hitches up his pants, and lumbers toward the driver's side of the F250.

Sara leans over, slaps the glove box, and retrieves her .357 magnum. Shoving the pistol into the back of her pants, she straightens up and cranks down the window.

A low growl rumbles deep in Rocko's throat as the Chief arrives at her door. Sara gives Rocko a hand signal and tells him, "Off."

Ignoring Rocko, the Chief leans his beefy forearms on her window frame, pinning her with a piercing glare. "You, again," he says with a grunt. "You're a real troublemaker, aren't you? I thought I told you to stay off Hualapai land."

Wamaya's eyes flash as she flings open the door, jumps down from the truck, and runs around to confront Chief Watonami. With a fierce stare, she gets in Chief's face. "She's with me," she barks. "My guest. I invited her. She has every right to be here. Now leave her alone."

The Chief sneers as he turns to face Wamaya. "You... What do you know? You're nothing but a drunk, a disgrace to your people. Your son's death is on you, your fault. You don't deserve to be a mother."

Rocko leaps through the window, almost knocking the Chief down. He rushes to Wamaya's side, hackles up, growling.

Sara turns bright red, her blood boiling. "You can't talk to her that way," she yells.

Wamaya waves her off, inching up on the Chief. "I am NOT a drunk," she snaps. "And I did NOT kill my son! Don't you ever say that again!" She starts poking his chest with her index finger. "Now get off my land!"

Brought To Light

Dry and breezy, the night sky hazy with a rising moon. Rocko leads the way as Sara joins Sam on the back patio. With a Salty Dog in hand, she scooches into her chair. She takes a sip and leans back, smiling contentedly.

"You should have seen her," she says. "I was flabbergasted. I couldn't have been more proud."

Sam takes a swig of his Seven & Seven, glancing at Sara. "Wamaya actually told the Chief of Police to leave you alone?"

Sara chuckles. "Then she told him to get off her property."

Sam nods "And he left... Amazing. Who would've thought she had it in her."

Sara rubs Rocko's ears as she sips her drink. "More amazing was the *way* she told him: she said she was NOT a drunk. The way she said it, I knew she was gonna be all right."

Sam nods thoughtfully.

"I would have never believed it." Gazing at her husband, she says, "You should've been there."

Sara turns her gaze to the distant traffic on 66. Headlights, taillights: pinpoints of white light punctuated with dots of red, calming, reassuring, as though they have always been there, and always will be. The only hesitation she had was leaving Wamaya all alone. But Wamaya is a grown woman who knows her own mind. However, without Rocko...

Sara worries, a niggling little doubt. Wamaya will learn to deal with it, in time, and in her own way. She flinches at a twinge of guilt. Rocko was Wamaya's steady companion, pulling her through the toughest episodes, refusing to leave her side. For Wamaya, sober, starting over without her best friend... It can't be easy.

Sam leans down to rub Rocko's neck. "You did a heck of job, boy," he says as though hearing her thoughts. "Didn't know you had it in ya."

Sara watches Rocko while Sam rubs him. "I'm glad Timmy couldn't take care of him."

"I can see why the dorm has a 'no pets' rule." Sitting back in his chair, Sam reaches for his drink. "Most of those kids can't take care of themselves."

Sara scrunches her lips. "I think Timmy's doin' okay."

"Jack's about got things worked out," he says. "Ol' Timbo's still gotta ways to go."

"He'll get there." Sara nods. "In the meantime, Rocko can stay here and take care of me." Out of habit, she reaches down and rubs Rocko's ears. "Wamaya's gonna miss him, though."

····•··•····

Another week slips by with no response. Dalton is not returning Sara's calls. Busy with a million things, she lets it slide. And it is too bad, Sara was outraged when she first found out about the cyanide bombs, but her passion waned after filing three more complaints with the BLM. That was two weeks and three meetings ago and the practice of "cyanide devices" for "so-called" varmint control continues unabated. When Sara met with Dalton last, she insisted he investigate the newest complaint, taking into account the evidence associated with the death of Bryant Watachka, and the updated ME report from Doc Pratt. Why she thought that would change things, she hasn't a clue.

At her downstairs desk, Sara records the latest receipts, double-checking the numbers as her mind wanders between Dalton at the BLM, and his highness, Dennis Drake. Off and on, she has toyed with the idea of paying the cattle baron another in-person visit. As hard-headed as he is, she doubts it would do any good. But Dalton keeps using the Drake Ranch as an excuse. She is not buying it. As far as she is concerned, it doesn't matter whose ranch the cyanide bombs are on, they are still inhumane. Sadly, she is convinced the BLM is not going to change its cruel practices of its own accord.

Sara keeps an eye on the phone as she lays down her pen and closes the ledger. She tidies up the stack of receipts and tucks them in May's envelope.

The phone stays still, playing dead. Sneering, she picks up the handset and dials. Now that she has Wamaya's permission, Sara is out of excuses.

"Director Dalton, please," she says, forcing politeness.

Recognizing Sara's snotty attitude, Judy Torbert replies, "Director Dalton is unavailable. May I take a message?"

"By all means," Sara snaps. "Take a message."

Judy rolls her eyes as she twiddles a pen above a note pad.

"Tell the Director, he has thirty minutes to call me back before I call the Miner." Sara hangs up without waiting for a reply.

Judy Torbert frowns at the handset and hangs up. Tearing the message off the pad, she trots to the Director's door and knocks, message in hand.

·····•·•····

Sara works her mostly empty coffee mug with tense fingers, her stomach gurgling, her nerves taut as piano wire from three mugs of Yuban black. Trotting down the stairs, she checks her watch for the umpteenth time. It has been forty-seven minutes and not a peep out of Dalton and the BLM. That tears it.

Dropping into her office chair, Sara swivels to grab the phone.

"Mohave County Miner," a girl's voice says.

"Owen Rivers, please."

"May I tell him who's calling?"

"Hi, yes. It's Sara Wayland."

"Oh hi, Mrs. Wayland." The girl's voice lights up. "It's Amanda. Let me get Dad for you, hold on."

Sara mulls how best to broach this with Owen, wondering how much influence Dennis Drake wields when it comes to the local newspaper.

"Hi, Sara. Did that crazy mutt of ours jump the fence again?"

Sara chuckles. "Hi, Owen. I haven't seen Curly. But if I do, I'll send him home. Have you thought about a taller fence?" she says, teasing.

Owen gives a short laugh. "I've thought about a better dog."

"Curly is a good dog. He just likes to ramble. Can't blame a dog for that," she says with a grin.

"Of course, you're right," he says. "But if you didn't call about Curly, what can I do for you?"

"When can we meet?" she asks.

"For you, neighbor, any time you like."

"I'll come there," she says. "Gimme about thirty minutes."

"See you then," Owen says.

Sara hangs up the receiver to stare at the phone, arguing with herself. Should she try the BLM one last time? She lets the question hang like a gallows noose, considering the consequences of a news story. It is bound to affect Wamaya, Dennis, Doc Pratt, and the Tribal Police. Things will change, but for the better? She doesn't want to hurt anyone. Yet, if she fails to hold the BLM practices up to the light, how many more innocent lives will be sacrificed?

Land Of The Free

Pushing up from her chair, Sara grabs the BLM folder and tucks it under her arm. "Let's go, Rocko." She whips her purse off the desk and digs out her sunglasses and her keys on her way out the door. In the pickup, with Rocko at shotgun, she backs out on Spring St. and heads down the hill. She glances at her neighbors' homes on the way downtown: the Tucker place, the Goodwins, old Miss Moser. She wonders if they'll still be talking to her after this.

Sara navigates the Grandview jog, sticking to Spring St., the high school annex to her right, the new junior high gym to her left, contemporary in red-brick and glass. Kingman is growing up. Her little city has changed a lot in the last twenty or so years. She smiles, remembering Jack's senior year as a first-string guard on the varsity basketball squad. They won their division, beating Holbrook and Winslow in away games. He was always so serious, so gung-ho, taking after his father. Glancing toward the junior high campus, she remembers how proud Timmy was of the ashtray he made in shop class. He hid it until Christmas then gave the turned-brass prize to his father, beaming when Sam was both surprised and impressed. She and Sam made a good life for the boys here.

At 1st St., Sara switches through the dogleg back to a older residential stretch on Spring St. Diagonal parking lines both sides of the deteriorating street, tall curbs crumbling, sidewalks broken and tilted. Ancient cypress, spruce, and mature shade trees overpower the tiny yards. The homes date to well before her time, a simpler time: boxy little houses with tongue-and-groove siding or smooth stucco, painted in unassuming hues with pitched roofs of asphalt single. She envisions the quaint dwellings as caches of untold stories—the families, the lives they shared. How to capture that spirit on canvas remains a mystery to Sara—something she intends to work on.

Determined to put the BLM hassle behind her, she daydreams of her paintings featured in a fancy New York art gallery: opening night, long flowing evening gowns and tuxedos with tails, caviar and champagne, a collection of her best works cover the walls, pictures of people and places she has yet to paint.

Sara downshifts, slowing for the stop sign at 3rd St. Through the intersection, the quarried stone of the Catholic Church adorns the corner. At the head of 4th St., the tall pillars and the glazed silver dome of the County Courthouse shine in the sun. Reminded, she silently questions Sheriff Bailey and his allegiances. Jurisdiction: what a strange approach to law enforcement, a more convenient view of right and wrong, fighting over turf like feral dogs. And Chief Watonami, throwing his weight around like a Sumo wrestler. The Arizona Territory was tamed with hard work by conscientious people. How discouraging to witness community leaders behaving with such silly self-importance—like kindergartners. She wonders how to set it aside, get on with her life. Now that she knows—seen it first-hand—her beloved little city will never look quite the same.

Spires of tall Italian cypress, fifty-sixty years old, reach into the sky, towering over the Episcopal Church, the Bonelli House, and the Methodist Church at Spring and 5th. Sara doesn't often appreciate Kingman's history, but its monuments, its institutions, like the Bonelli House and the Courthouse, bring it into focus. If she remembers right, the Bonelli House was built in 1916, shortly after Arizona gained statehood. Mrs. Bonelli was Jack's high school English teacher his senior year. She imagines the first settlers: the railroad men, the miners, the ranchers, their families, these people tackled life's opportunities head on. They forged a town out of a hard-bitten wasteland, ramrodded new industry and built businesses from the ground up, carving lives out of the barren volcanic terrain. Strength of character; she is proud to be a part of that tradition.

At the stop sign, Sara turns right, the Mohave County Miner ahead on the left. She loops a U-turn to park diagonally in front. Rocko bounds out of the truck, and she locks up with the BLM folder under one arm. She holds the entry door as Rocko follows her into the Miner building.

Behind a small reception desk, Amanda Rivers, a thin and wide-eyed seventeen-year-old, looks up from a schoolbook with a toothy smile. "Hi, Mrs. Wayland." She turns her smile on Rocko, holding out a hand. "Hey, Rocko," she says as she pets his head.

Sara returns the smile. "Hey, Amanda. How are you?"

Amanda twists her lips as she holds up her geometry book. "Finals."

"You graduate this year, don't you?"

Amanda nods, proudly.

"Good for you," Sara says. "Congratulations." She glances around the smallish front office. "Is your dad around?"

Amanda pops up. "He's in the back room, setting up the presses." Holding up an index finger, she walks toward the door marked 'private' in the back corner. "I'll get him for you."

Sara slides her purse off her shoulder, sets it on a corner of the narrow desk, and pulls the BLM file out from under her other arm. Rifling through the folder contents, she wishes she was more comfortable with this whole thing. Why can't the BLM act more responsibly?

"Sara," the owner/publisher/editor of the Mohave County Miner says, following his daughter out of the back room.

Glancing up, Sara waves and smiles. "Hey, Owen."

Short and wiry with thinning hair, Owen Rivers walks up, vigorously wiping ink-stained hands on a red shop rag. "Good to see you." Smiling, he sweeps a hand toward a large desk and worktable on the other side of the room. "Let's go over there, where we can talk," he says, leading the way. "How's Sam?"

With Rocko at heel, Sara follows him across the room. "Sam's doing good," She grins. "Though I never see him at the breakfast table. He's always got his nose buried in the Miner."

"That's what I like to hear," Owen says as he swings around behind his desk.

Sara takes a side chair, handing him the BLM folder as he sits behind his desk. "Before we dig into this stuff, you should know, you are my only hope."

Intrigued, Owen meets her gaze. "I'll do what I can. What are we talkin' about here?"

Sara scrunches her chin. "It's not pretty."

Owen nods. "I assumed as much. It has to do with that dead boy you found on reservation..."

"How did you know?" she asks, tucking her chin.

Owen gives her a big grin. "It's my business."

Flummoxed, she narrows her eyes as she cocks her head. "I'm surprised, is all. I thought only a few people knew about this."

"I wish I could take credit for an exclusive," he says. "But it's common knowledge—all over town."

"Oh no." Averting her eyes, Sara covers her lips with her fingers.

Owen gives her a sympathetic look. "Kingman is no Peyton Place, but it *is* a small town in a lot of ways."

Sara lifts her eyes to meet his as it sinks in.

Laying the folder down, Owen props his elbows on the desktop. "Maybe you should tell me your side of the story."

She points at the folder. "The facts are all there, but they don't tell the whole story."

"Hold on a sec," Owen says as he grabs a legal pad and hunts a pen.

·····•••••····

Sara glances out her kitchen window, the morning sun bright in a cloudless sky. It's another windy day: the oleanders whipping against the wall outside, tumbleweeds racing across the road, a dust devil siphoning dirt into a tiny tornado as it wanders down the hill. And it's getting hot, Spring is almost over. She sighs. Not exactly ideal weather for painting in the field.

Apprehension hangs in the air as she refills her mug. She turns to the table and Sam engrossed in his Miner. "I saw the headlines," she says as she sits.

"Top story." Sam pokes his nose above the newspaper. Snapping the front page, he reads, "Do Cyanide Bombs Cause More Harm Than Good?" He shakes his head, incredulous. "That ought to drive the worms outta the woodwork."

"When I showed this to Owen, I didn't know he was gonna do all this," she says. "Do you think his news story will do too much damage?"

Sam drops the paper to give her a wink. "I think it will cause people to think—probably hack off a few folks, too." He cocks his head and gives her a look. "Did you read the whole thing?"

Sara slowly shakes her head. "After that headline, I was too afraid. Is it bad?"

He snaps the paper up in front of his face. "Ol' Owen did his homework. I'll bet until they read this, most people never heard of a cyanide bomb. He gives dates and locations of cyanide device accidents: A small boy in Idaho, a hiker near Prescott, a prize hunting hound in Texas, and it goes on. It says, 'local BLM Director, Mr. Simon Dalton, declined to be interviewed.'" He chuckles. "I wonder why?"

Sara takes a sip of her coffee and presses her lips tight. "Who else does he mention?"

Sam scans the front page, then turns to an inner page. "There's you, Wamaya and Bryant, Sheriff Bailey and Chief Watonami—he doesn't refer to Doc Pratt by name, just as the Medical Examiner. I don't see Dennis or the Drake Ranch in here anywhere." He looks up from his paper, grinning. "He must like you; you are in here a few times."

Sara twists her lips and hangs her head. "He offered me a job."

Sam raises his eyebrows, intrigued.

"He wanted to hire me as a freelance field reporter." Sara narrows her eyes. "I told him I never want to get involved in a mess like this again; and I sure as heck won't go hunting for them."

"Yeah, but you're famous," Sam crows.

"Very funny. Just what I need," she grouses. "The question remains: did it do any good."

"Too soon to tell." Sam purses his lips. "Give it time. The federal government moves slower than glacial ice."

"I'm not getting my hopes up," Sara replies, flatly.

·· • • •· • ···· ·

At her desk downstairs, Sara files the last of the receipts for S.W. Vending. It has been an interesting few days since the piece in the Miner. George Bailey gave her the cold shoulder at the Country Club last Saturday night, but most folks went out of their way to congratulate her. Sam said he felt like an armpiece for his celebrity wife. The appreciation was a nice surprise, but all those compliments felt like a bit of a hollow victory. Last she heard, the BLM still refuses to acknowledge the situation, much less do anything about it.

The ringing phone snaps Sara out of her reverie. "Hello?"

"Am I talkin' to Sara, that pretty little wife of Sam Wayland?"

She recognizes Dennis Drake's gravelly twang instantly. Secretly pleased, she says, "Hello, Dennis."

"How're ya getting' along?" he asks.

To her recollection, the only time Dennis called, he was looking for his buffalo. He certainly never called to chat. Catching him beating around the bush, she has to smile. She gives him just enough slack to hang himself. "We're doin' fine. Ever find your buffalo?"

He barks a quick laugh. "That critter is long gone. I'll never see him again."

The line goes quiet, Sara can almost hear him switching gears.

"Listen, here's the deal," he says turning serious. "I called off the dogs."

Taken aback, Sara raises her eyebrows. "The BLM?"

"The BLM has removed all varmint control devices from the Drake Ranch. That's the cyanide bombs on all BLM land leased by the Drake Family Land and Cattle business."

"Dennis..." Stunned, she can't find the words.

"I had a change of heart—happens every hundred years or so." he chuckles. "You're right. And my attorney agrees with you. The risk isn't worth it. Besides... You can't put a value on your neighbors' goodwill. Owen Rivers is gonna run a follow-up story. I hope you're willin' to help him with that."

Sara almost drops the phone as she squirms with glee. "Oh my Lord... Of course!!!"

After she hangs up, Sara bounces up from her chair and does a little dance while Rocko bounds around her, barking. She can't wait to tell Wamaya.

Epilogue

L ATE-DAY SUN SHINES THROUGH a notch between peaks, shimmering through the trees. Entering Peach Springs, Route 66 curves, dropping into dappled shade beneath the leafy oaks and cottonwoods, magically transforming from highway to shady lane.

As Sara downshifts for the turn onto Diamond Springs, she glances at the little black ball of fluff with the yellow bow curled up next to Rocko. Amazing, Kingman to Peach Springs, the puppy slept the whole way. Passing the entrance to the Peach Springs Market, she checks the time and wonders what Wamaya will think. She should be home by now.

Approaching the Hualapai Police Station, Sara watches her speed. She checks for the Chief's silver Jeep with a furtive glance as she motors by at five miles under. While Wamaya got him off her back, Sara doubts the Chief will cut her any slack.

Sara turns into the rocky drive, pulls up next to Wamaya's rusty pickup, and shuts down her truck. The cooling engine sighs and ticks as the moment takes her. She hasn't seen Wamaya face-to-face since the young Hualapai woman was promoted. Sara swipes at her eyes with the back of her hand. She couldn't be prouder.

Sara gently wakes the pup as she picks her up. Squirming, the puppy licks Sara's cheeks. When Sara finally opens the door, Rocko leaps out. Turning in circles, he bounds around as she works her way to the trailer door.

Up the steps, Sara knocks and waits, the puppy wriggling in her arms. The trailer door swings out, forcing Sara down a step. She holds the sweet puppy out to Wamaya. "I brought you a present."

Wamaya cranes her neck, sticking her head through the doorway, her mouth moving wordlessly, her eyes as round as moon pies, her smooth skin dark as coal dust. "A puppy?" Tentatively, she backs into the trailer, cupping her hand as she motions Sara in. "Oh my, Rocko!" she says. Rocko bounces his front paws off Wamaya's thighs as she squats to hug him. Tears trickle down her round cheeks as she meets Sara's gaze.

"Look what I brought you," Sara says, holding up the black furball with the yellow bow.

Wamaya stands, her hand stroking Rocko's head. The look on Wamaya's face as she reaches for the puppy, melts Sara's heart.

"She's yours," Sara says, beaming. "I think you two will get along fine." She gives Rocko the eye. "What do you think?"

Wamaya hugs her puppy, turning around as Rocko barks his approval. Turning back to Sara, she meets her eyes. "I don't know what to say," she says in a hoarse whisper. "Thank you."

Before You Go...

T HANKS FOR READING. I hope you found Sara and Rocko's journey entertaining. I'm sure every book you read these days asks for your review, but the cold hard fact is, without reviews a book dies. If you've enjoyed *TRUXTON WHISKEY: A Route 66 Mystery*, please take a moment to rate and/or review it. Even a one-liner or a simple star rating would be much appreciated.

········•······

For exclusive access to discounted book offers, free stories, excerpts, giveaways, early releases, first reader opportunities, upcoming events and insights into my process get your behind the scenes "Access Pass." Go to https://subscribepage.io/UdooFA.

········•······

Thank you for your interest. This work would be impossible without you and others like you, supporting us indie authors.

········•······

Please join me: **Amazon.com Author Central:** https://www.amazon.com/-/e/B00AB4ETQ6; **YouTube Channel:** https://www.youtube.com/channel/UCiORGuAMx_IWhQ9lefY1tKQ; **BookBub:** https://www.bookbub.com/authors/michael-allan-scott; X: https://twitter.com/MAllanScott; **Meta:** https://www.facebook.com/AuthorMichaelAllanScott; **Instagram:** https://www.instagram.com/mallanscott/

What Readers Say

bestselling author of *Broken Places* and the award-winning *Broken Pieces*, as well as *A Walk In The Snark*, and *Mancode: Exposed*.

Flight of the Tarantula Hawk:

"If you thought the first book—Dark Side of Sunset Pointe—was any good, this book will blow your mind. The writing is mesmerizing and the execution of each separate theme is good enough to keep you thinking about the story long after you have finished... Highly recommended read for any mystery lover who enjoys twists, characters you'll love or hate and writing that will leave you salivating for more." – ***Quality Reads UK Book Club***

Grey Daze:

"An action-packed page turner based on real events, this murder mystery/thriller is layered with plot twists and alarming details, along with voices of the dead and visions of imminent peril. Grey Daze is sure to please already entrenched Underphal fans and draw new ones to the fold. Highly recommended for thriller/suspense fans." – ***Chanticleer Review***

Cut-Throat Syndrome:

"Cut-Throat Syndrome is a perfect entry point to the series, featuring a compelling storyline, deftly written action scenes and real emotional heft. ...a highly entertaining conspiracy thriller. But the real reason you'll reach for Scott's other books? To spend more time with Lance Underphal and his singular take on the world. The bottom line: A searing action thriller featuring an unforgettable psychic. Highly recommended." – **BestThri llers.com**

On Predation Road:

"Exceptional! To say that it is an exceptional read is not an overstatement of the fact that this book is the best one to date. Author Scott brings the characters together for a riveting adventure with breathtaking scenes from border to desert. Often, this reader has said, reading a Scott novel is like being next to the main character no matter the setting as the details are so vivid. Talk about HOT stuff in more ways than one. I enjoyed every word of this page turner and without a doubt, I fell in love with Chopper. How could I not? He was such a charmer." - **Zoe**

The Jena Halpern Mystery Thriller Series:

Blood-Red Mist:

"The most frightening thing about this story is it is based upon facts. The characters are realistic and well-described. The style of writing is easy to read, and the author demonstrates how external items can be beautifully described with a minimum of well-chosen words. The story includes violence, suspense and food for thought. Definitely a great book." – Amazon 5 star review by Kayak Jay.

"...a mystery that feels all too real. It made me think about every pill I've ever taken. This story kept me interested from beginning to end." – Amazon 4 star review by Reader of the Pack.

"...the tension winds the reader up like a spring." – Amazon 5 star review by Zee.

"Straight from today's headlines. ...scenes are well-paced and the detail of the writing is almost Dickensian. The author's research is clearly evident." – Amazon 5 star review by Tom.

"Mr. Scott did not fail to perform once again. His ability to take the reader into the world of the paranormal is outstanding. Blood Red Mist is a page-turner." – Amazon 5 star review by Zoe.

The Jack-O-Lantern People:

"What a ride! Plots within plots. My genre is everything this book is all about. I know when I buy one of his books to set aside time to finish it all at once. Or I stare at the ceiling trying to sleep while my Kindle awaits me in another room." – Amazon 5 star review by Deb H.

"Wow! This book gripped me from the very beginning. I didn't want to stop reading and when I had to stop all I did was think about it. What really happened? It kept me guessing until the very end. I found it to be a great story." – Amazon 5 star review by Karen.

"Best yet! If you enjoy a good detective story, add a stealthy dose of the supernatural and you have your new favorite character, Jena. Do yourself a favor and check out this writer's exceptional ability to paint pictures with words." – Amazon 5 star review by Patrick.

The Blind Puppeteers:

"It was amazing—read 2 times. Mr. Scott took his prose to the gym and returned with tight, hard-working words depicting one soldier's nightmare. I glued my eyes to every sentence of this novel, as the scenes and descriptions were so vivid that I couldn't look away. I felt as if I was looking through the gauze-like haze of Jena's visions while she unveiled the mystery. By far, this is Michael's best writing and best book in the series. Be prepared for many sleepless nights." – Barbara Daniels Dena's 5-star Goodreads review.

Breakfast of Scorpions:

"Masterful writing! Prepare for a magical mystery tour while reading *Breakfast of Scorpions*. Michael Allan Scott sends Jena straight out of the starting gate, visions whirling in her mind clear to the last pages. A real white-knuckle ride! This novel is similar to Scott's previous works. It has it all, intrigues, suspense, and unparalleled imagination." – 5-star Amazon review from Zoe J.

"I read it in one night. The book was hard hitting & eerily prescient considering all the research into AI these days. There's something about the author's writing style that I wish I had a word for... besides great. Really good reading, I highly recommend the entire series." – 5-star Amazon review from Susan Watts.

About the Author

Michael Allan Scott, his wife, Cynthia, and their rescue Doberman, Roxie, live with coyotes, bobcats, and javelina in the Arizona desert.

For more from Indie Author, Michael Allan Scott, click here.

A Big Thank-You

I'D LIKE TO TAKE this opportunity to personally acknowledge the people who helped me with this project:

First, my wife, Cynthia, for all her help and support. Our daughter, Julie, for her back up and handling our bookkeeping. Julie and Cynthia's work in building and maintaining my social media presence is nothing short of stellar. Alicia Fuller for her unparalleled care and guidance. Michael Manoogian of Michael Manoogian Logo Design for the ultimate in logos. My dedicated crew of "Alpha" readers—Dawnie Lynn McCraley, Theodore Shinkle, Barbara Daniels Dena, and Mrs. Terry Monk—who keep me on the straight and narrow. My "Trail Blazers" launch crew for phenomenal blastoffs. Then, of course, all the thoughtful reviewers and wonderful readers who make this dream job possible.

Legal Stuff

Made in the USA
Las Vegas, NV
21 November 2024

12265754R00118